Between The Worlds

Witches of the New Forest, Book 2

Joanna van der Hoeven

Witches of the New Forest

Copyright

© Joanna van der Hoeven 2024

All rights reserved to the Author

No part of this book may be reproduced, or stored in a retrieval system, or transmitted in any other forms or by any means electronic, mechanical, photocopying, recording or otherwise without the express written permission of the author and publisher except in brief quotations embodied in critical articles and reviews. Without in any way limiting the author's and publisher's exclusive rights under copyright, any use of this publication to 'train' generative artificial intelligence (AI) technologies to generate text is expressly prohibited. The author reserves all rights to license uses of this work for generative AI training and development of machine learning language models. Note however that the author will never, ever, ever, EVER give away or sell those rights to license work for AI.

Let's keep our human authors in business.

Published by Joanna van der Hoeven

This is a work of fiction. Names, characters, businesses, organisations, events, and incidents are the product of the author's imagination. The setting of this book is in Burley, a real village located in the New Forest, England. The village of Burley is used as inspiration for this book along with some of the myths and legends that surround the area. The characters in this work are completely fictitious. Any of the characters' resemblance to actual persons either living or dead is entirely coincidental.

Burley is a very real, very witchy place and the author urges you to visit if you are able.

Acknowledgements

Thank you to my mother, who is, and always has been, my biggest fan and supporter of everything that I do. I love you.

Thank you to my lady, Brighid, who has guided my thoughts and my hands throughout this work.

Lastly, I thank the village of Burley and the New Forest for providing me with the inspiration for this book, and for the entire series. May all the stories, myths, legends and folklore stay alive through the telling of its tales.

Dedication

I dedicate this book to my sister. I love you, and I'll be Ryder to your Hunter any day.

The Veil Between the Worlds

This book is intended as a fictional work only. The rites and rituals, herbs and other magickal practices are intended solely for the purpose of enjoying this fictional work. To understand more about Witchcraft and Druidry, please see the author's other non-fiction works. The author and publisher disclaim any liability arriving directly or indirectly from the use of this book.

Other Titles by Joanna van der Hoeven

WITCHES OF THE NEW FOREST SERIES

Hedge Witch, Book 1

The Veil Between the Worlds, Book 2

The Witch's Compass, Book 3
(Out late spring/early summer 2025)

NON-FICTION

The Old Ways: A Hedge Witch's Guide to Living a Magickal Life (published through Llewellyn, 2025)

The Path of the Hedge Witch: Simple, Natural Magick and the Art of Hedge Riding (published through Llewellyn, 2022)

The Book of Hedge Druidry: A Complete Guide for the Solitary Seeker (published through Llewellyn, 2019)

The Hedge Druid's Craft: An Introduction to Walking Between the Worlds of Wicca, Witchcraft and Druidry (published through Moon Books, 2018)

The Crane Bag: A Druid's Guide to Ritual Tools and Practices (published through Moon Books, 2017)

Zen for Druids: A Further Guide to Integration, Compassion and Harmony with Nature (published through Moon Books, 2016)

The Awen Alone: Walking the Path of the Solitary Druid (published through Moon Books, 2014)

Dancing with Nemetona: A Druid's Exploration of Sanctuary and Sacred Space (published through Moon Books, 2014)

Zen Druidry: Living a Natural Life, With Full Awareness (published through Moon Books, 2013)

"Above all, watch with glittering eyes the world around you because the greatest secrets are always hidden in the most unlikely places.
Those who don't believe in magic will never find it."

- Roald Dahl

Prologue

Jack's heart broke when he saw the hurt in Hunter's eyes. There was nothing he could do. "Goodbye, Hunter. Stay safe. And remember." He leaned forwards, kissing her gently on the forehead before turning and walking down the shadowy path back to his sister's house.

Tears fell down his cheeks as he walked away from the love of his life. Hunter was a woman like no other. She was a goddess to him; a beautiful, smart, passionate goddess. The memory of the first time he saw her on the heath, holding the deer antler up to the rising sun was forever imprinted on his heart. He would never be able to let that image go. Her tall, slim body, her long red hair flowing in the dawn breeze and her elated expression was a moment in time that shook his world forever. And as he got to know her better, his world had re-formed around her, for she was everything now.

And it was for that very reason he must stay away.

He wiped his hands across his face, and walked deeper into the night.

Chapter One

Hunter lay in bed, not wanting to open her eyes. She didn't want to face the world, not now, not without Jack. Hadn't she told herself to be careful with her heart? She had ignored her own advice, and look where that left her now. She was broken, utterly heartbroken, and facing possibly the most difficult challenge in her life. All in a strange, foreign country. Though she loved England, right now all she felt was how much she wanted to be back in her own home in Canada, where she could try and forget any of this had ever happened. She turned over and buried her face in her pillow, weeping as the hurt came in another great wave across her heart.

She heard a soft knock at the door. "Hunter?" Her sister, Ryder, opened the door gently and poked her head in. She was still in the clothes that she had worn the night before. Her blonde hair was sleep-rumpled, and her pale blue eyes had dark circles beneath them. "Hunter, what's the matter?" Seeing her sister in distress, Ryder came through the door and sat on the edge of the bed. "Hunter, talk to me."

Hunter just shook her head, still weeping into her pillow.

"Did something happen between you and Jack last night? I didn't feel anything, but I was out like a light as soon as I lay down. Hun, what's wrong?"

"I can't-"

The Veil Between the Worlds

Hunter's much younger sibling stroked her sister's long, red hair. "Hun, please. I can feel your heart breaking, but I don't know why. Please tell me what's wrong."

Hunter pulled away from the pillow and turned over, looking up at her sister. Ryder saw her red-rimmed eyes; eyes that had been crying all night. Her complexion was very pale, and her hair was twisted about her head. "Jack left me," Hunter said in a small voice.

"He what???"

Hunter turned her gaze to look out the window. "He left me, Ry. He said that he needed to do some things, and have the space to do them in. He said he couldn't be in a relationship with me right now."

"Are you fucking *kidding me*? After everything, after the way that you two have been loved up together for nearly two months now, he says and does this? *Really?*"

"Yes," was all Hunter said.

"That sonofabitch," said Ryder. She stood up. "I'm going to kick his ass into next week."

Hunter sighed, turning over onto her back, tears oozing out of her eyes and falling down into her hair. "It's not worth it, Ryder. You were right."

"Huh?"

"He just wanted to get me into bed. And now that he's had that from me, he's done with me."

Ryder shook her head. "As much as I may have suggested that earlier, I don't actually believe it. Not from Jack. I can't believe that."

Hunter closed her eyes, tears still falling.

"Oh sis, please stop crying. If that is true, then he's totally not worth it." Ryder went back and lay down beside her sister, holding her. "Don't waste your tears on that asshole. We've got more important things to do now."

Hunter gave out a long, shuddering sigh. "Mom will be expecting us soon," she said.

"That's right. We've got to welcome Mom home. And figure out how we are going to help her."

Hunter put her arm across her eyes. "I can't even think about that now. What am I going to do? How can I even look at, or talk to Elspeth now?"

"Just because she's Jack's sister doesn't mean that she still isn't our friend. I'll bet she's just as pissed as I am about the whole thing, if she even knows about it."

"Ryder, I really can't face anyone right now."

Ryder looked at her older sister. Hunter had always been the strong one, the one who had carried their family when their mother had gone missing; the one who had been like a mother to Ryder when she was just a toddler. The fifteen-year age difference meant that Hunter was already a young woman by the time Ryder was born. Hunter had kept the family together while their father fell apart after their mother's disappearance twenty years ago. It had taken him years to find his way out of a deep grief and depression at the loss of his wife. Ryder had never seen her sister like this, so despondent. It was heartbreaking. Hunter's emotions and thoughts kept rolling over Ryder, who was sensitive and who could hear her sister's thoughts when they were in close proximity to each other. And she just couldn't bear this pain, this hurt.

A hurt shared certainly did not lessen the pain.

Ryder patted her sister's arm and leaned up on her elbow, looking down at Hunter. "Then don't. You've been the one who has carried others for so long now. You need time to heal, so you do that. I can take care of stuff for you."

"But I don't want anyone to know," said Hunter, her voice trailing off.

Ryder could feel waves of embarrassment from her sister. "Don't worry. And don't be embarrassed. When people find out, it's going to be Jack's problem, not yours. He's the one who's going to look like an idiot."

Her sister rolled over and away from Ryder, not wanting to talk further. Ryder stood up and looked out the window. "I'll make you some coffee and bring it upstairs. Don't you worry about anything today. We can wait until you are better. It will be okay, Hun."

Ryder went to the door and stopped, waiting to see if there would be a response. When there was none, she gently closed the door behind her and made her way downstairs.

Jack's broken up with Hunter, Ryder texted to Elspeth.
What???
Just as I said. He broke up with her last night.
I'll be right over. Should I bring Abigail?
Probably not just yet.

Ten minutes later there was a gentle knock at the door. Ryder answered, and Elspeth stood in the little thatched porch of the cottage, her face calm but her eyes flashing with anger. "May I come in?"

"Of course." Ryder opened the door wider to let the older woman in. She walked in and turned to look at Ryder, studying the young woman for a moment. She noted that Ryder was still dressed in the clothes that she had worn last night, and her long blonde hair was still messy from sleep.

"Tell me everything that happened," said Elspeth.

Ryder led her to the kitchen, where she had a pot of coffee on. She put the kettle on for some tea, knowing that it was the older woman's preference. Elspeth sat at the table, calmly waiting for an answer even as her eyes held the anger that was being restrained. As Ryder was spooning the loose-leaf tea into the pot, she said simply, "Jack dumped Hunter last night. I don't know why. He said that he had stuff to do, and needed space or some other crap like that."

Elspeth folded her hands on the table before her. Her long, greying hair was neatly done up in a half-twist, and she looked as polished and elegant as ever. But Ryder could feel the barely contained angry energy that brewed beneath the calm, elegant exterior. She couldn't hear Elspeth's thoughts or emotions like she could her sister, but she could feel the energy radiating off the older Witch.

"Does this have to do with the hedge riding ritual from last night?" asked Elspeth.

"I have no idea."

"Did Hunter use her powers in some way against Jack?"

Fury crossed over Ryder's usually cheerful features, and she slammed a hand down on the table. "No, my sister would *never* do that. What the hell would make you even think –"

"Ryder, my dear, I'm just trying to establish the situation. Please, sit down and let's talk through this calmly."

Ryder's studied the older woman for a moment, and once she had calmed down, she knew that Elspeth hadn't meant it as a slight. She was merely trying to get more information before she came to a conclusion. "Hunter told me that Jack had said that he needed some space, and that he couldn't be in a relationship right now. That is all my sister told me," Ryder said evenly.

Elspeth shook her head slowly. "Jack never said anything about it when he got back. He simply came in, said goodnight and Thomas drove him home."

"Probably too embarrassed by his own shitty behaviour."

"Indeed."

"I thought he loved Hunter."

Elspeth sighed. "I thought he did too. He had never seemed so happy as when he was with your sister. Something must have happened recently, something to change the situation."

Ryder snorted with contempt. "Yeah. He slept with her."

Elspeth looked at Ryder disapprovingly. "I don't think that is it. I know my brother, and he is not that sort of man."

"Well then, how do you explain it?"

Elspeth sighed. "Honestly? I can't right now. But I will figure it out. Leave this with me. Now, what I'd like to discuss is what *you* did yesterday evening. Specifically, how you threw that lightning bolt at Lanoc."

Ryder grinned. "Yeah, that was pretty cool, wasn't it?"

"It was impressive. Was that your own ritual knife?"

Ryder scrunched up her face as she thought. "Well, yes and no. We think it was Aunt's Ivy's knife. Hunter found it when she did a hedge riding to see if there was anything in the house that we could use in our ritual. She found a whole bunch of tools, including the broom that got Mom back from between the worlds."

"Hmmm. Interesting."

"Yeah. Hunter and I did a small ceremony to consecrate and attune the knife with my own energies. It rose up in the air and glowed pink. It was totally awesome."

"Yes, it seems like it certainly does want to work with you. But how did you summon that blast of energy?"

Ryder shrugged. "Beats the hell outta me. I was just really pissed off, you know? That guy comes in and starts throwing down magic and lightning bolts, and I guess I just snapped. I was drawing up energy from the earth anyway, for whatever really, and then I saw him point his staff at you. And I guess I just kind of lost it. I shouted and pointed the knife, and the energy just shot out."

Elspeth nodded slowly. "Interesting. Very interesting."

They heard the creaking of the little staircase that led to the upper rooms, and then Hunter came into the kitchen. Ryder looked up at her sister. "Hun, what are you doing up? I thought you were going to do some self-care today."

Hunter stopped dead in her tracks when she saw Elspeth. Tears immediately sprang up in her eyes as she saw the family resemblance to Jack. She took in a deep breath and pushed those feelings down, then turned away to pour herself a cup of coffee and collect herself in front of Elspeth. When she was certain her voice wouldn't tremble, she said, "Mom needs us right now."

"Hunter," said Elspeth, "I had no idea that Jack had ended his relationship with you last night. I don't know what is in my brother's head at the moment, but I will find out."

Hunter's shoulders tensed, but she forced them back down and turned around to sit at the table. "Do not bother. We have more important things to do right now."

Elspeth reached across the table and touched the back of Hunter's hand. "If you need time, my dear, we can give you that. We can take care of some things for you. It is no trouble at all. Abigail can stay with me until you are ready."

Hunter shook her head, her curls falling forward around her face. "No, it's fine. Really, it is. I'd rather get all this sorted sooner rather than later. Mom went missing for nearly twenty years, lost between the worlds. My birth father is still out there, somewhere. I'd felt like time was running out before we even found Mom, and now it feels like we are still on the clock. We need to find my father, if he is still alive."

"Whatever you want, my dear. We will support you."

Hunter's gaze fell upon the rose that Jack had given her two nights ago, which stood in a little vase with a note next to it that read: *Everything I do is for you*. She sniffed and steeled her gaze, looking back at Elspeth. "Mom needs us right now."

The sisters moved in together into Ryder's room. Hunter gave her mother the room that she had been using, assuming that it has been her mother's room many years ago when she was younger. *Or not younger, actually*, she thought. When their mother had returned after they had found her in a hedge riding ritual and freed her from her imprisonment between the worlds, she had not changed, had not aged at all since she had gone missing. She looked to be in her late-thirties, which was just a few years older than Hunter was now. It was strange, and not a little confusing to welcome back a mother who was roughly the same age as you were.

But strange was pretty normal here in the village of Burley. Known for its modern history of Witchcraft, deep beneath the layers of a kitsch and touristy area lay a legacy of Witchcraft that spanned for hundreds of years. There were very real, very powerful practitioners of the art here in Burley, and it was with their help that Hunter and Ryder had managed to locate and free their mother. With the aid of Elspeth who had tutored them ever since they arrived, the sisters had increased both their knowledge of their heritage, and their Craft. Living in the next property along the road, there was a connection between the two families that ran deeper than most, with family friendships and strong bonds. At the moment, Elspeth was housing their recently returned mother, Abigail, while the sisters got the cottage ready for her return.

Elspeth had let them borrow a travel cot and Hunter set that up in Ryder's room, leaving her sister the double bed. Ryder argued, but Hunter simply held up her hand and thought a very loud *No!* towards her sister. She saw her sister flinch, and Hunter immediately apologised. "I'm so sorry, Ry. I'm all over the place right now, emotionally."

Ryder shrugged it off, "Don't worry, it's cool. You're allowed to be bitchy right now. You have three days to wear out all your bitchiness before I call you out on it. Deal?"

Hunter gave her sister a small, half-smile. "Thanks, but I will try and keep it to myself."

You don't always have to carry everything and keep everything to yourself, you know, she heard her sister say in her mind as Ryder stood across the room, looking at her.

I know. But for now, allow me this coping mechanism.

You got it.

They set up the rooms and then went to fetch their mother from Elspeth's cottage. They took the car as they couldn't let anyone outside their small circle see their mother. She had to be kept hidden, her return kept a secret. If people found out that she had returned and hadn't aged in nearly twenty years, there would be even more questions than usual, as well as the immense risk posed to the magickal families and practitioners here in the New Forest. Whatever happened, they must protect the magickal community's secret, so that they could live a quiet and 'normal' life. They wrapped up Abigail in one of Elspeth's pashminas, covering her head and shoulders and then quickly bundled her into the car for the very short drive to the next cottage along the road. They then hastily ushered her into the house. Abigail took off her head covering and stood in the living room, drinking it all it with her eyes and a smile upon her face.

"I wasn't sure I was ever going to see this house again," she said, her voice wavering slightly.

"Welcome home," said Hunter, going up to her mother and putting her arms around her. Ryder came up the other side and gave her estranged mother a hug. "Welcome home," she repeated softly.

Tears fell down Abigail's cheeks as she hugged her daughters in her ancestral home. "Oh girls, it just doesn't feel the same without Ivy. I wish you could have met her. Elspeth told me last night that she had passed away."

The sisters pulled away from their mother and Hunter spoke. "Yes, Mom, last September. I'm so sorry. It must be such a shock." Hunter and Ryder had never met their aunt, and were beginning to learn more about her as they had inherited her cottage. Ivy had been a Witch, who ran the local coven for the legacy Witches in the area who wished to work together. As she got older she passed leadership of the coven over to Elspeth, who was the daughter of Ivy's best friend and whose magickal proficiency and steady manner made her an ideal candidate.

"It is such a shock. It's like I expect to see her sitting there, in her favourite chair by the fireplace."

"Aunt Ivy left the cottage and all its contents to both me and Ryder," said Hunter. "Of course, the house is yours, without question."

"Oh girls," their mother said, sitting down on the sofa and staring into the empty fireplace. "I can't live here anymore. Not after everything that has happened. I must find a new place to live. I talked to Elspeth about it earlier this morning. I can't go back to my old life, not now. That would expose the magickal community here in the New Forest, and that is not something that I can accept. Hopefully I will be able to find someplace far from here, where no one knows me. I cannot go back to Daniel in Canada, my loves. I assume that he has rebuilt his life without me by now."

Ryder sat down next to her mother. "Yes, he remarried around five years after you disappeared. A lovely woman named Dawn. She's really great, I love her."

Abigail looked at her daughter beside her and stroked her long, blonde hair. "I guess she was the mother to you that I couldn't be," she said softly. Ryder simply took her mother's hand in hers and gave it a small squeeze.

"So, what are we going to do to get my father back?" asked Hunter. It felt strange referring to someone she had never met as her 'father'.

"I don't really know," replied Abigail. "Last night I was just processing the fact that my sister has passed away. It all feels so strange to me. And so sad. I have missed her so much." Her mother's eyes once again filled up with tears, but she wiped them away quickly. Her face set with determination, she said, "I think we should have a long discussion with Elspeth about that before we make any decisions. This is something that requires her knowledge and experience. I have already made a huge mistake in my hedge riding, with not taking the proper precautions. I will not put myself in that situation ever again. Nor endanger you two."

"We know, Mom," said Ryder, a little awkwardly. She was used to calling her stepmother, Dawn, 'Mom' and now she had two 'Moms'. "We will be careful and plan all this out properly. We will need lots of time to prepare as well, no doubt. Hunter and I are still learning the Craft. We knew nothing about our magical heritage until we came here last month."

"I am so sorry that I never told you girls. That I never told *you*, Hunter, of your heritage. I felt that after what I had gone through with your birth father, I couldn't or didn't want to expose you to that world, for it only led to heartbreak and pain for me."

"Heartbreak and pain are in any world, Mom," said Hunter softly, looking away.

"Yes, I suppose you are right, my dear."

"Let's get you settled in, and then then maybe tomorrow we will have a conference with Elspeth to discuss our plans going forward," suggested Ryder. She pulled her mother up by the hand. "Come on, we've set up your old bedroom for you; at least we assume that it was yours. The last one on the right?"

"Yes, oh how wonderful, my girls. You are so beautiful, so grown up now, so strong. Words cannot describe how proud I am of you both."

"We know, Mom," said Ryder, leading her mother towards the steep little staircase. She cast a quick glance at Hunter, who remained downstairs, sitting on her chair and trying to repair her broken heart. "Tell me all about what it was like growing up here," Ryder said to her mother as they climbed the steps, leaving Hunter to her deal with her pain in the silence that she knew her sister preferred.

As Hunter sat in front of the empty fireplace, she went over and over again what had been said the night before, when Jack had left her. She still had trouble believing that it had actually happened. Had she done something to push him away? She went over everything from the last few days, and couldn't find any reason for his behaviour. So maybe, just maybe, it wasn't her. Maybe Jack was like all the other men she had ever been in a relationship with: once they got what they wanted, they turned elsewhere. Hunter felt a deep betrayal in her heart. She had deliberately waited before she had slept with Jack, and then shortly afterwards he dumped her. She had thought he was different. Special. He had made her feel like no one had ever done so before; he made her feel magickal, powerful, confident. He had always encouraged her to come into her own power. And then, just like that, he was out of her life.

Hunter deliberately turned her mind from thinking about Jack. Instead, there was a whole new revelation to consider which had changed her life forever. She had just found out that she was half Fae; that her father was one of the magickal beings from the Otherworld. What did that mean for her?

Hunter thought back to everything that she already knew about the Fae, from her folkloric studies. A lot of things resonated with her: the liminal times and places, that sense of otherworldliness, of feeling set apart and not quite fitting in with the people around her. She wondered what other effects her heritage had on her life.

So, faeries were real. Or the Fae, as Elspeth called them. Hunter had learned that her father was a Fae, and was the brother to some sort of tribal king, named Lanoc. It was Lanoc who had tried to harm them during the Midsummer ritual that they had performed, and it was Lanoc who was responsible for trapping both her father and her mother between the worlds. It was also Lanoc who had attacked Hunter, Ryder, and Jack in the forest, and who had tried to separate Hunter from her body just as he had done with her mother, Abigail. Lanoc held great power, and it was only through the work of Elspeth's coven who had aided them in the ritual, that they managed to fend him off and free Abigail from her imprisonment. Hunter had seen her mother beckon to another trapped soul nearby, trying to help him break free, but he was struck down by Lanoc before anything could be done. That trapped soul was Hunter's real father, Aedon. Which would make Lanoc her uncle. How could someone want to harm his own family so viciously and vehemently?

She was, by birth, half Fae. Just what did that mean? It kind of made sense to her, as she had never truly felt like she belonged to this world. She had always felt separate in one way or another. Things mattered to her that didn't matter to others. Liminal times and places were like home for her. She had always known that she was different from others, but now that difference was overwhelming. The reality of the magick of this place and its inhabitants was going to take a lot more getting used to than she thought. As well as her own magick and legacy.

For a long time, Hunter simply sat in front of the empty fireplace.

Chapter Two

Late in the afternoon Hunter roused herself from her musings and went upstairs to tell her mother that tea would be ready shortly. She was still getting used to calling supper 'tea', but she went with it anyway. She knocked on her mother's door; however, there was no answer. Knocking again, she put her ear to the door to see if she could hear anything. There was only silence. She opened the door slightly and peered inside.

Her mother sat at the little window seat, looking out over the back garden and the forest behind it. "Mom? Tea is almost ready."

Her mother's gaze never turned, and her body was still. "Mom? Mom, can you hear me?" Still there was no response. Hunter went up to her mother and took her gently by the hand. "Mom? Mom, please, you're starting to scare me."

Abigail's eyelashes fluttered, and then she took a deep breath and turned towards Hunter. "Hunter, my lovely, what are you doing here? I didn't hear you come in."

Hunter had a million questions at that moment, the first was wondering if it was possible to be asleep with your eyes open. She presumed it might be, but concluded that it was much more likely her mother had been hedge riding. She smiled at her mother, pretending nothing was wrong. "You must have dozed off. It must be so overwhelming for you, being back."

Her mother smiled, and patted Hunter's hand. "It is, and it isn't. Sometimes I feel the weight of the years that have passed, and other times I feel like no time has passed at all. It's all very peculiar."

"Well, you've got to eat at any rate, so come down with me. Ryder and I are going to do a little food shopping for you afterwards."

"Thank you, Poppet."

Hunter's heart warmed to hear her mother call her 'Poppet'. No one had called her that for decades, as it was her mother's special nickname for her. She stood and pulled her mother up by her hand, and they went downstairs to eat at the kitchen table.

"Girls, this is so lovely. Thank you both so much." Abigail tucked into her little sandwiches and cake with relish. "I'd almost forgotten what food tasted like while I was trapped between the worlds. There is nothing more grounding, more earthy than eating. Well, eating and sex," she said with a naughty smile.

Ryder laughed, while Hunter quickly stood up and went to the fridge for another drink. As she leaned in to grab a can of soda, she took a deep breath and willed herself not to cry. She straightened and squared her shoulders, closing the fridge door and wiping top of the can with her shirt. She popped the lid and took a long drink, still with her back to the table as she pulled herself together.

Ryder immediately caught on to Hunter's emotions and thoughts, and diverted her mother's attention away from Hunter. "So, Mom, what are your favourite foods? We can go and pick them up tonight from the shop, if they've got them."

Abigail smiled. "Well, do you know, what I craved the most while I was trapped was a Cadbury Flake, and a Curly Wurly."

"A what and a what?"

Her mother laughed. It was something that Hunter had missed for nearly twenty years. At that sound Hunter's heart eased, and she turned around to look at them. "Chocolate, my darling. Those were the two chocolates that I loved the most as a child here, and which I could never get in Canada. I would love to have some of those again."

"Not a problem," said Ryder with a grin.

Hunter looked over at her sister. *Ryder, can you offer to stay here with Mom? I'm a little worried about her*, she thought.

She heard her sister's reply in her mind. *Yeah, sure. What's up?*

I'm not sure, but I think Mom was hedge riding earlier. She may not even be aware that she was doing it.

No way. Okay, yeah, I'll stay and keep an eye on her. See if you can have a quick word with Elspeth too before you come back.

Okay. "Alright Mom," said Hunter. "We'll pick those up for you."

Ryder spoke up. "Actually, would it be okay if I stayed at home with Mom? There's so much I want to ask her, to talk to her about." Hunter gave her sister a slight nod.

"Yeah, sure, that's no problem," replied Hunter. "You two have to get to know each other; there's a lot of missed time there. It's no trouble at all."

"Come, my dear," said Abigail, standing up and taking their plates. "You can help me with the dishes while your sister is out, and then we can have a proper girly chat."

"Sounds good to me," said Ryder, genuinely pleased to be able to spend some time with her mother.

"Right, I'll be off now. See you both soon," said Hunter as she picked up her bag and keys from the sideboard and headed towards the door. *Don't let Mom out of your sight until I get back.*

What if she needs the bathroom?

The loo, you mean?
Yeah, whatever.
You'll manage.

Hunter closed the cottage door and walked out towards the car. Her car. Her little yellow Beetle, that Jack had chosen for her. She pushed past the lump in her throat and opened the car door. *Not now*, she thought. *I have things to do, people to take care of. I cannot let myself fall apart every time I am reminded of him. There is work to be done.* She steeled herself and sat down, pulling the door shut. She got out her phone and texted Elspeth.

Are you home? There something that I need to talk to you about, regarding Mom. Something important.
I'm at the shop, just closing up.
I'm on my way into the village now, shall I meet you there?
I'll put the kettle on.

Hunter parked in the main car park for the village, and walked the short distance to Elspeth's shop, The Covenstead. It was one of three witchy shops in the little village of Burley, and it was the best of all three. Here in the New Forest, Burley had gained notoriety in the 1950's from the witch, Sybil Leek, who had lived here alongside her familiar, a jackdaw named Mr Jackson Hotfoot. The media loved it, and the ensuing chaos proved too much for the little village of Burley, which began to suffer because of her fame. The non-magickal community began to turn against her, wanting their peace and quiet returned, whilst those from magickal families in the area urged her towards more caution and discretion. Sybil wanted none of that, but was forced to leave when her landlord evicted her. And so she went to America, where she could be as open and flamboyant with the press as she liked. The little village gave a sigh of relief as the media circus ended, and the magickal community's secret was kept. For magick was real, and Burley in the New Forest was a very special, liminal place where myth and legend were a part of everyday life. Families of Witches had lived there for hundreds of years, and they knew the importance of watching their backs even as they watched over the community.

There were five magickal families that lived in Burley, and had lived there for generations. Hunter and her sister came from the Appleton line. Then there were the Caldecottes, which included Elspeth, her daughter, Rowan, and Jack. There were also the Sandfords, and the Inghams. The sisters knew of one of the Inghams, who worked with Elspeth's own coven. His name was Thomas, and he was currently working as their Guardian. And then there were the Hardwicks, who were rich, powerful, and according to everyone asked, just not very nice to anyone, believing themselves to be superior in both the magickal and non-magickal community.

Newer Witches had moved into the village in the last hundred years, and so new covens established themselves amongst the older five families. One of these covens, the New Forest Coven, had links to the famous, or infamous depending upon whom you asked, Gerald Gardner: popularly known as the Father of Modern Witchcraft. He claimed to have studied with the New Forest Coven, a group of occultists many of whom had Masonic and Rosicrucian backgrounds and who began to work in the area at the start of the 20th century. Gerald Gardner then went public in the mid-century after the repeal of the Witchcraft Laws in England, and made elements of the Craft known to all who had an ear to listen, much to the annoyance of the five established magickal families, as well as the New Forest Coven itself. Then later in the 1990's an even newer coven established themselves: Brightstar Coven, a Gardnerian coven with a lineage from the man himself. The older families had very little to do with the newer covens, not wanting them to know the true power that resided within the little community, nor have others become aware of the work that they did in the area. They enjoyed their anonymity, and their quiet lives. The Witches of the New Forest were a secret to be kept safe for all concerned, a secret that was kept close.

Burley was a village surrounded by the New Forest, a mix of heathland and woodland areas. These lands contained lots of flora and fauna, as well as magickal beings of all kinds. Burley was a liminal place, where the veil between the worlds was thin, especially between the times of Beltane and Midsummer, as well as at Samhain, popularly known as Hallowe'en. Myths and legends of all manner of creatures were intertwined with the little village and the surrounding countryside, but were seen as just that: collected bits of interesting and amusing folklore, and nothing more. But those of true, magickal blood knew differently.

Hunter considered the little village and its secrets, all hidden beneath a veneer of modern witchy tourism. It was now the twenty-second of June, and tourist season had just begun. The village was much busier than usual during the day, and the sisters were told that this would continue through to November. New Forest ponies roamed freely throughout the village, much to the delight of visitors. All kinds of horses, pigs and cattle still had the right to roam on the common land around the area, which included Burley. That, as much as Witchcraft, was a huge draw for the village.

Elspeth ran the biggest and most authentic of the three Witchcraft shops, refusing to sell mass-produced items and 'tat' as she called it, imported from the Far East. Instead, her shop was a place that contained hand-made items including herbal teas, incense, and all manner of magickal paraphernalia. She had a large apothecary section with its own counter, as well as a book section of both modern and used books, some of which were hard to find in ordinary bookstores or online. She worked with local craftspeople to stock hand-crafted tools of all kinds for all magickal traditions. And Elspeth herself reflected her beautiful business: calm, elegant and knowledgeable.

Hunter opened the door and entered. The shop smelled wonderful, with strange scents from the apothecary blending with the smoke of the incense that was burning in a tiny iron cauldron near the till. Elspeth stood behind it, counting down the drawer. "Turn the sign over, will you my dear?" she asked without looking up.

Hunter turned the shop sign over to 'Closed' and locked the door. She wandered around for a few moments, not wanting to distract Elspeth. Finally, the older woman shut the till drawer and gave a large sigh. "Hello, my dear. Fancy some tea?"

"Yes, please," said Hunter. Elspeth waved her to follow, and they went into the back room which held a small kitchenette. Elspeth poured some tea from a large teapot into two proper teacups with saucers; no mugs in this space, she had often said to the sisters. Elspeth was adamant that tea should always be served in china cups, to get the full flavour. Today, Elspeth was wearing a dark grey boho style dress, with long balloon sleeves and a full skirt. She had a light grey silk scarf around her neck, and her long dark hair streaked with grey was done up in a French plait. A large ginger cat jumped up on one of the available chairs. "Hello, Mr Tom Greediguts," said Hunter, giving him a pat. The cat leaned into her palm, and then sat back and winked at her.

Elspeth sat down across from Hunter. "So, my dear, what did you want to talk to me about regarding Abigail?"

Hunter took a sip from her cup, savouring the herbal blend of mugwort and catmint. She sat back and sighed, looking at the older Witch. "I think I caught Mom hedge riding."

Elspeth shook her head. "Damn. I noticed that she kind of drifted off at breakfast this morning, but I just assumed it was because she was tired. We've all been through a lot."

Hunter looked down at her teacup. "She was sitting on the window seat upstairs in her room, looking out over the back garden and the forest. Her eyes were open, and she was completely still. I called out to her, but she didn't respond. It was only when I took her by the hand and called to her again that she came around. She thought she had fallen asleep, but I don't think people sleep with their eyes open."

"Some do," said Elspeth with raised eyebrows, "but it is very rare. No, it is far more likely that your mother was hedge riding. Remember what I told you during your training? You shouldn't hedge ride more than two times a week, because the link between your body and your spirit can weaken the longer they are separated from each other. And Abigail's spirit has been separated from her body for nearly twenty years. No, this is not a good thing. We must do something about it."

Hunter swallowed down her fear. She had just found her mother, and now something was very wrong. "What – what can we do about it?"

"I will have to think on that. This is a very unique situation, and not something that I have dealt with before." Elspeth took a sip of her tea, considering her options. "Perhaps we should treat it like an addiction, and try to ease her from it gently. Provide her with distractions as well, to keep her occupied and grounded. Get her to perform groundings throughout the day."

Hunter half-smiled as she remembered what her mother said that morning. "Mom says food and sex are the best things for grounding."

Elspeth's lips curled up slightly. "Yes indeed, they are."

"Well, I'm off to get some food after this, so we will be stocked up with plenty of goodies for her."

"I'll pop by on my way home, and have a chat with Abigail before I drop off Rowan back at university, in Portsmouth. We will figure this out." Elspeth looked at Hunter, and then took her hand. "I'm sorry, but I haven't heard from Jack at all. He is not responding to my messages. But I will keep trying."

Hunter looked away, pushing down her sadness. "It's his choice," she said. "Right now, I've got other things to focus on."

As Hunter pulled into the driveway, she saw Elspeth's car outside the cottage. She picked up the two bags of groceries from the boot and carried them into the thatched cottage. "I'm home!"

Ryder came out of the kitchen and took one of the bags. "Elspeth is here, talking to Mom."

"Good." The sisters went into the kitchen. They unpacked while listening to the conversation between Abigail and Elspeth.

"I can't remember hedge riding at all today. It is just so strange. But you say it has happened twice now?"

"Three times," interrupted Ryder. Everyone turned to look at her. She cleared her throat and looked down. "Um, sorry Mom, but when you were looking at the photo album downstairs with me about an hour ago, you kind of drifted off. I had to shake you quite hard to bring you back."

"Oh," said Abigail, bringing a hand to her heart. "I'm so sorry, I thought I was just lost in a memory, a little 'away with the faeries' as they say."

Elspeth's eyes narrowed. "That may indeed have been the case, Abigail. Remember, you are very much involved with the Fae around here. The saying 'away with the faeries' stems from a much older knowledge of the dangers of traversing into their realms. And some of the Fae would very much want you separated from your body so that they can trap you once again between the worlds. Or worse."

Abigail's eyes widened. "I hadn't even thought of that. I was just so happy to be back, to be home. I thought everything was going to be okay. And now I am dealing with my sister's passing. It's all a bit overwhelming. Being here, in Ivy's house, without her. I haven't even thought about the Fae, really. I hadn't even considered that I would still be a target for them, not while I was in this world, at least."

"Well, you are, my dear, and we are going to have to deal with it immediately."

Hunter turned and fished out two chocolate bars from the bags. She had heard last night of what Elspeth and the others had to contend with during her hedge riding ritual. "Here, Mom, you said these were your favourites. Chocolate helps most things." She didn't want her mother to feel guilty about her condition and situation, and so she pushed the sweets towards her.

"Oh, wonderful, Poppet! She peeled back the wrapper from a Curly Wurly and took a bite, savouring it. "Delicious."

"What's in it?" asked Ryder, leaning over to look. "Oh, it's chocolate covered taffy."

"That gives me an idea," said Elspeth, a finger to her lips as she contemplated.

Witches of the New Forest

"You want to cover Mom in chocolate?"

Elspeth shot Ryder a withering glance before saying, "We can use something she loves to anchor her here, to bring her back should she go wandering."

"So, like, we need to have candy bars on hand at all times?"

"No, my dear, let me explain. We find something that will act as a trigger for your mother to come back from any involuntary hedge riding that she does. We can instil a trigger word in her mind which, when used, can bring your mother back quickly. Something that in her mind differentiates this world from the Otherworld."

"Like a self-hypnosis kind of thing?"

"Yes, something like that. Abigail, what do you think?"

"I think we need to try it."

"Excellent. Come with me into the living room. Girls, can you please set up a circle for us?" The sisters nodded, and got to work.

Once the ritual was over, Elspeth and Abigail came into the kitchen where the sisters sat, giving their mother and friend some privacy while they worked together. Elspeth had done some training in hypnotherapy, and so she took charge of the ritual and led Abigail through it. When the women returned to the kitchen and sat down, they smiled at each other.

"I think it will work," said Abigail hopefully.

"Only time will tell, but I too am hopeful," replied Elspeth.

"So, do we have a trigger word that we can use to bring Mom back?" asked Hunter.

"Yes, yes we do indeed," said Elspeth with a little smile.

"What's the word?" asked Hunter.

"Curly Wurly."

Chapter Three

The sisters and Abigail spent the next two weeks getting to know each other again. They talked about many things, including what had happened in the family since Abigail's disappearance and how the world had changed in the last twenty years. They also began discussing how they were going to proceed in the near future with finding Hunter's father.

Abigail and Hunter also worked in the gardens, planting up and restoring them to their previous splendour. Abigail worked in the back gardens so that she wouldn't be seen, while Hunter focused on the front roadside aspect. They discovered that when Abigail was working with the plants, her hands dirty from the soil, she was much less apt to drift off into hedge riding mode. They surmised that the gardening had a grounding effect on her, and so she spent most of her time in the garden, working.

The flowers and plants brought new life to the cottage, and Hunter often simply stood and looked at the beautiful cottage, wondering what she was going to do with her life. She loved this place dearly, perhaps even more than her home in Canada. Would she stay, what with all the magickal threats and dangers? Not to mention Jack. Could she stay, and casually come across him on a regular basis, in the village or on the heath? What if he was seeing someone else? That thought crushed her the most, and she pushed it down day after day, focusing on the cottage gardens when she wasn't studying. She avoided working in the vegetable patch, however, where she and Jack had worked together one morning. The memories that it brought back were just too painful.

Abigail and Elspeth decided that more training was required for both Hunter and Ryder. Abigail showed them the tools that she and her sister had used in their work, and with Elspeth's aid the sisters worked hard to learn how they could better protect themselves from Lanoc as well as to prepare them for Aedon's rescue. It was Ryder's first time learning from her birth mother, and it was a special time for the both of them. Aunt Ivy's cottage was filled with magickal paraphernalia, even more than Hunter had found when she had looked for such items before. It was a huge learning curve for both the sisters, but they dove into their studies headlong. Ryder learned more about the ritual knife that she had inherited, which Abigail informed them was used by their aunt to direct energy in rituals. Ryder tried a few attempts in the back garden to recreate what she had done on the heath, but to no avail. She just shrugged and brushed it off, as both she and her sister were still learning. For Hunter, the studying was a welcome distraction.

They also decided that they needed to learn more about the Fae. Hunter knew a little about them from her folkloric studies, but there was a wealth of information that she needed to familiarise herself with before she even thought about entering into their realm to help her mother find her father. She did online searches and spent hours in the local libraries.

They had also discussed whether Abigail should even go with Hunter on this quest, but it quickly became clear that Hunter would have a much more difficult time finding her father without her mother's aid. Abigail was still on strict instructions to avoid hedge riding at all times, but sometimes she 'wandered' with no warning. The sisters managed to call her back quickly using the trigger words each time. And so, they began to learn how to work both in a magical and in a mundane capacity as a family unit. The sisters kept to their studies while the hot summer sun beat down upon the surrounding forest and heathland, and Abigail learned how to surf the internet (with many, many warnings and strict 'parental' controls put in place first).

Hunter watched as Jack's rose in the little vase began to droop after a week, the edges of the petals going brown. She didn't know why, but she took the rose and hung in upside down in the airing cupboard upstairs, so that it would dry. She wanted to preserve the rose, even though it pained her terribly. She also kept the little note that came with it, that said, *'Everything I do is for you'*. She still couldn't get her head around the message. Why would he break up with her for *her* sake? It just didn't make any sense. The pain that he was causing her was most definitely not for her benefit. At times she felt a rage rising within her. She wanted to rip apart the rose and the note, and then stomp them into the ground, grinding them beneath her heel. At other times the rose reminded her of the special, magickal moments that she and Jack had shared, and which she knew she would never forget. After the rose had dried out she took it, and the note, and placed them in an empty shoebox in the closet of the room that she now shared with her sister.

Elspeth had told her that she still hadn't had any contact with Jack. She had even tried to go over to his cottage several times in the evenings, but there was no one there. She had called the ranger station, to see if Jack was still working. They confirmed that he was. Elspeth tried to contact Dougal, but discovered he was away in Scotland with his brother, and so couldn't offer her any advice until he got back.

Ryder had been out most evenings, sometimes even doing double shifts at the pub as the tourists poured into the village.

Hunter stayed with her mother at these times, both to prevent her from slipping into hedge riding and also to study and learn from a real-life Hedge Witch. When Ryder was particularly late coming home, she would sleep on the sofa downstairs so as not to wake her sister. They were all getting on as best they could with this new way of life.

One morning Hunter and her mother were outside, drinking their coffee in the shade while taking a break from gardening. Hunter turned to her mother, and asked, "What is the Otherworld like?"

"Oh, it's a marvellous place, Poppet. You can meet all manner of beings there. It's very much like our world, and yet different. The light, the colours; there is a slight difference to it that is more magical, more ethereal." Hunter reached out and held onto her mother's hand as she talked about the Otherworld, and gave it a squeeze every now and then to remind her mother to stay in this world even as she spoke. "The Fae are utterly enchanting, though rather standoffish. The few I had come across after I had met your father wanted nothing to do with me. They looked down their noses at me and treated me like I was some sort of strange animal in their midst. Before I had been a novelty to them, someone that they were kind of interested in, I guess. I even traded stories and songs with a few of them. But after your father and I fell in love, the attitude shifted rather quickly."

"I wonder why that is?" asked Hunter. "Surely they would have seen how much you loved each other." *Even if, perhaps, you loved him more than he loved you. Men can be deceiving,* she thought to herself.

"What was in our hearts mattered little to them. Though some of the Fae had been known to have a dalliance or two with a human, I have no idea how love works in the Fae realm, in all honesty. All I know is that your father and I wanted to be together, forever."

"Did you want to live in the Otherworld?"

"This world, the Otherworld, it would make no difference as long as we could be together. That is what your father said. But it was his family that caused us so many problems. It became harder and harder for us to meet. And then one day he never came to me. And so I went searching for him, tired of waiting to see if he would come to me. I would have been happy to live with him in either world, you see. But when I went to the Otherworld to find him, well, that's when it happened."

"That's when his brother, my uncle, trapped you between the worlds."

"Yes. And also trapped your father. I couldn't believe it; I had finally found Aedon! But Lanoc was there, waiting for us. He had planned the entire thing. He magicked us away somehow into separate realms. We were both trapped, unable to see each other or be together. But we managed to find a way. For a brief period of time we could at least see each other between the time of Beltane and Midsummer. When the sun set during that liminal time, we could see each other from across the barrows, neither dead for alive, but existing between the two. Also at Samhain, because these are the times when the veil between the worlds is thin."

Hunter's stomach gave a slight lurch. *Neither dead nor alive, but existing between the two.* These were the words that had popped into her mind when she had done her first hedge riding, at the very spot where her mother had been all those years ago when her mother had ridden the hedge, and had been separated from her body. Her mother had told her that the yew tree was her favourite spot to ride the hedge, and that was the place where her body had lain when her soul became trapped. Abigail's body had been taken in by some Fae and kept safe, and later brought back when Abigail's spirit had been found by Hunter in a hedge riding ritual.

"But some Fae *were* on your side, it seems, as someone kept your body safe," said Hunter.

Her mother blinked. "Yes. Yes, I suppose you are right. I had almost forgotten how I had come back, in that regard. Elspeth's coven said that three Fae had appeared and brought my body back at the end of the ritual."

"Perhaps we need to try and contact those Fae, to see if they can help us again," said Hunter.

Abigail tapped a finger to her lips, something she had always done when she was thinking. That small gesture from her childhood made Hunter smile. "Yes, that is indeed a possibility, Poppet."

The two looked at each other, and then said at the same time, "We need to talk to Elspeth."

A week later Elspeth accepted their invitation to come round for tea. She had been exceptionally busy with electrical and plumbing repairs to her store, and so came at the earliest opportunity. She rolled her eyes as she told them of the woes of working in a Grade 2 listed building. Things which they would find out first hand, when they needed repairs on the cottage themselves. Later, when the sisters began clearing away the plates, Abigail leaned towards Elspeth and touched her hand. "Ellie, there is something that I need to ask you; a favour, if you will."

The older Witch looked at her for a moment, studying her face for two long breaths before saying, "You may ask."

Abigail blinked, uncertain at the tone in the older woman's voice. But she gathered her courage and asked, "Can you contact those of the Fae who returned my body?"

She saw a flicker of something pass across Elspeth's features, before she picked up her cup of tea and took a sip. "I'm afraid that is not very likely," she said, putting the cup down carefully.

"Why?"

The two sisters in the kitchen were paying close attention while seemingly not to, and looked at each other as they stood by the sink. Ryder raised an eyebrow, and Hunter merely gave her a small shrug in reply. Elspeth had always been eager to help them before.

"Abigail, dealing with the Fae always, *always* has its consequences. Now, I don't know why they kept your body safe, nor why they returned it to us when we needed it. I am very grateful for their intervention on your behalf, but to seek them out and ask more of them would be dangerous. Not only because it might alert those who could be actively seeking you out to destroy you, but also because the Fae are simply unfathomable. You never know where you stand with them. Just like in this world, there are those who are beneficent, and those who would wish us harm. The Fae all have their own agendas, and we all may simply be pawns in one of their many games. I for one have no wish to seek them out and expose myself to their whims and fancies. It is just too dangerous."

"But there are those who are good and trustworthy on the Other Side as well, Ellie," said Abigail earnestly. "Aedon was one of them. I can't believe that he is the only one."

Elspeth sighed. "I'm sure he was, my dear, but you said yourself that the other Fae you met turned against you. Did you have any other ally in the Otherworld, apart from Aedon?

"From the Fae? No. But I did have my familiars."

At this the two sisters turned around, left the kitchen, and sat right back down at the table. "Tell us more, Mom," said Ryder eagerly.

"I had two familiars: one a fox, and the other a small, wizened old man only a foot high. I guess you would call him a pixie, of sorts. I met him at the Puckpits Inclosure."

"How long have you known this piskie?"

Ryder interjected. "I thought she said he was a pixie."

"Same thing," said Elspeth, Hunter, and Abigail at the same time.

Abigail leaned back in her chair, and thought for a moment. "I think I first met him when I was around thirteen years old. He was a nice old fellow, and later he began appearing in other places in the forest too. He told me to call him 'Puck'. But after a few years I didn't really see him again. I guess as I got older, we just were on different paths, literally and figuratively. But he always had some wise words for me at the time, when I needed them the most."

"And what about the fox?" asked Ryder.

"The fox, well, he was a handsome fellow. Soft, orange fur and a big bushy tail. He came right up to me one day, sat down and began to talk to me. I thought I had finally lost the plot. He didn't speak with words, but I understood his thoughts in my mind. He told me secrets of the forest, such as where to find the liminal places. I used that knowledge when I was older and became proficient in hedge riding. As with Puck the pixie, when I grew older I saw him less and less, until he was just a flash in the evening's light darting in the undergrowth every now and then. But I knew he was still there, watching me, I suppose. But I guess he is long gone now."

"Was it a real fox? Or a creature from the Otherworld?" asked Hunter.

Abigail shook her head. "I was never really sure."

Elspeth sat up straight and smoothed out her long skirt. "Whatever they were, you might be able to reach them again, but I would advise against it. You are being sought out, Abigail, by a very powerful foe. Lanoc could have caused us all very serious harm during the ritual we performed to help Hunter get you back. I would not want to expose the girls to that again."

Hunter and Ryder looked at each other, and then faced the Witch. "Don't you think that should be *our* choice?" asked Hunter softly.

Elspeth studied her for a moment. "It is always your choice, my dear," she said evenly.

"There is nothing to say that even if my familiars are still around, that they would be able to help us find Aedon," interjected Abigail, wanting to keep the peace. "They were more like childhood friends than Otherworldly aides. As I got older I simply did the work myself, without anyone else's help."

Elspeth turned to Abigail. "You found Aedon by yourself that first time, and every other time until his brother spirited him away. I'm sure that you will be able to do so again, without the aid of anyone but Hunter here. It is the safest route, in my opinion. Contact with those from the Otherworld is just too risky."

Abigail sighed. "You are probably right, Ellie. We must be careful in how we work this out."

Elspeth nodded. "I have some more books, and can share articles and essays on Fae lore with you. Some of it is academic work, some of it has been passed down through the magickal families."

"What, really?" asked Ryder. "Which families?"

Elspeth poured herself another cup of tea from the teapot. "The Caldecottes and the Sandfords have retained some Fae lore and passed it down through the generations. I believe the Sandfords have an oral tradition of local Fae lore, and I have a couple of manuscripts dating back to the 17th and 18th century."

Hunter's heart began to beat a little faster. As a history professor, she itched to take a look at these documents. "Please may I see them?"

Elspeth nodded. "Yes you may, though I'm not sure how much information they will provide."

"We should also ask Harriet over and pick her brain on some stuff," said Ryder. "I can give her a call now."

"Sounds like a plan," said Hunter. "Mom, what do you think?"

"I think it all sounds marvellous," said Abigail with a smile.

Ryder called Harriet, who entreated the sisters to go out for a drink with her. She said she needed to blow off some steam, and so the sisters went down to the pub with her. Hunter prayed that she wouldn't see Jack, as she didn't think that she could deal with that right now. Elspeth stayed to watch over Abigail and catch her up on the goings on of the magickal families in the village. "You have a nice time, girls," she said.

Abigail gave them a hug each. "I wish I could join you. How I'd love to be at the pub again," she said with a sigh. "It's been so long since I've had a proper pint. The beers in Canada were just not the same."

"We'll get some nice beers for you tomorrow, Mom, when the shop re-opens," said Hunter, giving her mother a kiss on the cheek. She grabbed her keys and went out the door with Ryder in tow.

"Man, I need this too," said Ryder. "Although on my one night off this week, I'm going to the frigging pub where I work. Ah well, I guess there are bigger problems in the world."

"Mm hmm," said Hunter as she got into the car. Her mind was completely elsewhere, trying to prepare for how she would react if she saw Jack there.

"Jack hasn't been at the pub since the break-up," said Ryder.

"What did I say about staying out of my head?"

"Can't help it when you shout your thoughts and feelings to the world, you know."

"I've *got* to talk to Elspeth and get a grip on this. I just hope no one else can hear them."

Ryder shrugged. "I don't think so. No one has said anything, so far."

Hunter just sighed and started the car, pulled out of the driveway, and drove carefully down the road that ran across the heath and into the village. It was a quiet night in Burley, for which she was thankful. They parked up and walked into the pub, spying Harriet immediately at the bar with a gin and tonic in her hand. "Hey ladies! Nice to see you, Hunter."

Hunter smiled at the young woman. Harriet was a couple of years older than Ryder, with short dark hair and beautiful curves. She was dressed casually, as they all were, in jeans and a t-shirt. She had lived here all her life, and looked so comfortable as she stood leaning against the bar. Hunter wished that she could find a place like this to call home, but after the Jack fiasco she had no idea if she even wanted to stay here come September. Before he had broken up with her, she had been contemplating staying on and living at the cottage, and perhaps even seeing if she could get a job at the university in Portsmouth. But now? Just the thought of him made her stomach drop and a well of sadness fill her heart.

Easy sis, she heard her sister say in her mind. *We aren't making any long-term plans yet. Just enjoy right now. Live for the moment.*

Hunter blew out a long breath. *Okay.*

Harriet looked at them quizzically. "Something going on over there?" she said, gesturing with her drink at the sisters.

"Just some sisterly chat," Ryder said quietly as she sidled up the bar. Harriet raised her eyebrows but said nothing. "I'll have what she's having," Ryder called out to Jenny, the bartender. "Hunter?"

"Just a lime and soda, please."

After they had been served their drinks, they went to sit at a little table in the corner. "So," said Harriet, looking at Hunter. "How are you holding up?"

Hunter looked down at her drink. "Not very well. I guess Ryder told you," she said softly.

Harriet studied her for a moment. Her gaze was directed just over Hunter's head, and her eyes became unfocused. She held that gaze for a few breaths, before taking in a deep breath and returning to look Hunter in the eyes. "Yeah, your energy is a mess. It's all over the place, with holes everywhere."

"Holes?" asked Ryder.

"Yeah, holes. Big gaping ones, around the heart and head. I've seen it before. Psychic wounds, we call it in my family. I never would have believed Jack would do such a thing."

"You think Jack did this to her?" asked Ryder

"Well, no, not per se. But the result of his actions has caused Hunter to lose parts of herself and leave her open and vulnerable, as well as a bit scattered and emotional. Does that make any sense?"

Hunter stared at Harriet. She had nailed it right on the head. "You can see how I feel?" she said.

Harriet nodded as she took another sip of her drink. "We Sandfords are a type of energy worker, remember? When I first met you, I read your auras."

"Yeah, I remember," said Ryder. "Mine was yellow, with orange around my head, and Hunter's was golden, but shifting around all the time."

"Yes, and there weren't big holes or discrepancies; just healthy, fairly happy if somewhat mysterious auras, at least in your case, Hunter. But knowing your heritage now, it makes sense. But it seems that this Jack situation has really done a number on you. It may even have opened up old wounds that you've already dealt with for the most part. I'm so sorry." Harriet reached out to take Hunter's hand. "I can help patch up the worst holes for you now, so that you are better able to cope and heal yourself, if you'd like."

Hunter blinked. "You – you can do that?"

"Yup."

"How?"

"By using some of my energy to help yours flow better, and to provide some temporary fixes, like psychic bandages, if you will, until you can 'regrow' those parts more strongly yourself. It's a simple process, and should only take about fifteen to twenty minutes."

"That's incredible!" said Ryder.

Harriet shook her head. "No, it's pretty normal for those in my family," she grinned.

"Where should we do it?"

Hunter held up her hand. "Hang on, Ryder, I haven't agreed to it yet."

"What's not to like? Harriet can help. Take it. You've always sucked at both asking, and taking help, you know."

Hunter studied her sister for a moment. What Ryder had said was completely true. Hunter saw herself as kind of a lone spirit: self-sufficient and capable. But this situation was all just a bit too much for her to handle right now. She needed to receive help if she was to be able to offer help her mother. She also had choices to make regarding a life here, or in Canada. It was just too overwhelming to do it all in her broken state. "Okay. Where should we go?"

"Let's just finish our drinks, and then we can go to my place. It's only five minutes from here."

The ladies stayed for one more round, Harriet telling them about the crazy day at Lymington that she had at the market with her refill van. "I tell you, I can't wait until the First Harvest Dance at the end of next week."

"First Harvest dance?" asked Ryder. "What's that?"

"Just before the first crops are taken in, the local community celebrates with a First Harvest dance. The wheat, rye and oats are doing well this year, especially the heritage wheat and rye. We always have a dance at the Village Hall to celebrate the beginning of the first harvest. It also raises money for charity."

"That is so awesome. What kind of dance is it? Like a ball?"

Harriet laughed. "No, not this one. This is country dancing; folk dancing some people call it. Kind of like a Scottish cèilidh, if you've ever heard of those before."

Ryder furrowed her brow. "Is that where they have callers telling people what to do, in big group dances? Kind of like square dancing?"

Harriet nodded. "Yup. There's a band and a caller, and they tell you what the dances will be and call out directions for those who aren't familiar with the dances. It's a hell of a lot of fun."

"I'm so up for that," said Ryder, looking at her sister.

Hunter looked at the two women with her, who both seemed so excited about this event. "I – I'm not sure I'll be going," she said softly.

"Why?" asked Ryder. "Because of Jack? Who knows if he'll even be there. Come on Hun, you've got to live your life your way."

"I – I'll think about it."

They finished up their drinks and left the pub. Harriet showed them to her apartment, just on the edge of the main row of the village shops. She had a small loft above the ice cream parlour. "It's nice in the summer, because they keep it cool down there, obviously. And in the winter when it's closed, it's nice and quiet here." She walked them up the stairs to the apartment, and showed them in. It was a one-bedroom place with character: some oak beams in the ceiling, and white plaster walls. It was minimal and uncluttered, and seemed bright and airy even though it was a small space, with small windows. Hunter commented on that fact, and Harriet smiled at her.

"An energy worker's home is usually kept pretty clean, physically and energy-wise," she said, motioning the two sisters to take a seat on a two-seater sofa. She plopped down onto a beanbag chair. "That's why it feels light and airy. I do a daily cleanse, both of the space and myself, especially after interacting with so many people in my line of work. Can I get you anything to eat or drink?"

The sisters waved away her offer. Ryder leaned forwards and asked eagerly, "So, what can you do for Hunter? How do you do it? Can I learn that stuff too?"

Harriet laughed. "Easy, tiger! So, what I can do for Hunter is to cleanse her aura energetically. I do that by separating what is her own energy from energy that is 'stuck' on her, for lack of a better word. Sometimes other people's energy clings to a person and needs to be shifted so that you can be yourself again. I take the stuff that's clinging to someone and throw it out, usually out through an open window if I'm working indoors. Once in the open air, the energy disperses without causing harm to anything. I then lay down some of my own energy as a temporary bandage over the open spaces, until the person's energy can heal themselves. And yes, you can learn to do this for yourself, though it does take some time to learn."

"Cool," breathed Ryder.

"Hunter, does that sound acceptable to you?"

Hunter considered it for a moment. If some of Jack's energy were still stuck on her, she wasn't sure if she wanted it removed. She wanted to keep a hold of him somehow, even if it was painful. He had believed in her, had supported her throughout her steps into coming into her own power as a Hedge Witch. "What if there is someone's energy we don't want to let go of?"

Harriet leaned forwards and took Hunter's hand. "You have got to live your life for *you*, Hunter. Not for others. When energy that is not yours clings to you, it can cause blocks to your own flow. It's their energy, not yours. You need to release what isn't yours in order to return back to yourself. You are not throwing away everything that you may have had with a person in the process. That's what memories are for; they are there to retain the beauty of a relationship within your heart and mind, while allowing your body to function clearly. Sometimes the emotions that come with memories tend to get a bit sticky, and need to be cleansed energetically over and over until you can accept what has happened, transition through the pain, and then find the good and also the lessons involved in the situation. Then you can continue to live your best life."

Hunter nodded slowly as the young woman spoke. It all made sense, but she was still hesitant. Harriet could feel

Hunter's hesitation, and so she said, "Hunter, letting go of the energy that is blocking you is not the same as letting go of love. Love always remains."

Ryder leaned over to hug her sister, and a wellspring of tears shone in Hunter's eyes. "Yes, you are right, Harriet," she said softly. *'Tis better to have love and lost, than never to have loved at all.*

Ever has it been that love knows not its own depth until the hour of separation, Hunter heard her sister say in her mind. Shocked, she looked at her sister. Ryder smiled at her. *Kahlil Gibran.*

"Okay, whatever witchy thing you both are doing, have you decided, Hunter?" asked Harriet with a grin.

"Yes," said Hunter. "Let's do it."

Harriet motioned for Hunter to lie down on the floor. She threw down a blanket and gave her a pillow to make her comfortable. Ryder sat on the beanbag chair to watch. Harriet put on some soft, meditative music and opened the windows in her apartment to get a breeze flowing through. "Ready?" she asked Hunter.

"Ready," she said, lying down on the floor.

"I'm going to get into your personal space with my hands, Hunter. Is that okay?" Harriet held a hand over Hunter's belly, a few inches away from it. Hunter thought about it, and said, "Yes, that is okay."

"Alright. Just close your eyes and relax. Oh, and try not to drift off and hedge ride while I'm doing this. Best to stay here, with us. Focus on how your body feels as I'm doing the work. In fact, considering who you are and your abilities, it's probably best to do a grounding first, please."

Witches of the New Forest

"Okay." Hunter took a few moments to ground and centre, and when she was ready she released a deep breath. "I'm ready, Harriet."

"Let's do this." Hunter tried to relax. She listened to the music, and focused on her breath. She began to feel her own energy as Harriet's hands moved over her aura, starting from her feet, and moving up towards her head. She began to notice places where Harriet hands lingered, places where the energy was stuck. Hunter was surprised, as these were places where she often had aches and pains. She had just chalked that up to the work that she had been doing in the gardens, but realised that it was also the places where energy had become trapped.

Hunter could also begin feel the places where there were holes in her aura as Harriet moved her hands over her. She felt very vulnerable each time Harriet's hands approached one of these places. Harriet spent some time around Hunter's heart, moving her hands over and patching up holes in her aura with her own energy. Hunter could feel Harriet's energy as a blue light that soothed and covered up the raw, aching points like a salve and bandage would for a bodily wound. She accepted that energy into her own, and felt it blending in at the edges. For some areas simply having this blue light shine on the place for a moment was all that was needed for Hunter to pull up her own energy and cover up the hole herself. When she did this, Harriet said softly, "Well done."

Around Hunter's head took the longest, and she tried to work with Harriet as much as possible. Hunter was surprised that it was her head area that was most affected; she would have assumed that it would be her heart. But as she felt the energy that wasn't hers lifting away, and then any holes being covered with Harriet's own healing energy, she realised just how much she carried energy in that part of her aura. And how her thoughts about so many things lingered and created their own, sticky energy in that part of her body. Finally, after nearly half an hour, Harriet gave a deep sigh and said, "Okay, Hunter. Open your eyes when you are ready."

Hunter opened her eyes slowly, her attention shifting from her auric self to her bodily self. She felt lighter, more energised, and more herself. She smiled up to Harriet. "Thanks."

Harriet squeezed her hand. "Don't mention it. Get up slowly, and take your time. I'll put on some tea."

Hunter lay there for a few more moments, before getting up slowly. She felt much better; she actually felt more like her old self. A self that she realised that she had been losing steadily over the years. She felt a return to a more magickal self, where awe and wonder overrode the mundane worries that life brought along with it. Everything appeared slightly different: lines were clearer, sharper. Colours were more vibrant. Plants that dotted the apartment had a glow to them.

"How are you feeling?" asked Ryder.

"Awake. Aware. Amazing."

"That's so awesome. I watched what Harriet did. I could almost see the energy that she removed from you, and sent it out the windows. With each pass you looked more and more... alive, I guess you would say."

"Hey!" said Hunter, suddenly noticing something. "You had to ask me how I felt. Can you not feel how I feel?"

Ryder shook her head. "Nope. You're quiet now. Which I guess is a good thing."

But can you still hear me when I talk to you in this manner?

Yes. I guess you're just not broadcasting your emotions everywhere now.

Harriet came back in, having overheard the sister's verbal conversation. "Hunter's big, gaping holes in her aura were letting a lot of stuff through," she said, echoing Ryder's summation. "Her own energy, her emotions, and her thoughts were coming out, as she didn't have enough of her own personal energy to stop them from escaping from those wounds. Now that she's patched up, she'll be more self-contained, and the energy won't leak out so much."

"That's good," said Hunter.

"I'll second that. Living with her had been a friggin' nightmare recently."

Hunter smiled at her sister. "Thank you, sis, for being there."

"Right back at you, Hun."

Harriet handed over a book to Hunter. "Try reading this. There are some good exercises in there for controlling your energy, emotions, and all that stuff."

Hunter took the book and flipped through the pages. "Thank you, Harriet. I will."

They drank some tea, and then Ryder suddenly snapped her fingers. "Holy shit, I almost forgot the reason we needed to talk to you in the first place, Harri."

Harriet smiled. "Which was?"

"We need to know more about the Fae, and Elspeth said that your family has an oral tradition with information that we may be able to use for our next big ritual in helping to recover Hunter's father. Is that right?"

Harriet nodded. "Yup, we have lots of stories in our family about the Fae. We are even rumoured to have some Fae blood. It might be why we are able to do what we do, as energy workers."

"Really? That's so awesome," said Ryder.

"So, what can you tell us?" asked Hunter.

"Probably best to come around to my parents' place sometime this week, and have them talk to you. I'll give them a ring and see when they're available, and then have you over. Would you like that?"

"Yes," the sisters said at the same time, and smiled at each other.

Chapter Four

The next day Abigail got up early to work in the back garden. The girls were still asleep having been out late with Harriet, and so she let them be and made her way silently to the back door. There, she slipped on a pair of wellies and walked out into the misty morning pre-dawn light. It had rained overnight and so the moisture from the earth rose up into the air, creating a beautiful ground mist that would only last until the sun rose. She stepped out into the garden, took a deep breath, and smiled.

She loved the smell of the early morning. Nothing could quite compare to it. She turned to look at her ancestral home and thought of the life that she had lived there before she had gotten into all that trouble with the Fae, simply for falling in love. She sighed wistfully, thinking about Daniel: that lovely young man who had come to her rescue, taking her and Hunter in when many here in the small community would have shunned them for Abigail's indiscretion and having a child out of wedlock. She supposed it was very different now, with the little village of Burley having caught up with the modern world in many respects. She still loved her husband, Daniel. She was coming to terms with the fact that her life in Canada was over, and that he had remarried a long time ago. She still didn't know what awaited her here in Burley, and so instead she took it one day at a time. Her mission right now was to find Aedon, free him, and tell him of his daughter. What happened next was in the lap of the gods.

She sighed and went to the perennial flower bed to do some weeding. She knelt down onto the damp soil and starting pulling up the little shoots. As soon as she touched the earth she felt more grounded, less apt to wander both mentally and magickally. She hummed softly to herself as she worked, the mist curling around her in gentle drifts.

Suddenly she felt like she was being watched. She raised her head and looked around, noting that the mist had increased. It had become difficult to see anything, even the nearby cottage. Her breathing became more rapid as she recognised one of the signs of the Otherworld.

"Curly wurly, curly wurly, curly wurly," she said to herself. The mist remained.

Suddenly she saw a figure in the mist, walking towards here. She knew instantly that it was a Fae. She took in a breath to cry out to her daughters, but the figure raised a hand and Abigail felt a sort of energy bubble surround them.

"No one can hear you, Hedge Witch," a soft, male voice spoke.

"Who are you?" asked Abigail, rising up to stand with her garden trowel clenched in her hand. She watched as the figure approached her. He was clad in shades of grey, and slowly his hands reached up to pull down a hood. The Fae man stalked up to her like a big, predatory, sexy cat. Abigail's breath caught in her throat as he approached. He was quite beautiful. His blond hair framed his face as it curtained at his forehead and swept down to his jaw. Grey eyes watched her, and pale lips turned up in a mocking smile. He leaned in close to Abigail. "Who do you think I am?" he said.

"You are Fae."

"And?"

"You tell me."

The man began to circle her, and she turned to keep her eyes on him. "I am your saviour. I am your gallant hero. I am your protector."

Abigail raised an eyebrow at these declarations. "Really? What is it that you have done for me?"

The strange, eldritch man came close. She could smell his scent, of fallen leaves and mist. "I have kept you safe while others sought you out. For many years I have watched you. You and your kind hold the key."

"The key to what?"

"You shall see," he said and stepped back, disappearing into the mist.

Abigail blew out a breath that she didn't know she had been holding. The sun had risen and the mist was quickly evaporating in the early light. She realised that she was still holding onto the garden trowel tightly, and so she unclenched her fingers, dropping the tool down to the ground. Shakily, she bent down and thrust her hands into the earth, feeling its cool, comforting energy grounding her after that encounter.

I didn't ride the hedge. I didn't ride the hedge, she repeated over and over again. After a few moments, she lifted herself back onto her haunches and looked around. Everything seemed normal, the cottage in plain sight and the birds singing. *What had just happened?*

She slowly stood and went back into the house. Taking off her wellies at the back door, she slipped silently into the kitchen and put on the kettle for tea. She leaned against the counter as she went over the encounter in her mind.

I hadn't ridden the hedge. I was still here. He must have been the one to come over, she thought. *But why?*

She heard the steps from upstairs creaking, and soon Hunter entered the kitchen. "Oh, hi Mom. You're up early," she said brightly.

Abigail studied her daughter for a moment. "Yes, I like to be up early sometimes. You look well today, my dear."

Hunter stood there and smiled. It was the first genuine smile her mother had seen on her daughter's face since they had been reunited. "Yes," said Hunter. "I'm feeling much better than I have in a long time."

"So, what happened?" asked Abigail as the kettle started to whistle. She took it and poured it into the teapot.

"Harriet did some energy clearing and healing on me," replied Hunter, moving to the coffee machine and filling up the pot. "I feel… lighter. Almost like years have fallen off me."

"Ah," said Abigail with a smile. "And why would you need energy healing, Poppet?"

Hunter looked at her mother a little sheepishly. "Um, well, I was having some problems with a relationship ending," she said a little lamely. She felt guilty about not talking to her mother about her breakup with Jack, but she didn't want to overload her mother with her problems, not when her mother had just returned from years of imprisonment between the worlds.

"Yes, I know of it, my dear. Elspeth told me shortly after it happened."

"Oh," said Hunter, not knowing what to say.

Abigail came over and wrapped her arms around her eldest daughter. "Don't worry, dear. It's okay. You were trying to protect me. And it's your life to live. I want you to know that you can come to me for anything, but I will not pry. Do we have an agreement?"

Hunter turned around in her mother's arms and looked into her deep blue eyes. "Deal," she said, smiling and giving her mother a big hug.

"Oh, it's so good to be back with you and Ryder," her mother said, giving her a squeeze. She let go of her daughter, and went to the fridge. "Pancakes?"

"Sounds great."

As Abigail made the pancakes, she debated telling her daughter of what had happened in the back garden this morning with the Fae. She wasn't sure if she should tell her, but she was also wondering why she was holding back. As she thought about it, she realised that she was trying to protect her daughter from whatever and whoever it was that she had met this morning. Just as Hunter had tried to protect her from her problems. Abigail worried that Hunter might try and seek out the strange Fae man, to get more information from him. She knew, in her heart of hearts, that he was trouble, and so she remained silent.

They were so alike, mother and daughter.

Several hours later, Ryder came downstairs. Her hair was sleep-rumpled, and she blinked blearily in the mid-morning light that streamed through the kitchen window. She saw Hunter out in the front gardens, weeding the window boxes. Hunter felt Ryder's gaze on her, and she looked up and waved with a smile. Ryder gave her a wave back, still not awake enough to smile back. She went to look out the back door, to check in on her mother. She opened the door and poked her head out, and saw her mother whistling as she walked towards the compost heap with her arms full.

"It's like a whole different species," grumbled Ryder as she softly closed the door. Mornings had never been her friend. She helped herself to some coffee and pulled her phone out from her pyjama shorts pocket. She saw a message from Harriet, and clicked on it.

My parents are free today, after 2pm.
OK.
Just get up?
Yup.
Talk to me after you've had some coffee.

Hunter came in to find her sister at the table, a stack of pancakes before her. "Hey Ry! Lovely day, isn't it?"

"Mmm," said Ryder, taking a bite of her breakfast. "Harri asked us to come over at 2pm."

"Sounds great," said Hunter, going to the coffee pot and pouring herself another cup of coffee. "Are you working tonight?"

"Mmm hmn."

Hunter sat down and looked at her sister. "I feel so bad about you working all the time while I stay here, study, and keep an eye on Mom. I do have money set aside, and we have some inheritance as well to help maintain us while we're here."

"I know," Ryder shrugged, talking with her mouth full. She chewed and swallowed before carrying on. "I don't mind it, actually. I'm getting to know the local people here. It's work, but it's fun work. Best way to integrate and all that."

Hunter looked at her sister intensely for a moment. "So, are you thinking of staying here longer term?" she asked.

Ryder shrugged again. "I don't know. Too early to decide. I'm just having fun getting to know people and seeing how life works here in England. It's a big learning curve, but I'm enjoying it. What about you?" she asked, waving her mug towards her sister.

Hunter chewed on her lower lip for a brief moment. "Honestly? I don't really know. I love this place, as much as I do Canada, I think. The history is amazing. The magickal families, the myth, the folklore, it's all just so amazing. It feels like home."

"Buuuuut?"

"But what about Jack? Will I be able to stay here long term if he's around in the village all the time? What if he starts to see someone else? Will I be able to cope?"

"You can cope with anything, sis. After what you've gone through with Mom, you can handle anything."

Hunter smiled at her sister. "Thanks, Ry." She took a sip of her coffee. "I guess I'm still just taking it one day at a time."

"Best way to do it."

The sisters decided to bring along their mother to see Harriet's parents. They got Abigail into the car and she lay down under a blanket as they drove to the Sandford's property. It was located on the opposite end of the village, in a thatched cottage similar in style to their own. Ryder had texted Harriet to let her know that all three were coming, and she told them to drive up and around to the rear of the cottage where they could all come in through the back entrance. Harriet's father worked on cars as a pastime, and he often had cars parked up in the back garden to work on. They pulled up next to a vintage pickup truck and got out. Abigail had a pashmina over her head and large sunglasses as she made her way to the cottage with her daughters. Harriet opened the door, waiting for them.

"Hey, you're here! Nice outfit," she said as she waved them through. Abigail took off the disguise and smiled at Harriet.

"Thank you so much for having us over. It's nice to get out of the house, actually. Even though it's lovely to be back, I am going a little stir-crazy with this whole 'staying hidden' malarkey."

Harriet nodded "I get it. Maybe you and Elspeth should do a road trip somewhere for a few days, some place where no one knows you. Rent a cottage in Cornwall or something."

"Oh, that's a marvellous idea! Why didn't I think of that?" said Abigail enthusiastically.

"You should totally do that, Mom," said Ryder as Harriet showed them through the kitchen to the living room. "Hunter and I still need time to prepare, and you could have some fun before things kick off again."

"I might just do that," said Abigail with a smile.

Hunter looked around at the interior of the Sandford's cottage. It was cosy and modern while retaining its character. Unlike the Appleton cottage, this one was free of clutter, painted white and had beautiful sleek furniture and fittings. Hunter preferred her aunt's cottage with its horse brasses, knick-knacks, and old furniture, but she could appreciate the loveliness of Harriet's parents' home.

"Mum, Dad, they're here!" called Harriet.

They entered a bright living room with a large conservatory extension off to one side. "Coming!" they heard a woman's voice answer from deep inside the sun-filled room. In an opposite doorway a man in his mid-fifties appeared, wearing an old-fashioned waistcoat complete with pocket watch and chain. "Abigail, oh my! How long has it been?"

"Nearly twenty years, Roger," Abigail replied going over to him, giving him a hug, and then a kiss on his cheek.

"Too long, too long," he said, smiling at her.

"Abigail!" A woman with long dark hair tied up into a messy bun on the top of her head came into the room and stood in shock. She was wearing denim overalls with some paint splattered over them, and had a paintbrush tucked into her bun. "You haven't aged a bit! Oh my, how wonderful it is to have you back!" She ran up to Abigail and threw her arms around her. "You must tell us everything, my dear," she said, a few tears escaping. She pulled away, still holding Abigail, and studied her for a moment. "I can't believe it. I just can't believe it. How do you feel?" she asked.

Abigail laughed. "I feel fine, Constance. Better than fine, now that I'm back with my daughters." Abigail waved the two sisters up. "Have you met Hunter and Ryder?"

"No, I haven't! Hello my dears, aren't you both just gorgeous." Constance pulled them both into a hug. Hunter wasn't a huggy-type person, but she accepted this woman's warm embrace. She felt comfortable in her presence. "You look just like your mother," Constance said to Hunter. "You could be sisters!"

Hunter smiled. "Yes, it's pretty amazing, isn't it?"

Constance turned to Abigail with a knowing look. "Time just does not work the same in the Otherworld, does it?"

"That's what we are here to talk about," said Harriet, turning the conversation to the Fae. They all sat down, and Roger went to make them some tea. The three Appleton women took the sofa, while Constance and Harriet took the two chairs.

Abigail nodded. "We are planning to go into the Otherworld in order to find Hunter's father."

Constance nodded. "Harriet mentioned that briefly. Now, you must tell me everything first, from the beginning."

Abigail began to recount the story, and Hunter filled in the gaps along the way from her and her sister's perspective. When they were done, Roger had come back. He placed the tea on the coffee table before them, and gave a low whistle. "That's a pretty powerful thing that you have managed to do, bringing

The Veil Between the Worlds

your mother back," he said to the sisters. He went and grabbed a chair from the dining room to sit on, next to his wife.

Ryder nodded. "It was mostly Hunter here, as she's the Hedge Witch like Mom. I'm the supporting act and comic relief," she said with a grin.

Abigail put her hand on Ryder's knee. "Darling, don't sell yourself short. Your magic saved Elspeth from Lanoc's attack, from what she told me."

At the mention of Lanoc's name, Constance sat upright. "Lanoc! It was he who imprisoned you between the worlds? Oh my. Oh my."

"What can you tell us about him?" asked Hunter.

"Just a little from the stories my grandmother used to tell," said Constance. "He was, or *is* I suppose, a King of the one of the Fae realms. He's very proud, and magically quite powerful."

"Why is he so intent on keeping my mother between the worlds?"

Constance looked at Hunter, her eyes dark and knowing. "Because some of the Fae are not very nice at all, my dear. Because that is their nature."

"While others are willing to help."

Constance nodded. "For their own reasons, yes. The lore in our family goes that a Fae will never do anything unless it benefits them in some way. Mind you, that's how a lot of humans are acting these days as well," she said ruefully.

"Is there mention of any other Fae in your lore?" asked Ryder.

Constance shrugged. "Burley is such a liminal place. All we do know is that one Fae realm, for certain, borders these lands. There may be more."

"Do you think those other Fae who kept my mother's body safe while she was imprisoned are helping out us humans, in some fashion?" asked Hunter. "Elspeth said that after her coven had sent us power, three Fae entered the circle and brought back her body. Unchanged from when she had gone missing."

"It is possible, but I do not know who they are. They could be a group that opposes Lanoc in some way. For what reason I do not know, other than Lanoc is a prick from all accounts. If he is as much an arse in the Fae world as he is in this world, he would have enemies for certain." Ryder giggled at Constance's words. "All I know from our family lore is that Lanoc despises humans, feels that they are inferior and any child born to a Fae and human parentage is 'tainted' in some manner. But we Sandfords, of course, believe very much otherwise, what with the Fae blood that runs through our heritage. We have gifts that we can use to help and to heal that the other magickal families do not. It has very much worked in our, and everyone else's favour." She looked at Hunter. "And you, my dear, would have gifts as well from your Fae lineage."

Hunter looked at her mother, and then back at Constance. "Yes, I suppose I do," she said. "I hadn't even thought about that very much. I wonder what abilities I might possess due to my Fae heritage."

"Your work as a Hedge Witch may simply be augmented by the fact that you are part Fae," said Constance. "You have only recently come into your powers, have you not?" Hunter nodded. "And yet you performed a very difficult ritual and found your mother's spirit. That's not something that a novice hedge rider could do. Your Fae heritage most likely had a lot to do with that."

Hunter considered the older woman's words for a moment. "That, and my love for liminal places and times most likely comes from my Fae heritage," she mused softly.

"Oh yes," said Constance. "Are you drawn to dawn and dusk, the turning of the seasons? When things are neither one nor the other, but hold a multitude of being in the same moment? That is part of what it is to be Fae. Neither in one world nor the other, but able to walk between the worlds, to cross the veil between the worlds. To have a foot in both worlds, in all worlds. It's your nature."

Constance's words all rang true for Hunter. She knew that she loved the liminal, as all Hedge Witches do. But there was something deeper there, something that allowed her to kind of live in both worlds at the same time. She had suppressed that feeling over the years; that feeling of possibility, that there was always something more to life, something magical, something that lay just beyond what the five senses could perceive. As a child, she knew and felt and lived that reality. But as an adult she had pushed that down and in doing so, denied her true nature. This revelation shocked Hunter, and she remained silent as she digested it all.

"It's also in your nature to feel energy," said Harriet. "When we were doing an energetic healing on Hunter, she easily helped out and understood without much prompting. Hunter, do you sometimes see or feel energy in other people?"

Hunter's mind immediately went to her time spent with Jack. How she could always feel his energy, strong and green like the oak that was so sacred to his Druid path. How she had often felt their energies merging and blending in ritual, and in other, more intimate times. "Yes," Hunter said softly. "Yes, I have."

Ryder sensed Hunter's sadness, and diverted the conversation. "What else can you tell us about the Fae?" she asked.

"Only that they are able to work with and channel energy. It's second nature to them. They can call up storms, lightning, water, wind, fire; they are masters of elemental and natural energy. They can harness the earth's energy and use it to their advantage in a multitude of ways."

"Anything else?"

"It's been said that the Fae cannot lie. While they may not always tell the direct truth, they cannot lie." Constance looked at Roger briefly, and gave him a wink. "And that they are beautiful and charming. Especially those who are descended from them."

Ryder laughed out loud, and Hunter and Abigail smiled. Harriet leaned forwards and looked at her mother. "What could we use to our advantage, should Lanoc and his kind come around again?"

Constance shook her head. "I don't really know, darling. It seems you all fended him off before, so just keep doing what you are doing. The Fae have power, but they are not the only ones. We are not weaklings easily intimidated by some arrogant Fae king. We Witches of the New Forest have our own power too. Each of the magickal families has certain gifts and abilities that are unique and special. All we have to do is to stand strong in our own power and be true to ourselves."

The next day Hunter went to Elspeth's to look over the old manuscripts that contained local Fae lore which dated back hundreds of years. She touched the old parchment as little as possible with her hands, wishing that she had her cotton gloves with her to handle the material properly. In the manuscripts she saw a few accounts of people in the New Forest who had encountered some sort of Fae being. But just who the Fae were in particular was still a mystery. The manuscripts briefly mentioned all manner of magickal beings, from the beautiful and mysterious Fae to the weird and wonderful creatures such as dragons, giants, and ghosts. Hunter sighed as she sat back in her chair at Elspeth's dining table, frustrated by the lack of information. *Someone, somewhere, must know more about these other Fae*, she thought.

But it seemed that the only way that they would find out would be when they went to the Otherworld itself.

Chapter Five

That night, after she had gone over the manuscripts at Elspeth's house, Hunter decided to pay her sister a visit while she worked at the pub. She still felt bad about Ryder working while she was studying, and wanted to show her support and thanks for all that her sister was doing. She was nervous, in case Jack showed up, but she steeled herself and was determined to be there for Ryder. She felt bolstered by the energy work that Harriet had done, and decided that it was now or never. It was time to be social, even if it was awkward and difficult for her, and totally against her natural introvert tendencies. Plus, there was a folk band playing that night, and as Hunter loved folk music it made it all the more appealing.

Elspeth came over to watch some movies with Abigail and talk about a secret getaway. They made some popcorn and got cosy in the living room, with a small fire burning merrily in the fireplace. The air had turned cooler during the week with a steady northerly wind. Hunter thought it was nice to see Elspeth relax a little. She was actually wearing jeans. It was the first time she had ever seen Elspeth in trousers of any sort.

Hunter went upstairs and picked out what she was going to wear tonight. She decided on her favourite slim leg jeans and a white, bell-sleeved blouse as well as her low-heeled ankle boots. She threw on a large green pashmina over her shoulders and put on a new, long, beaded boho-style necklace that her sister had picked up for her at the Portsmouth market. Hunter decided to let her hair hang loose, and put on some mascara and lip gloss to a make a bit of an effort.

She drove down to the pub, even though ever since the car crash, she was very wary of that road when night fell. She pulled into the pub car park, turned off the engine, grabbed her bag and went in. It was busy for a Wednesday, as the band were playing. Tourist season had also begun. There were still a couple of places open at the bar. She grabbed an empty barstool and took a seat. She nodded to the older gentleman next to her, and caught her sister's eye. Ryder smiled and waved at her while pulling a pint.

"Hey, Hunter! Wow, nice to you see here! Slumming it now, are you?"

"Way to insult your patrons, sis," Hunter said with a smile, waving at the people around the bar who laughed.

"These guys? They know," her sister said with a grin and a wink at her regulars. She walked up to her sister and leaned against the bar. "So, what'll you have?"

"Um, I think I'll take a glass of rosé, please."

"Small, medium or large?"

"Medium. No, large. What the heck. Let's live a little."

"Large it is," said Ryder, and she went to pour the drink. Hunter looked around the pub. No sign of Jack, thank goodness. There were some tables free, but at the moment most people were clustered around the bar to drink. A few elderly people sat together at a table near the unlit fireplace, playing card games. A table of young lads were drinking beer and watching Ryder as she worked. Hunter watched her sister as well. She seemed to be in her element, being sassy and witty with the 'punters' as they were called here in England, and serving up drinks like a pro. "Here you go, sis. This one's on me. It's just so nice to see you out and about," she said with a smile. She was drawn away as a man called for another pint from the other side of the bar.

A loud laugh came from the games room, a laugh that Hunter recognised. Soon enough, Dougal and another man came out into the bar area. The Scotsman slapped his friend on the back and congratulated him on playing terribly. They laughed together, and then the other man wandered off to a table. Dougal spotted Hunter and made a beeline for her. "Hunter! Och aye, lassie, how've ya been?"

Hunter half-smiled at the tall, brawny, redheaded Scotsman. "I'm doing better."

Dougal looked a little puzzled. "Better than what?" he asked.

"Didn't Jack tell you?"

"Tell me what?"

Hunter swallowed against a rising pain in her heart. She would not let this ruin her night. "He broke up with me."

Dougal actually took a step back, a look of astonishment on his usually jovial features. "Ya dinnae say, lass. Are you sure?"

Hunter laughed a short, bitter laugh. "Yes, I'm sure Dougal."

Dougal sidled up next to her at the bar, and pulled an empty barstool a bit closer, planting himself upon it. He lowered his voice as he said, "I haven't seen Jack for a couple of weeks now. He took a few days off back towards the end of June, and then I've been away back in Scotland with Mackenzie on family business. As I hadn't seen either of you since I got back a few days ago, I thought you both were off somewhere together. Last month he had talked about taking you on a trip to Ireland, you see."

Hunter shook her head, looking into her drink. "He broke up with me at the summer solstice."

Dougal studied her face for a moment, then turned and waved to Ryder. She nodded and proceeded to pour Dougal a pint. He turned back to Hunter. "I cannot believe that. That lad was head over heels in love with you."

"Apparently not," said Hunter, and took a few large swallows of her wine. She thought that she had come to terms with the pain, but it reared its ugly head with ferocity once more. As well, she felt her old wounds opening up from her previous relationships. All the times that she had been dumped. She felt like she and Jack were just another blip on her love life's record. Another instance of a man falling head over heels for her, and then losing interest. None of them ever stayed.

Ryder approached them and handed over Dougal's pint. She could see her sister was unhappy. "I guess she just told you about Jack," she said quietly to Dougal.

"Aye," he said softly. "I would ne'er have believed it."

Ryder looked at her sister. "Dougal hasn't been in for a while – he's been up in bonnie Scotland, as he says. Man, I'd love to go up there one day," she said, placing her arms on the bar and putting her chin in her hands as she dreamt of a Scottish vacation. "Castles, mountains, lochs, bagpipes, men in kilts…"

Dougal laughed. "Everyone needs to go to Scotland at least once in their lives. It's an amazing place."

Ryder straightened and looked at Dougal. "Is it true what they say about men in kilts?"

Dougal laughed softly. "That's something one has to find out for themselves, lass."

"Wouldn't it chafe against the wool of the kilt? Is it the itchy, scratchy kind of wool? Do *you* have a kilt? Does your family have their own pattern?" Ryder's questions flew thick and fast.

Hunter was grateful that Ryder had steered the conversation away from her and Jack. She wasn't ready to go there just yet. She drank her wine and listened as Dougal gave her sister the low down on kilts. She soon found her glass empty, and asked Ryder for another.

Ryder looked at her for a moment, and then nodded. "Guess I'm giving you a ride home, sis," she said with a smile. Hunter gave over her keys to Ryder as her sister poured another glass. Ryder pocketed the keys and then handed over the large glass of wine. "Go easy, sis," she advised.

Hunter merely nodded. She turned to Dougal. "So, Dougal, what made you decide to call the New Forest home?" Dougal flushed a little, which Hunter thought was intriguing. Something was keeping him here, or *someone*, she surmised.

"My job in the New Forest is great, and what with Mackenzie over at Portsmouth, I figured he needed someone to keep an eye out for him. After I got placed here in my training a couple of years ago, when a job opened up, I decided to take it and I've been here since."

Hunter felt like Dougal wasn't telling her everything, but she wasn't one to pry. "Tell me what it's like, to work in the New Forest day in and day out."

Dougal smiled and regaled her as they sat almost shoulder to shoulder at the bar. Hunter was halfway through her second glass when she heard her sister communicate with her telepathically. *Heads up, sis.*

What?

Dickhead at two o'clock.

Hunter's eyes turned to the doorway, where she saw Jack enter the pub. He looked as handsome as ever, his dark hair tousled and falling over his forehead. He was clean shaven, having foregone his usual short, stubbly beard. He was also not alone. On his arm was a petite, dark-haired woman. Her hair was cut in an angled bob, and her clothes were designer-made. Her dark eyes scanned the pub, a look of disdain mixed with arrogance on her perfectly made-up face. She would have been very pretty, had she not had such a supercilious look about her. Her eyes honed in on Hunter sitting at the bar across the room, and her features swiftly changed to a mocking smile. She looked up to Jack and said something to him, pulling him closer to her. He bent his head down to say something back, and the woman looked back at Hunter, smirking openly as he spoke.

Hunter turned away, feeling the heat flush to her face. She took another large gulp of wine, willing herself to remain calm. Dougal saw that she was in some sort of distress and turned to look at Ryder, who was now facing the door with her arms crossed over her chest. He finally spotted Jack with the other woman.

"Now what the hell is that feckin' eejit doing with that woman?" said Dougal.

Jack straightened to look in the vicinity of his date's gaze, and saw Dougal and Hunter sitting at the bar looking at him. He quickly looked away, and led the woman to a table in the corner. The woman sneered at everyone in the bar as she passed, her eyes throwing daggers at Hunter especially. Ryder came over to stand with her sister in solidarity.

"Feckin' Courtney Peterson," grumbled Dougal. "She looks like a dug licking pish off a nettle."

"I'm guessing that was an insult," said Ryder, whipping out her phone and typing in that phrase. She snorted and handed the phone over to Hunter.

Scottish slang: *A face like a dug (*a large dog*) licking pish (*piss*) off a nettle.*

Hunter gave a similar snort and handed the phone back to her sister. Ryder reached out to touch her sister's hand. "I'm so sorry, Hunter. I had no idea he'd be here tonight. Hasn't been in since before... you know," she said quietly.

"It's fine, really, it is. I'm good."

"Ya don't look so good, lass," said Dougal softly, putting his arm around her shoulders and giving her a gentle hug of support. Hunter took another large gulp of wine.

Jack came up to the bar to order drinks. He stood on the other side of Dougal, who pulled his arm away from Hunter but studiously ignored Jack. Ryder came up, recrossing her arms in front of her and a grim look on her face. "You've got some nerve, Jack," she said quietly, not wanting to make a scene for her sister's sake.

"Hello to you too, Ryder," said Jack softly. He turned to Dougal and Hunter. "Dougal. Hunter."

"Away 'n shite," was all Dougal said quietly, not even bothering to look at him.

Jack looked away for a moment, before returning his gaze to Dougal. "I must remind you, I *am* still your boss," he said.

"An' I'll deal with that tomorrow at work," Dougal said, pointedly not looking at Jack and lifting his pint to his lips.

Jack turned to Ryder. "A pint of bitter shandy, and a large glass of shiraz," he said.

Ryder simply stood there with her arms crossed, studying Jack's face. Finally, she nodded stiffly. "I'll bring it to your table," she said, dismissing him. Jack left and went back to the table where Courtney sat.

"So, that's Courtney, eh?" said Hunter softly to Dougal.

"The one and only. I can't believe he'd break up with you to go out with that woman again."

Hunter took another swallow of her wine. She leaned in to Dougal and said quietly, "He told me that he had some things he needed to do, and the space to do them in. I guess he meant her," she said, gesturing vaguely with her glass, a little sloshing down the side.

The band began to play, and people started to move away from the bar to sit at the tables. Hunter and Dougal remained at the bar, turned away from Jack and Courtney as much as possible. Ryder went to Jack's table to serve them their drinks without a word, simply placing them down and turning to leave. "The service has really gone downhill here," they heard a woman's voice cut across the room. Ryder's shoulders twitched, but she kept heading back to the bar without a word.

"She's one nasty piece of work," said Dougal.

Ryder came up to Hunter and leaned in. "Don't let it get to you, sis. Don't let this ruin all the good work that you and Harriet have done over this last week. Stay strong."

Dougal looked up at the mention of Harriet. "What's this?"

Hunter turned to look at Dougal. His dark blue eyes held hers intently as he waited for her answer. "Harriet did some healing work on me," she simply said.

Dougal nodded. "She's a fine woman, that one." He turned to his drink and took a long pull from his pint. Ryder watched this with interest, but was then called away by another patron.

"Dougal, I don't know what I'm going to do," said Hunter. He put an arm around her again and gave her shoulders a squeeze, holding her. "Dinnae worry, lass. Ye've got friends here, you'll get through this."

The sound of glass breaking had heads turning in the direction of Jack's table. Jack was bent over, picking up large shards of glass by his feet while the rest of the bar applauded his clumsiness, as was customary. Ryder heaved a large sigh and got out an old rag, a broom and a dustpan and went to help him clean up the mess. Dougal dropped his arm as he leaned back to get a better look. Hunter watched out of the corner of her eye and saw Courtney say something to Ryder, who ignored her. She could almost feel her sister's temper rising from here, and hoped that Courtney would shut up soon before her sister decked her. Ryder managed to keep it under control, and returned to the bar to dump the broken glass into the glass recycling bin behind the bar.

Hunter was desperate to get out of there, but did not want to concede defeat to this woman who was now with Jack. She sat up a little straighter, squaring her shoulders. At that point a member of the band came up to her and tapped her on the shoulder.

"Pardon me, miss, but I remember you from karaoke night. You've a fine voice. Would you like to sing a song with us tonight?"

Hunter turned to look at a middle-aged man with glasses and short, curling brown hair. Behind his glasses were warm brown eyes, and he had a fiddle and bow in his hands. "Um, I don't know," she said unsurely.

"It'd make our day," he said with a smile.

Hunter took a deep breath, and made up her mind. "Sure. What would you like me to sing?"

"Do you know As I Roved Out?"

"The Deluded Lover? I sure do," she said, somewhat sardonically.

"That's great. We'll call you up."

"Okay."

Hunter sighed, wondering just what she had done to deserve such a fate. She finished her second glass of wine. No sooner had she begun to feel sorry for herself than the band ended the song that they were playing and Hunter was called onto the stage. She turned and hopped off the barstool with only a slight wobble, Dougal's arm shooting out to steady her. She made her way to the stage, ignoring Jack and Courtney as she picked up the microphone. The band smiled at her, and she gave them a false smile in return.

Don't do anything stupid, sis, she heard Ryder's voice in her head.

Hunter didn't reply. Instead, the band started and the music rolled out across the pub. Everyone had turned to watch Hunter as she stood on the stage. Her long red curls shone in the little spotlight, and she held her head down until she began to sing. The song rolled out of her, filled with the sadness and bitterness that dwelt in her heart. She could almost feel some of the holes in her aura opening again, and so as she sang she allowed the anger of betrayal to boost her energy and cover up the holes with a fierce red fire. The song's words echoed the sentiments in her heart. She would not let Courtney or Jack know that they were causing her unimaginable pain. Instead, she sang in spite of them being there, and letting Jack know especially just who she thought he was. She otherwise kept a check on her powers, not allowing the song to kick in a hedge riding experience like last time.

As I roved out on a bright May morning,
To view the meadows and the flowers gay,
Whom should I spy but my own true lover,
As she sat under yon willow tree.

I took off my hat and I did salute her,
I did salute her courageously,
When she turned around and the tears fell from her,
Saying: "False young man, you have deluded me."

"For to delude you, how can that be, my love?

Witches of the New Forest

*It's from your body I am quite free.
I'm as free from you as a child unborn
And so are you, my dear Jane, from me."*

*"Three diamond rings I own I gave you,
Three diamond rings to wear on your right hand,
But the vows you made, love, you went and broke them,
And married the lassie that had the land."*

*"If I married the lassie that had the land, my love,
It's that I'll rue until the day I die,
When misfortune falls sure no man can shun it,
I was blindfolded I'll ne'er deny."*

*Now at night when I go to my silent slumber,
The thoughts of my true love run in my mind,
When I turn around to embrace my darling,
Instead of gold, sure it's brass I find.*

*I wish the Queen would call home her army,
From England, Ireland, from America and Spain,
And every man to his wedded woman,
In hopes that you and I will meet again.*

    The slow, mournful strains of the song played out through the guitar, fiddle, and Hunter's voice. Halfway through the song a tin whistle came softly in, weaving in and out with Hunter's voice like the plaintive call of a bird across the heath at twilight. Hunter did her best not to look at Jack and Courtney, but failed as soon as the woman's accusations in the song came up. She just glanced briefly at Jack as she sang the woman's accusatory words, and saw that Jack was looking back at her, his beautiful green eyes full of pain and sorrow. Hunter tore her gaze away from him then, not allowing herself to see his pain. Not when hers was so raw. He could rot in his choices for all she cared.

As the song ended, Hunter gave a small bow as the pub erupted in loud whistles and cheers. Avoiding Jack's table, she made her way back to her seat at the bar where Ryder stood with Dougal. "Nice one, sis," said Ryder with a grin.

"Aye, you sure told him," said Dougal with a smile, patting her on the shoulder.

"Another glass of wine, please," said Hunter to her sister.

Ryder looked at her for a moment. "Are you sure? You are kind of a lightweight, you know." Hunter simply stared at her sister until she shrugged and got another glass of wine. As she passed it to Hunter, Ryder shot a quick glance at Dougal. He nodded to her briefly, letting her know that he'd take care of her. Ryder nodded back and was called away to the other side of the bar.

Dougal leaned back to take another look at Jack and Courtney. They seemed to be having some sort of argument. Jack briefly glanced their way as Courtney turned her head to the side and pouted, and he gave Dougal a slight nod of his head before turning away. Dougal's eyebrows raised for a moment, wondering what that was all about. He turned back to the bar and focused on his pint as he pondered.

The band switched to a lively tune, which got the pub singing and clapping along. Hunter focused on her drink. She was a little embarrassed by what she had done, and hoped that the people at the pub didn't know the underlying context of the situation. She heard Ryder's voice in her head. *No one has a clue, sis. Don't worry. It's all good. Went right over their heads.*

Thanks, Ry.

Hunter got up to use the loo. The bar stool was getting more difficult to disembark from, for some reason. Dougal helped her down again and watched her as she made her somewhat wobbly way to the back of the pub where the toilets were located. He then kept a surreptitious eye out on everyone else in the pub as he hunched over his pint. Sure enough, he saw Courtney rise from her seat and start to make her way to the loos where Hunter had gone. Dougal edged out of his seat, now standing at the bar with his pint. As Courtney came up to walk behind him, he turned with his drink in his hand and hit her square on, spilling his drink all over her.

"Och, aye, I'm so sorry!" he said.

Courtney glared up at him. "You idiot! What the hell were you thinking? This is a Dior!"

"Nay," said Dougal with a look of confusion. "That's a jumper. The door's over there," he said, waving at the pub entrance. A couple patrons nearby laughed softly.

"*Dior*, you fool. Argh!" She clenched her small hands into fists and stamped on the floor. "This whole village is full of idiots."

The people at the bar turned around at the insult. Courtney glared at them for a heartbeat, and then stomped back the way she had come and gestured to Jack to follow her as she stormed out the door. Jack tossed Dougal a quick glance, and Dougal could almost have sworn he saw laughter flash in Jack's eyes for a brief second before he turned and, with his hands in his pockets, followed Courtney out the door.

"I'll just put that on your tab then, Jack!" Ryder shouted after them as they left.

The punters returned to their pints with a shrug of their shoulders, muttering about 'townies' before turning their attention back to the band. Ryder walked over to Dougal and handed him another pint with a large grin on her face.

"On the house, my good man."

"Aye, thanks lass."

Hunter emerged from the loos and joined them at the bar. She looked at Dougal and Ryder smiling at each other. "Did I miss anything?"

"Nay, just a little pub humour is all."

Hunter nodded with an uncertain half-smile, and climbed back on the bar stool. She could swear it was getting higher each time. She finished her wine quickly and asked Ryder for another.

Um, I think you've had enough, sis.

You're not the boss of me.

How old are you, like ten?

Just give me a glass of wine, Ryder.

Ryder nodded and when Hunter's gaze turned to look at Jack's now empty table, she crooked a finger at Dougal to follow her round the bar. "Be right back, lass," he said to Hunter as he hopped off the stool. He followed Ryder around to the other side of the bar which was hidden behind a corner of the kitchen wall. It was much less crowded here as there wasn't a good view of the stage. Ryder poured her sister another glass and then leaned in towards Dougal. He met her halfway across the bar and suddenly found his shirt collar in the younger woman's grasp.

"If you do anything to take advantage of my sister, I will kick your ass all the way back to bonnie Scotland," threatened Ryder.

Dougal nodded, trying not to grin. "Aye, understood lass. Just give her this one more, and then I'll take her home. She'll throw up, feel like shite tomorrow and have lessened some of the grief held in her heart in the process."

Ryder stared at Dougal for a moment, not expecting such insight from him. She let go of his shirt collar. "Okay then," she said, not having a comeback.

Dougal grinned at her and made his way back round the bar. Ryder brought Hunter her glass. She had poured a medium size amount into a large glass, hoping her sister wouldn't know the difference. Hunter picked up the glass and took another large gulp. Ryder shook her head, knowing that Hunter would be paying the price tomorrow morning.

They listened to the band for another few songs. The players mixed it up with slow, lamenting tunes and bright, cheerful melodies. As Hunter finished her fourth glass, she found herself swaying in her seat with the music. Other people from the tables got up and pushed the tables to one side, making room for a small dance floor. A few couples began to dance merrily, and Hunter sighed in longing. She loved to dance. She turned to Dougal. "Dance with me," was all she said.

Dougal looked at her in surprise. "Ya want to have a dance with *me*?"

"Yes, I do," she said with a smile.

Dougal's face flushed red as Hunter turned and got ready to get down from the barstool once more. *Why do they make them so damn high?* she thought to herself. She felt Dougal grab her arm again as she nearly toppled over.

"Right, okay. I've got you," he said. He put his arm around Hunter's waist as they navigated along the length of the bar. When they neared the makeshift dance floor, Dougal grabbed Hunter into a tango pose, and tangoed her to the door. She laughed at first, not realising what was going on until they got to the door. As she opened her mouth to protest, Dougal laughed a loud, roaring laugh that drowned out her protests even as he put an arm around her waist and led her out the door. As the door swung closed behind them, Hunter turned in his grasp and pushed him away.

"Just what the hell do you think you're doing?" she said with anger, slightly slurring her words.

"Seeing ya home," said Dougal softly.

"I don't want to go home. I want to dance." Hunter then swayed on her feet, and Dougal put an arm around her again.

"I don't think that's such a good idea," he said firmly. He led her out into the carpark.

Hunter pulled away and stood before him with her hands on her hips. Dougal was glad that there was no one in the car park to witness this little debacle. "I'll have you know, Dougal Walker, that I have full control of my facilities."

"Don't ya mean faculties, lass?"

"That's what I said." Hunter's hands dropped from her hips, as she swayed once more.

"Right, that's enough," said Dougal, and walked towards Hunter. He picked her up in a fireman's lift and carried her to his truck. She protested the whole way, banging her fists on his back. He ignored it and put her back on her feet by the passenger side of the truck. As Hunter stood, she swayed again and looked decidedly green.

"Oh god, I don't feel so good," she said, and leaned over to throw up in the empty parking space next to Dougal's truck.

"Better out than in," said Dougal, his hand on her back to steady her and his other hand holding her hair back. Hunter had her hands on her knees, shaking as a sheen of sweat came out all over her body. "Dougal, take me home please," she said in a small voice.

"Aye lass. Come on then," he said, helping her to straighten up and practically pouring her into the passenger seat. He clipped her in with the seatbelt and went round to the other side to get in. He started up the truck and slowly pulled out of the car park. "If'n ya feel sick again, let me know and I'll stop," he said. "Remember, this is my work vehicle." Hunter just nodded, her eyes closed and head leaning back on the headrest.

They made the short journey back to the cottage. Dougal helped Hunter out of the truck, and carried her more gently in his arms this time right up to the door. Hunter had her arms around his neck and her head on his shoulder. He shifted Hunter slightly so he could knock on the door, and Elspeth answered.

"Special delivery," said Dougal.

Elspeth took one look at Hunter and sighed. She waved Dougal in, and closed the door behind him. "Abigail!"

Abigail came out from the kitchen. She saw Hunter in Dougal's arms, and cried out, "Hunter! What happened?"

Dougal's jaw dropped when he saw a woman who looked very similar to Hunter. He quickly closed it, and lay Hunter down on the sofa. "Four glasses of wine is what happened," he finally managed to say. "She got a bit mad wi' it."

Hunter groaned softly and apologised to everyone in the room.

Dougal said quietly, "She just needed to let loose a little bit. Let off some steam. It's nay to worry about."

"Oh, my poor Poppet." Abigail then turned and looked up at the tall Scotsman. "Thank you. I'm sorry, I don't know your name."

"My name's Dougal," he said, running a hand through his red hair.

"Thank you, Dougal," said Abigail, gently leading him towards the door. "We will take it from here. Thank you for getting my daughter home safe."

"And Dougal?" said Elspeth. He turned around. "This stays quiet. Do you understand?"

Dougal looked over to Abigail. "Aye, dinnae fash. I'll tell no one."

"You're a good man, Dougal," said Abigail.

"Aye, that's what they all say," he replied softly, waving behind him as he went to his truck.

Dougal pulled up outside Jack's cottage. There was a light on, and Jack's jeep was there. Slamming the truck's door, Dougal stomped up to the little porch. He knocked, but there was no answer. Dougal just kept knocking until finally the door was pulled open violently, and Jack stood there, glaring at his friend.

"Aye. Are we alone?"

"Go away, Dougal," said Jack, trying to control his temper.

"Answer my question," Dougal replied. Jack simply nodded. "Good," said Dougal, and then he stormed past Jack and barged into the cottage. He looked around the living room and ran his hands through his red hair. "Just what the hell do ya think you're doing, you feckin' eejit?" he shouted.

Jack closed the door softly. "What do you mean, Dougal?" he said evenly.

"You broke up with that bonnie lass! You broke up with Hunter, the love of yer life, or so ya kept telling me over and over again for nearly two months. Why, Jack? Why would ya do such a fecking stupid thing?"

Jack looked down for a moment, before he looked into Dougal's eyes. "I have my reasons. Please do not ask me anything more."

Dougal moved swiftly and got up in Jack's face. "I'm not letting this go, Jack," he said threateningly.

Jack's eyes flashed with green fire. "I see. That's how it is. You two were pretty cosy together at the bar."

Dougal's fists clenched. "I'd ne'er do that to a friend, and you know that. Or you should. What the hell has gotten into you? And why are you back together with Courtney, of all people? Don't you remember what she did to you? Are you feckin' mad?"

Jack looked away as his friend's tirade washed over him. "Dougal, please, just leave."

The angry Scotsman just shook his head. "There's something going on here. I saw the look and the nod you gave me at the bar. What was that all about then, eh?"

"Dougal, please." Jack looked at his friend square in the eye. "Just leave it be."

It was then that Dougal saw his friend's pain. Jack's face was pale, and it looked like he hadn't slept for days. "That Canadian lass was the best thing that ever happened to you," Dougal said softly. "You were ne'er so happy as when you were together. She was a goddamned blessing, and you know it."

Jack simply nodded, not saying anything.

Dougal just shook his head. "Yer a feckin' bampot," he said, and stormed past Jack, pulling open the door. "You have totally messed things up, and hurt a damned fine woman in the process. You should be ashamed of yourself." He then stepped out and slammed the door behind him.

As he stood in the darkness and fished for his keys in his pocket, Dougal felt something on his foot. He looked down to see Dexter, Jack's big, fluffy, smokey-grey cat sitting there, staring up at him. "Och, aye, wee man. Yer owner's an eejit, ya know."

Dexter rose up on his hind legs and patted Dougal's knee, almost as if he was trying to reassure him. Dougal gave him a gentle pat on the head, and moved away to his truck. He got in and drove away. As the truck rolled down the little dirt track,

Jack opened the cottage door and Dexter came up to him. Jack picked him up and nuzzled Dex's soft head for a moment, and then turned back and closed the door behind him.

Chapter Six

Hunter spent the next morning in bed wondering if it was better to just die than deal with this hangover. Her sister came in and cheerfully told her that the tannins in wine were what often made people feel terrible afterwards. Hunter just threw a pillow at Ryder (which missed) and pulled the covers up over her head. Ryder placed a large glass of water and some ibuprofen next to her sister's bed. "Coffee's on downstairs when you can manage. Here, take these and hopefully you'll feel better soon."

When she heard her sister close the door behind her, Hunter emerged from the blankets to blink blearily around the room. It was raining outside, for which she was thankful. She didn't think she could deal with sunshine today. She grabbed the pills and water and drank them down, and then lay back upon the bed and stared up at the ceiling.

Jack and Courtney. Courtney and Jack. Together. After everything that Courtney had done to him. Hunter pondered this for a long time. It just didn't seem right. Jack had broken free from Courtney and was finally back to his old self, or so everyone had told her. He had told Hunter that he loved her. She felt his joy and his love when they had been together, as well as that wonderful energy that often passed between them. Had all this been a deception? She didn't think Jack was even capable of it, but the facts were stacked up against her after what she had seen with her own eyes last night.

Hunter fell back asleep for an hour, and awoke again. The rain had stopped, and the sun was trying to come out. The window had been opened, and Hunter was grateful for the fresh air in the room. She finished the last of the water in her glass, then pulled on some sweat pants and a t-shirt. Her headache was nearly gone, and she braided her hair down along one side of her head to keep it out of her face. She then went to the bathroom to wash up. As she came out of the bathroom she smelled something delicious baking downstairs, and so gingerly she made her way down the steep, tiny cottage steps.

She heard Ryder and her mother in the kitchen and stopped. They were talking about Aedon, Hunter's father. She sat down on the stairs to listen in on the conversation.

"So, Mom, why do you want to go back to Aedon so badly? What was wrong with my dad? He loved you so much."

Abigail sighed. "Your father is a good man, Ryder. I do love him and there is nothing wrong with him at all. It's not so much that I want to go back to Aedon, but I feel a responsibility to free him from the prison his brother had put him in, because of me. I also feel an obligation to tell him about his daughter. My love for Aedon, well, it was different from Daniel. With Aedon it was - I don't know. Just different. It was intense, and passionate, and a world of emotions. Your father was steadfast and wonderful and was perhaps just too good for me, in all honesty. He took care of me and Hunter when my world was falling apart, when I had no one to turn to except my sister. It was such a difficult time for me. But Daniel was a light in the darkness. I feel terrible for what I did to him, and for hurting him by coming here and trying to contact Aedon myself. I tore the family apart."

"Mom, don't say that. The heart wants what the heart wants." Hunter could hear her sister move over to give Abigail a hug.

"It's okay to love someone else, really, it is. I just want to know why Aedon is so important to you."

Hunter heard her mother sniff softly. "Aedon was my everything. The bond that we shared was so deep. It's difficult to explain. All I know is that I have to find him again and free him from his imprisonment. It's all because of me that he had been trapped all these years. When I could see him every now and again for brief moments during those liminal times, I could still feel his love for me. His love *never* faltered. I don't know, maybe I felt guilty for having moved away and marrying someone else after he disappeared. At the time I thought Aedon had just left me, or lost interest, or even started listening to his brother. It was all such a mess.

"When your father, Daniel, came along, I was offered something new from a good man. I took it with both hands. My heart was so broken. Hunter was so young. It just felt like the right thing to do at the time. But when I came back, I felt I had to give it one more try, as Aedon deserved to know of his daughter. I don't know why, I just felt like I had to do it. And then I got myself trapped in the process."

"I get it, Mom. You don't have to justify your actions to me. I was just curious to know what it was about Aedon that made him your true love."

"That's something I think you can't explain, my love. It's something that you can only feel."

Hunter wiped away a tear at her mother's words. It made all kinds of emotions batter her heart and she willed herself to calm down. Her situation with Jack was very different than the love her mother had for her father. Jack had left her, had broken up with her. Aedon had been imprisoned by his brother. The two were not analogous.

"Well, I hope one day I'll feel something like that," said Ryder.

"You will, darling. You will."

"Lord knows I've already felt up my fair share of men," her sister said laughing. Abigail joined in.

Hunter smiled and went down the last of the stairs and into the kitchen. As she entered the kitchen the two women stopped in their tracks. "Igor, it's moving. It's alive! It's alive! It's aliiiiive!!!!" cried Ryder.

Their mother burst into a fit of giggles, even as Hunter held up a hand to her head. "A little louder, why don't you?" she said to her sister.

"Here, darling, have some coffee and a fresh-baked scone." Abigail poured a cup for Hunter and pushed a scone, some jam, and clotted cream across the table to her. Hunter found she was famished, and devoured two scones laden with jam and cream, washing it down with two cups of coffee. She felt more human once she had eaten.

"What time did I get in?" Hunter asked.

Ryder grinned at her. "You were out until the wee hours of 10.30pm, you rockstar, you."

Hunter sighed. "I didn't make a fool of myself in front of Jack, did I?"

"Nope," said Ryder. "In fact, he soon left while you were in the loo, remember?"

"Oh," said Hunter. "Yeah. Oh shit. Dougal had to drive me home, didn't he?"

"Yup. I brought the car back."

Hunter put her head in her hands. "I'm so embarrassed."

Ryder sat down next to her and patted her on the arm. "Nothing to be embarrassed about. You held your own and rocked the pub when you sang that song with the band."

"Oh god, the band!"

"What did she sing?" asked their mother.

"Um…" Ryder shrugged, not remembering.

"As I Roved Out," said Hunter.

"The Deluded Lover?"

"That's the one."

Abigail smiled. "Nice."

Hunter looked up at them both. "I made a fool of myself."

Ryder shook her head. "Nope. In fact, I think you did brilliantly. You were amazing."

Hunter stood up and rinsed her dishes in the sink. "I hope you're not lying to me."

"Hun, I wouldn't lie about something like this. You held your own with dignity and style."

"Thanks, Ry."

Oh, and Jack whispered something to me as I was cleaning up the broken glass. He said something like 'remember the rose'.

Hunter stiffened as she rinsed her plate. She didn't reply to her sister's mental message. She needed to think about it first.

Abigail moved up to stand next to Hunter at the sink. "Hunter, darling, do you think you are up for a little hedge riding tomorrow?"

Hunter nearly dropped her plate in surprise. She turned to her mother. "Why?"

"Well, Elspeth and I discussed it last night, and we feel that you should dip your toes into the Otherworld, to get used to it a little. What do you say?"

Hunter looked at her mother. "Um, okay, I guess."

Abigail's face lit up. "Wonderful! Ryder and Thomas will watch over us, just to be safe. This will be fun!" Her mother clapped her hands and rushed out of the room to get her tools ready. Hunter had a strange, sinking feeling in her stomach but pushed past it and shrugged, setting her plate on the counter, and wiping her hands on a small towel.

"We've got your back, sis," Ryder said, patting her on the shoulder before going out to keep an eye on their mother as she got the preparations underway for tomorrow. Hunter stood at the kitchen sink and looked out over the front garden. A couple of rose bushes were heavy with blooms. *Remember the rose.* Why would Jack say that? The rose was just a rose. And the stupid note that came with it, which said, '*Everything I do is for you*'. Hunter wondered if there was some sort of hidden message encoded in those words, something that she just couldn't understand. But the hurt at seeing Jack last night with Courtney was just too powerful. The anger came back, the anger that she had used last night in self-defence. She let it wash through her, strengthening her resolve. She had preparations to make for tomorrow, and Jack could go to hell for all she cared.

The next morning Hunter awoke to another grey and blustery day. She had taken it easy the day before, still recovering from her night out. She resolved never to drink more than two glasses of wine in one sitting ever again.

She yawned and got up quietly, noting that Ryder was still asleep in her bed. She padded to the window to look out. The northerly wind continued, and blew the low clouds overhead in ragged sheets. Hunter threw on a cardigan and made her way downstairs to breakfast.

Her mother was already sitting at the kitchen table, drinking tea. "Morning," said Hunter as she walked in.

"Good morning, darling. How are you feeling today?"

"Much better, thank you."

"Wonderful. I'm very much looking forward to working with you in a hedge riding! This is going to be fun!"

Hunter sighed as she poured herself a cup of coffee. "Mom, I don't think that it's supposed to be fun. It's supposed to be research for me, to get me used to the Otherworld so that when we go and look for my father, it will hopefully be easier."

Abigail waved her hand. "Yes, yes, but my dear, this will be your first hedge riding in the *Otherworld*! You've only done hedge ridings to places in *this* world. It will be a totally new and magical experience for you."

Hunter blew on her coffee before taking a sip. "If you say so, Mom."

Abigail pushed a plate of pancakes towards her daughter, and gestured over to the pan on the stove. "Eat well. You are going to need your energy. There's scrambled eggs on the stove too."

Hunter nodded and helped herself to some breakfast. Abigail hummed as she worked around the kitchen, tidying up. The more she thought about it, Hunter could see the likeness between Ryder and their mother now that they were all together. Ryder was always up for an adventure, while Hunter usually needed to be coaxed into one. Abigail's whimsical nature belied a strong spirit, just like Ryder. Hunter smiled into her cup of coffee, watching her mother move about, reminding her of early mornings before school, with the radio on and her parents having breakfast in the kitchen with her.

"So, what time did you want to do this?" asked Hunter.

"Elspeth and I agreed that around 2pm would be a good time. Less chance of anyone who opposes us to be out and about around that time, not being a particularly liminal time. It may provide a bit more of a challenge for us to cross over, perhaps, but we can manage. The ritual circle will make it easier."

"So, are what all the stories say, true? That witches work mostly at night?"

Abigail smiled. "I suppose it is true. Evenings, or even midnight, are wonderful, magical, liminal times when you are less likely to be interrupted by the outside world. They are quieter times; times when you can go about your own business without attracting attention."

Hunter nodded. "Makes sense."

"We have a present for you, my dear."

"We?"

Abigail nodded, a huge grin on her face. She clasped her hands together before her, just barely containing her excitement. "Elspeth and I decided that it's time."

"Time for what?" asked Hunter cautiously.

"To have your own broom, of course, darling!"

Hunter inwardly moaned. *Of course. Witches have brooms.* Abigail rushed out of the kitchen and then came back in, brandishing a broom. This broom was different to Abigail's own, but still made in the traditional style of birch twig bristles, an ash handle and willow binding. Abigail handed it over proudly to her daughter.

"With many blessings, my dear Hunter," she said, beaming.

Hunter stood up and took the broom in her hands. The handle had been beautifully carved with images of fallow deer, oak leaves, and heather. She ran her hands down the handle, brushing the bristles. It was absolutely gorgeous. "Mom, I – I don't know what to say."

"Say, thank you," grumbled Ryder as she slipped into the kitchen.

Abigail put her hand on Hunter's arm. "Your sister gave us the idea for the decoration. She said you loved the deer and the heath."

And the oak leaves for Jack, Hunter thought with a pang. Though she knew that her sister wasn't really aware of the oak symbolism of the Druidry that Jack practiced, it still made her heart twinge despite its beauty.

"What's that?" asked Ryder, looking at her sister.

"Nothing," said Hunter. "It's very beautiful. Thank you both so much." She didn't want Ryder to know that the oak leaves pained her. She drew up energy from the earth to shield and cover her aura, so that her thoughts and emotions wouldn't leak out all over the kitchen. She had read about that yesterday in the book that Harriet had lent her when she had done the healing work. "The broom is truly stunning," she said, smiling at them both.

"And we can use it today in our hedge riding!" exclaimed her mother, clapping her hands in glee.

"As long as you don't ride it when you're angry," said Ryder. "You might fly off the handle."

"And as long as she knows how to drive a stick," said Abigail.

Hunter groaned as she turned the broom over in her hands. She tried to fake a little enthusiasm. "Thanks, Mom. I think I will dedicate and consecrate it first."

"Would you like Ryder and I to help?"

"No," said Hunter softly. "I'll do it on my own."

Hunter did a short consecration ceremony, to ready the broom for her work and also a little dedication to bind the tool to her own energy. When she was ready, she headed down for some lunch. The three women ate together, Abigail pushing food towards Hunter the whole time. "It's important, you know, so that you don't stray too far when we're in the Otherworld."

Hunter nodded and ate as much as she could. The doorbell rang, and Ryder went to answer it. "Hi, Thomas!" she said brightly, waving the man inside.

Thomas was the Guardian of Elspeth's coven. This entailed watching over the coven as they performed their rites, ensuring that there were no mundane interruptions as well as keeping an eye on the coven members themselves during ritual, seeing to their safety from anything otherworldly that might affect them in ritual. He had dedicated this entire year to working as the coven's Guardian, and he had already aided Hunter and Ryder when they had performed the ritual that freed Abigail from her imprisonment.

"Hello, Ryder." Thomas was a tall, slim man. He was twenty-eight years old and lived in the village. His blond, curly hair was cut short on the sides, and was longer on the top. He wore wire-rimmed glasses that rested on a strong nose. As he came into the living room, he saw Hunter and Abigail at the dining table. "Hello Abigail, Hunter." He had a soft voice and a quiet, but easy, laid-back manner about him.

"Hello, Thomas. Please, do come and sit," said Abigail. "Would you like some tea or coffee?"

"Tea would be lovely, thank you," he replied. He sat down across from Hunter.

Hunter leaned back in her chair, her tummy full. She wondered what Thomas would do in their ritual. "So, Thomas, can you tell me what role you will be playing in our hedge riding? This is all still so new to me."

Thomas nodded, pushing up his glasses further along his nose. His bright blue eyes smiled, and he nodded his thanks to Abigail as she handed him a cup of tea. "Essentially, I will provide physical and spiritual protection for you both as you ride the hedge. Along with Ryder," he added, glancing briefly at her as she plopped herself down next to him. "Elspeth has taught me how to provide magical cover for things that may intrude upon the ritual. It's very rare that anything actually does, you must understand," he said, noting the look of worry that appeared on Hunter's face. "It's just in your situation, with your past experience and this being called Lanoc, we must be extra vigilant. We wouldn't want to lose you both between the worlds."

Hunter swallowed past a lump in her throat. The way that Thomas described his role lent a gravitas to the ritual that she hadn't really been expecting.

Abigail put her hand on Hunter's arm. "Oh, don't worry my dear. We are just taking every necessary precaution. Better safe than sorry and all that." Hunter nodded, still uncertain.

"Abigail is right," Thomas said, sipping his tea. "Plus, it provides me with even more practice as I find my way in this role."

Ryder shifted in her chair, turning towards Thomas. "So how long have you been doing this?"

"I began at the Winter Solstice last year."

"Cool. And how long do you stay in this role?"

Thomas leaned back and took off his glasses, wiping them on his shirt as he spoke. "Well, usually the roles in the coven are swapped every year, so that everyone gets a chance to learn a different skill. The best way to learn something is by doing it."

Ryder nodded, looking at him thoughtfully. "I can't wait to see how all this works."

"You and me both," he said, his lips turning up into a small smile as he put his glasses back on.

They assembled in Abigail's room. At her instruction, they opened the window to allow Abigail and Hunter's spirits to fly freely, without hindrance. They had already shifted the bed to the middle of the room, and with chalk Ryder had drawn a large circle on the wooden floorboards around the bed. The circle was large enough that it encompassed most of the room. Ryder cast the circle and called in the elements. Her way of circle casting different from Hunter's way of hallowing the compass, but it was what Ryder was most comfortable with, and so she went with it. Abigail asked the Lord and Lady of the Witches to watch over them. Thomas stood in a corner of the room, just outside the circle and nearest to the door. Ryder stood within the circle by the window, opposite from Thomas. They had all grounded and centred, and were ready.

Abigail smiled at Hunter and then lay down on the bed, her broom next to her. She rested her hand upon it. Hunter copied her mother, lying down next to her with her broom on her other side. The feel of the ash handle tingled through her fingers, the broom's energy almost eager in its anticipation of the ritual. She stroked the wood and felt the carving of the graceful fallow deer, and took in their beauty to guide her heart. The heather she felt next, its enduring nature in the harshest of climes providing her with persistence. Lastly, her fingers brushed the oak leaves, giving her strength. She did not allow any room in her mind for Jack during this work.

With her other hand she reached out and took her mother's hand. They turned their heads to smile at each other and then closed their eyes, feeling the energy of the ritual flowing around them. A few moments passed, and then they began their chant in unison. The chant contained old, traditional phrases used in Witchcraft and hedge riding, combined with their own newer verses that they had rehearsed:

"Beyond the hedge is where we go

Secrets of the Otherworld to know
We ride the hedge with might and main
In the Lord and Lady's name
We set our spirits aloft, alight!
By our power and our might
Safe in this ring set about
Thout a thout and tout a tout
Horse and hattock, horse and go!
Horse and pellatis! Ho! Ho!
We cross the veil between the worlds
We cross the veil between the worlds
We cross the veil between the worlds"

As they finished the last line, Hunter felt her spirit lift from her body. Her etheric body still held her mother's hand, and she turned to look at her. Abigail smiled in her etheric body, and then nodded her head towards the open window. She watched as her mother placed her broomstick between her legs and Hunter did the same, though she preferred to sit side-saddle. It just felt more dignified that way, for some reason. With a laugh, Abigail took off, pulling Hunter with her out through the window and into the air. They rode higher and higher, through the grey clouds and into the mist.

Ryder looked over at her sister and mother, lying so still on the bed. She could have sworn she saw something fly out the window, a flicker of something, and assumed that it was their spirits shooting out towards the Otherworld. She looked out the window at the clouds, darkening in the skies and threatening with rain. She turned to look at Thomas, who was watching her intently. He nodded his head silently, and then walked around the circle's edge quietly, looking around the room for anything amiss.

The mist suddenly parted, and Hunter found herself flying over a beautiful forest that stretched for miles. She and her mother flew towards the centre of the forest where hills rose up from the wooded area, bare of trees but with a circle of standing stones upon the tallest hill. They flew to the standing stones and landed gently upon the ground. Abigail released her daughter's hand and looked around, an expression of sheer delight upon her face.

"Oh, I haven't been here for so long!" she exclaimed. "This is a wonderful spot, my darling Hunter. Your father and I spent some time here all those years ago, an enchanted evening under the stars. It may have even been the night you were conceived."

"Um, okay," said Hunter, not sure how she felt about that.

"Isn't it beautiful here?"

Hunter had to agree. There was a strange light all around them that wasn't quite daylight; more like a perpetual twilight. It felt comforting to her. It was not the harsh brightness of daylight, nor the deep darkness of the night. She felt strangely connected to this place.

She looked around, bringing her broom up and standing it on its head, bristles facing upwards. Her mother did the same as she began to wander around the stones, singing a song that Hunter was unfamiliar with. Hunter followed slowly, feeling how her etheric body moved in this world. It was different, almost like wading through water at times, while at other times it felt like she was floating. She reached out to touch one of the large standing stones, running her fingers along the rough surface and stroking the soft moss that grew upon it. The stone felt like it has many stories to tell, and she just wanted to sit with it and listen.

Her mother stopped singing abruptly, which made Hunter turn quickly to look. Her mother walked to the centre of the circle and stopped, looking down at something that lay upon a large, recumbent stone altar of sorts. Small quartz crystal flecks could be seen shining throughout the stone. Hunter walked up to stand beside her mother and looked down.

Upon the altar lay a small piece of metal with a seven-pointed star upon it. Abigail bent over to pick it up, but Hunter grabbed her arm. "Should we even touch it, Mom? We don't know why it's here."

Abigail turned to her daughter. "The seven-pointed star is a symbol of the Fae. It is the symbol that your father wore on his coronet when I first saw him. This might be a connection to him, in some way." She bent over to look at it more closely. "In fact, this could be the very one from his coronet."

Hunter looked down at the star. It may have been made of silver, but it was very tarnished. She tried to get a read on it, to see if it felt magical or strange in any way, or if it felt like some sort of trap. "I don't know, Mom."

Abigail waved her hand over the amulet and smiled. She looked to Hunter with her eyes full of hope and also tears. "It's his. I know it. I just know."

Back at the cottage, the wind began to pick up outside. Ryder turned back to look out the window and saw storm clouds rolling in. "I don't like this," she said softly as Thomas walked by her in one of his passes around the circle.

"I don't either," she heard him murmur as he continued to walk around the circle's edge.

"What should we do?"

Thomas stopped and looked at Ryder. "Wait," he said softly. "That's all we can do."

Abigail reached down and picked up the little star. A golden glow suddenly emanated from the star, and she smiled as she brought it to her heart. "Oh Aedon, we will find you. *Help us* to find you. Give us some more clues and information, and we will find you, my love."

A breeze kicked up and swirled around them. Flower petals rained down upon them, soft rose petals, daisies, and apple blossom. Abigail smiled and spread her arms wide, the flowers falling all around them. "I will find you, my love. But I need more information. *We* need more information."

The sharp crack of lightning sounded outside the cottage, and a long peal of thunder rattled the windows. The wind turned into a gale, and Ryder saw the trees in the forest that bordered their property swaying wildly. Rain came bucketing down in sheets, and another crack of lighting sounded, making Ryder jump with its sound. It was like it was coming from right over their heads. "Oh man, this isn't good," she said with trepidation. She looked over to Thomas, who was looking upwards to the ceiling. He pulled out his ritual knife and pointed it upwards. His voice carried above the thunder.

"Lady bless the house,
From site to stay,
From beam to wall,
From end to end,
From ridge to basement,
From balk to roof-tree,

From found to summit,
    Found and summit."

He then threw his knife down into the floorboards by the foot of the bed, where it quivered, embedded in the wood. "By iron and forge, by earth, fire and water, Lady be here now and protect your daughters!"

Ryder felt a mini shockwave of power come from the knife and fill the circle that she stood in. The sound of the storm faded, becoming somewhat muffled. She looked over to Thomas and smiled her thanks. He nodded in return and began to pace around the outer edge of the circle once more.

Ryder looked over at her mother and sister, and began to pray that they would come home safely.

Hunter looked up as the flowers swirled around them. Her heart was pounding, but she didn't feel any fear. Instead, a strange sort of excitement flowed from her, to dance with the petals flowing on the breeze. She then heard a soft voice whisper,

"At the rising sun,
A bridge there will be,
Where day meets night,
That is where I will be."

Hunter turned to her mother to see if she too had heard the words. Her mother nodded and then threw her arms up to the sky, shouting with joy: "Yes, my love! We will be there soon! We are coming for you!"

Another peal of thunder rattled the walls of the cottage, and even Ryder could feel it in the protected circle. She could see Thomas standing at the circle's edge now, his arms stretched downwards, palms facing the floor, and she knew he was drawing up energy from the earth. Ryder followed suit, and pushed that energy out to strengthen the circle from within even as Thomas strengthened it from without. When she felt her energy touch his, it gave her a strange tingling sensation. Thomas looked up with surprise, and then gave her a small smile. He nodded, and then spoke loudly so that he could be heard from within the circle and above the storm. "Now draw up more energy with me from the earth and push it out to encompass the entire cottage!" he said. Ryder immediately did so, sending the energy out and into the walls and ceiling of the cottage. Again, she felt her energy combining with Thomas', a pleasant tingling that made her feel good in some way. They pushed the energy out and felt it wrap itself around the cottage in a protective embrace, shielding it from the storm. As they finished, Ryder grinned at Thomas, grateful that they had the Guardian's help for their ritual.

She was shocked out of her thoughts when a lightning bolt hit a tree close to the house. Ryder spun around to look out the window as the oak tree nearest to the cottage glowed for a moment before exploding. She cried out in surprise, covering her eyes instinctively. She felt Thomas run around the circle's edge towards her. When she looked out the window again, she saw a cloaked figure come running out from the beech woods behind the house. It ran full tilt across the lawn and stopped near the oak tree, drawing out a knife from the folds of the cloak. It raised the knife high and then stabbed downwards into the earth, making a small hole. It then turned the knife upside down and thrust it into the earth, handle first, the blade facing towards the storm.

Ryder recognised this action. She had seen Jack do the same thing when the storm had hit them in the forest. He had split the wind and the storm itself, and sure enough the same thing happened for this strange, cloaked figure. The wind rallied one last time, and then there was a loud shriek on the air before everything suddenly stopped, and silence reigned as the sun came out.

"What in the hell," said Thomas quietly as he followed Ryder's gaze out the window.

The figure in the back garden withdrew the knife and ran for the forest edge, disappearing from sight.

Abigail's face suddenly became anxious. "Come, my love, we must return. Something is happening on the Other side."

"At the cottage?" asked Hunter, not knowing what to do.

"Yes, come on, we must go back. Now." They sat upon their brooms and Abigail grabbed her daughter's hand. Instantly they rose up into the sky. Flying straight to the clouds, they entered into the misty realm and came out the other side to see the cottage lying below them. Dark clouds rolled away in the distance, and the sun had come out. The large oak tree nearest the house which they often sat under had a large chunk of it laying on the ground, smoking, even as branches were strewn all around it in a tangled mess.

Abigail took them directly to the cottage. They could see Ryder and Thomas looking out the bedroom window. Ryder suddenly said something to Thomas, and they quickly moved to the side. Abigail and Hunter flew back in, landing on the floor at the foot of the bed. They disembarked and hurried up to where their bodies lay. Carefully they lay down and re-entered their bodies, taking a deep breath.

As they slowly sat up, they saw Ryder and Thomas looking at them. Ryder ran to them and jumped onto the bed, throwing herself into a group hug. "Mom! Hunter! You're back!"

"Oooof! Hello, dear," said Abigail, smiling. "Did we miss something?"

Chapter Seven

As they cleaned up the room and put it back to rights, Ryder told them of what happened while Hunter and Abigail were away hedge riding. As she spoke, she and Thomas pushed the bed frame back against the wall, while Hunter went to look out the window. The oak tree had stopped smoking, and the figure that Ryder described was nowhere to be seen.

Abigail wiped away the chalk circle with a damp rag. "I wonder who on earth was in the garden?" she asked.

"Whatever or whoever it was, it did the same thing as Jack did when we were trapped in the storm in the New Forest," said Ryder.

Thomas straightened from the bed frame and pushed his glasses back up. "Could it maybe have been someone from Jack's Druid group? Or Elspeth even?"

"Only one way to find out," said Ryder, whipping out her phone. She shot off a quick text to Elspeth, who responded almost immediately. "Elspeth says that it wasn't her. She hasn't been able to leave the shop. The plumbing's giving her all kinds of grief still."

"Maybe it *was* someone from Jack's group. Or maybe it was Jack himself," said Abigail softly from where she kneeled on the floor.

Hunter came over and took over from her mother, waving her away. "No," she said as she scrubbed away the chalk. "It wasn't Jack."

"Why not, dear?"

"Because he's too busy with someone else right now." Hunter had to fight to keep her voice level as the pain rose in her heart. She pushed it back down and continued to wipe away the circle's outline on the floor. "He's got other things to do."

Abigail looked out the window and saw the wreckage of the old oak tree. "That poor tree. It's been such a good friend to us at this cottage our entire lives. I guess we should call in the professionals to see what they can save."

Thomas walked up to Abigail. "I know some tree surgeons that can come and take a look. I could give them a ring if you'd like."

Abigail turned to the tall, slim man beside her. She gently touched his arm. "Thank you, Thomas. That's very kind of you."

Thomas left shortly after that. He had apologised for the damage to the floorboards where he had thrown his knife, and offered to patch it up. Abigail simply smiled at him and told him that it was perfectly alright, and that he needn't worry.

The three women now sat at the kitchen table, the sisters with their coffee and Abigail with a cup of tea. Hunter got out a plate of cookies, or biscuits as they were called in England. They went over what Hunter and Abigail had found in the Otherworld. Ryder was particularly interested in what the Otherworld felt like, and grilled her sister on it. Hunter described it as best she could, but words just seemed to fail the real experience of hedge riding, especially hedge riding in the Otherworld.

Abigail brought out the small, silver star. Ryder asked her how she could bring it back to this world when it was her etheric body that has gone to the Otherworld, not her physical body.

Abigail simply smiled and said, "Why, magick of course, darling. This item is magick. *We are magick*, all of us."

Hunter looked at the small seven-pointed star. "May I?" she asked. Abigail handed it to her. Hunter turned it over in her palm, not feeling any sort of energy emanating from it. "So, this was part of my father's coronet?"

Abigail nodded. "Your father was the younger brother of Lanoc. They both had crowns, of course. Lanoc's was larger and more ornate, because he was the King of their realm, tribe, or whatever it is that they call it over there. I never really paid much attention." Abigail sipped her tea and then looked away dreamily. "Aedon was so handsome, so tall, so… kingly. So much more than Lanoc could ever be. Aedon was wise and compassionate, quiet, and strong. He knew who he was, and never tried to be anything else. I'm sure that the Otherworld realm that they belong to would be better off under his rule than his brother's. But Aedon never sought the crown. He supported his brother as much as he could, before Lanoc changed. Or rather, before Lanoc showed his true colours."

"What do you mean, Mom?" asked Ryder.

"Aedon told me of his brother's utter hatred for humans. His disgust at his brother for loving me. Lanoc's high temper and cruelty. His delight in causing pain. His utter contempt for everyone and everything that was different from him."

"I guess the Fae aren't so different from humans after all," grumbled Ryder.

Abigail looked over at her daughter with a sad smile. "I guess not, Peanut."

Ryder looked shocked. "Peanut???"

Abigail laughed. "That's what your father and I called you when you were born. Hunter was Poppet, and you were Peanut."

Hunter laughed softly. "Alright, Peanut?"

Ryder just grinned at both of them and grabbed another biscuit. "I like Peanut."

They took it easy for the rest of that day, and as usual, Hunter was up early the following morning. The weather was fine, and she was soon out on the heath in the early pre-dawn light. She walked without a plan for a destination; she only wanted to get out and think about everything that had happened. She was still trying to process her feelings about what Jack had done, about her own heritage, and how she was going to solve this problem with Lanoc. As the first rays of the sun poked above the horizon, she came out of her own thoughts and found herself in the very spot where she had first met Jack.

She stood on the path and watched the sun rise. The deer were not there, and all was quiet on the heath. The sun's disc was pink as it crested the horizon, and then turned orange as it came up over the distant trees of the New Forest. Finally, as it cleared the horizon she was forced to look down, and a few sad tears escaped to roll down her cheeks.

Suddenly she felt she was not alone. Someone was on the path behind her. And then she knew.

Jack.

She could feel his energy from where she stood. He approached her quietly, and then stood behind her. There was silence between them for a moment, before he said, "Hello, Hunter."

Hunter, still facing away, did not reply.

"I had a feeling you would be out here this morning. I had to see you."

Hunter hugged her arms around herself. Finally, she spoke. "And why is that, Jack?" she said, still with her back to him.

She knew he was running his hands through his dark hair, like he always did when he was unsure. "I don't know. I – I miss you."

Hunter's heart skipped a beat, but then she felt anger flowing from it to envelop her in its warm embrace. She turned around, her arms still tight around her. "You missed me?" she said, incredulous. "You don't get to *miss me*, Jack." She felt more hot tears streaming down her face.

Jack sighed and looked down. "You are right. I guess I don't." He took another step closer to her. "Hunter, please. Remember what I said. Everything I do, it's all for you."

"Oh, really? Going out with Courtney is for *my* best interests? How is what you are doing with *her* benefitting me in any way, shape, or form?"

"I can't tell you, Hunter."

Hunter ignored the hitch in her heart when he said her name like that. That always got to her. She pushed the feeling down, and said bitterly, "Of course you can't." She had to look away.

"Hunter, it kills me know that you are hurting like this. That you are so angry with me."

The dam of her full anger burst, and she faced him again, dropping her hands to her sides and balling them into fists. "Oh, poor you, Jack! Poor you! It's killing *you*, is it? This is all *your* doing, you know! This is your choice, your decision. I thought we had something special. I thought that you loved me. But I was wrong. You are just like all the other men I've ever had the misfortune in my life to have been in any sort of relationship. You are all infatuated and *so in love* at the start, but none of you can *ever* stay the course. You just get what you want and then leave. Well, fine, Jack. You got what you came for, and now you can just leave."

The Veil Between the Worlds

Jack simply stood there, letting Hunter's tirade flow through and past him. He breathed deeply, grounding himself against her anger. He blew out a long breath, and simply said into the silence, "Hunter, this is something that I have to do."

"Why Jack? Why?" she shouted.

"To keep you safe," he said quietly, before turning and walking away.

Hunter stood there, breathing heavily as she watched Jack walk away. She wished that she hadn't blown up like that. She had wanted to keep her cool, should they ever meet like this. But her emotions had taken over, and there was nothing that she could do to stop the hurt and anger that flowed through her. Once again, she wrapped herself in her anger, drawing it close to her like a suit of armour, blocking out any of Jack's emotions or energy as he walked away. *He had done this. He did not get to feel bad about it.*

He turned off the path and disappeared behind the gorse. Hunter took in a deep breath and wiped her face with her hands. She waited a few moments longer before she began to walk home, if indeed the cottage here in Burley *was* her home. *Maybe I should just go back to Canada, where I have a life waiting,* she thought. She walked down the path, her mind in turmoil.

When she got back, she found her mother and sister talking animatedly in the kitchen. Hunter went in without a word and poured herself a cup of coffee.

"Morning, Poppet." Hunter grunted something noncommittal.

"Guess what, Hun? Harriet has three free tickets to the First Harvest Dance tomorrow! Please say you'll go."

Hunter took a long sip from the mug before she turned around. She was still in a bad mood from her confrontation with Jack. "I don't really feel like going to a dance, Ryder."

Ryder looked puzzled. "But this is a proper, oldy worldy tradition here in Burley. You've *got* to come!"

"I don't *have* to do anything, Ryder."

Abigail stood and touched Hunter's shoulder. "Is everything okay, Hunter?"

"Just peachy," Hunter snarked.

Abigail looked to Ryder for guidance. She could only shrug. She was usually the one who was surly in the mornings, not Hunter. Abigail tried again. "It really is a lovely dance. I used to love going to it when I was younger."

Hunter sat down at the table and blew out a long breath, easing some of the anger in her heart. "I don't know, Mom. I'm just not feeling all that social, right now."

Abigail went over and leant down towards her daughter, giving her a little hug. "It's okay, Poppet. You do what you have to do." She straightened up, and then declared, "Elspeth and I are going away tomorrow on holiday!"

"You what?" asked Ryder. "Mom, that's awesome!"

Hunter looked at her mother and frowned. "Is that such a good idea?"

"Why not?" said Abigail. "I've been cooped up in this cottage for weeks now. While it's nice to be back home after being trapped in the Otherworld, I would like to see something more than just the back garden. Elspeth and I decided to head out for a week, and go to Cornwall. We're renting a cottage right on the coast. It's going to be so lovely!"

Ryder went over and gave her mother a hug. "That's great, Mom. You both could use a bit of a holiday."

Hunter just drank her coffee, still feeling out of sorts. She barely listened as her mother and sister chatted about the cottage in Cornwall. Instead, she was going over what Jack had said on the heath. How on earth could leaving her equate to keeping her safe? What he had said just didn't make any sense. Hunter gave up and pushed those thoughts away, dismissing them as a cop out on Jack's part to not own up to what he did to her. She sneered into her coffee cup. *I hope he chokes on his false nobility.*

She heard her sister clear her throat, and Hunter looked up to see both Ryder and Abigail looking at her. "What?"

"Are you sure you're okay, Hun?"

Hunter stood and grabbed her coffee mug. "I'm fine," she said softly. "I'm going out into the garden, to do some weeding."

Ryder and Abigail stood in the kitchen, watching her leave. "I think she's still processing a lot of stuff," said Ryder softly.

Abigail nodded. "She was always so sensitive. She still is. It's what makes her special, you know. Though she never sees it."

"So, what's my superpower, Mom?"

Abigail studied her daughter for a moment. "Your wit, your intelligence, and your adaptability. I'm so proud of who you've both become, you know."

"Aw, thanks, Mom."

As Hunter got her hands in the soil, she instantly felt better. The smell of the earth was comforting, the warm sun on her shoulders and back felt soothing. She pulled up the little weeds that were beginning to grow in the vegetable patch. She figured what with being so emotionally raw after seeing Jack this morning, she might as well venture out into the place that held memories of him. She could hardly feel any worse than she already did at the moment. She refused to reminisce, however, and instead focused on pulling up the weeds and planning what it was that she wanted to do.

Now that she had calmed down a bit, she knew that she couldn't make any firm decisions yet about staying or leaving Burley. There was still too much up in the air, what with the quest to find her father and all that. It was still a case of living day to day, moment to moment, something which irked Hunter to no end. She liked to have things planned out; she liked to have order in her world. But the last two months here had forced her into a new way of life that made her think and react differently to her normal routine. And while it had its downsides, it also had changed her slightly, something which she could finally admit to herself wasn't such a bad thing.

Dealing with the different crises that had arisen over the last two months, not to mention her relationship with Jack, showed her that she could handle what life threw at her, without planning or forethought. Maybe she wasn't so unsuitable a candidate to go to the Otherworld with her mother to find her father. Yes, she was still new to learning magick and magickal techniques, but her Fae heritage had probably helped her in many ways that she hadn't yet realised until she had spoken with Harriet's parents. Elspeth and the Sandfords had said that Hunter's Fae blood was probably how she had been able to pull off the difficult task of finding and helping to free her mother from her imprisonment. Though she might be a 'newbie' in some areas, her bloodlines from both her mother and her birth father held something quite powerful, which she was only just learning how to tap into. She had to believe in herself more.

She drew up energy from the earth, and let it soothe her emotions. It felt good; a kind of balm against the heat of her anger. She drank in the dark, earthy energy and released some of her anger into the transforming nature of the earth. As she worked, she considered how she was going to proceed. *Take it day by day*, she thought.

Maybe she should go to the dance.

Chapter Eight

Hunter put on her new dress that she had bought that afternoon in Lyndhurst. It was a knee-length tea dress in dark blue. It had a wonderful light, floaty fabric that made Hunter feel good, and when she twirled around, it flowed nicely. She had also bought a cute new pair of ballet flats to go with it. She had washed her hair earlier that afternoon, and left it to air dry. Her long red curls bounced, and she decided to leave her hair loose for this evening. She put on some light makeup, with eyeshadow, mascara, powder, and a bit of blush. She topped it off with some lip gloss and her favourite perfume. She took one last look in the full-length mirror in her mother's room, smoothing out her dress. She breathed in deeply, psyching herself up. She *was* going to have fun tonight.

Harriet had assured her earlier that they were pretty safe tonight from Jack and Courtney. This kind of dance wasn't really Courtney's style. In fact, Harriet had never seen her at any community dance, ever, nor at any community charity event. It was, as Harriet said, 'beneath her'. And so, Hunter was determined to have a good time tonight, albeit without drinking. She didn't want a repeat of the last time she had gone out.

She heard her sister call her, and she came downstairs. Her mother waited with Ryder at the bottom of the stairs. Ryder was wearing a long, black skirt in a stretchy jersey fabric, that had slits all the way up the knee so that she could move easily. With it she had paired a black top that had slashes across the collarbone, and her sparkly purple Doc Martens. When Abigail

The Veil Between the Worlds

saw her eldest daughter, she was all smiles. "You look so beautiful, Hunter. You go and have fun tonight." She went up to Hunter, giving her a hug and then a kiss on the cheek.

"You have fun too, Mom. Should we wait for Elspeth to get here?"

As they said that, they heard Elspeth's car pull up in the driveway. She came to the door, and smiled at the girls who were ready to go out. "Have a nice time, dears. We will be on our way soon, as well."

"Yes," said Abigail. "As soon as it gets dark, we are out of here and on the road." She waved at the suitcase that Hunter had loaned her, along with some of her clothes. "All packed and ready to go! Just remember, my loves, no hedge riding or big magickal workings until we return. It's just too dangerous."

"We know, Mom," said Ryder, giving Abigail a hug. "You have a great time in Cornwall. I want photos!" Ryder then turned and bounced a couple of times before she grabbed Hunter's arm. "This is going to be so cool!" Hunter was pulled along to the door by her sister. "Okay sis, let's go dancing!"

"And don't forget to study!" called Elspeth after them. "You've got to prepare for your next hedge riding!"

"We know!" the sisters said in unison.

Hunter was starting to get a little excited. She did indeed love dancing, and it had been a long time since she had treated herself to a night of fun and dance. She used to go to a few folk nights at various places where she lived in Ontario, and they sometimes did folk dancing. She loved it so much: the atmosphere, the live music, the happy people. This was just what she needed.

They waved goodbye to their mother and Elspeth, and got into the little yellow bug. Hunter drove them to the village car park, which was free after 6pm. They could hear people laughing outside the village hall, and they made their way over. Harriet waited outside on the pavement, and when she saw them, she waved. The sisters went over and Harriet handed them their tickets.

"Okay ladies, let's go in and get some drinks before the band begins!"

They got into the queue to go in, and soon found themselves in front of a woman at a small, popup table by the door. She took their tickets and waved them in with a smile. As they entered the building, Hunter could see a stage at one end, where the band was setting up, and a bar in the opposite corner. The three women made a beeline for the bar, and as they stood waiting for their turn, quite a few people greeted Ryder. It turned out that these were regular patrons from the pub. Hunter watched her sister chat and get on with the locals. She felt a small pang as she considered her own social awkwardness, compared to Ryder's amiable and extrovert nature. Would she ever fit it? Hunter knew she was different, and after finding out about her heritage recently, those differences seemed even more acute, especially in these kinds of situations. She took a couple of deep breaths and forced herself to calm down and relax. She smiled at the people that Ryder introduced to her, and decided that even if she wasn't as gregarious as her sister, she could at least try harder.

They saw some members of Elspeth's coven dotted around the room. Doris was there chatting with a group of older ladies, and Bernard stood with his arm around a woman, smiling at a younger couple that had joined them.

"Well, if it isn't three of the bonniest lassies in Burley." The women turned around to see Dougal standing behind them. "Glad ta see ya here tonight, ladies. Are ya ready for a good reel and a hooch?"

All three of the women looked at each other blankly. Finally, Harriet said, "I think he means are we ready for a dance and a good time?"

Dougal barked out laugh. "Close enough, lass, close enough." He put an arm around her shoulder. "So, what can I get you hens to drink?"

"Is he calling us chickens now?" whispered Ryder to her sister.

"He lost me at hooch," replied Hunter.

Hunter was on soft drinks tonight. They got their drinks and Dougal led them to one of the many tables that were set up close to the walls of the building, to allow room for dancing in the centre. As it was the weekend, they saw Dougal's brother, Mackenzie, sitting by himself and watching the people around him. "Hey, Mackenzie!" said Ryder, plopping herself down next to him. "Haven't seen you for a while. How's it going?"

Mackenzie took a sip from his pint. He was much slighter than his brawny brother, quieter and somewhat withdrawn. "It's going well, thank you," he said, his accent thick like his brother's, but his voice softer and more musical.

"How are your studies going? This is your second year, right? And you're doing summer sessions?"

Mackenzie nodded. "That's right. I'm taking extra psychology classes to help broaden my knowledge a bit."

"What is it that you're studying again?"

"Forensic psychology."

"Oh yeah. That's so interesting. Tell me more."

Mackenzie took another sip of his pint, and looked at Ryder for a moment, almost as if he was deciding whether or not he wanted to talk about it. Hunter could sympathise with Mackenzie's social awkwardness. The only time she had met him before, her sister had pretty much scared him off with her outgoing nature. *Ease up, sis. Remember, he's a bit of a skittish kitten.*

Ryder shot a quick glance at Hunter. *Oh yeah, right.* "Um, only if you want to talk about it. No pressure."

Ryder smiled at him and took a sip of her drink.

With some of the pressure eased, Mackenzie actually leaned onto the table and began to talk to Ryder about what he was studying. Dougal looked over at Hunter and raised an eyebrow. Hunter just smiled back.

"It's nice ta see ya back out again, Hunter," said Dougal, much more softly than in his usual tone. He reached out to gently pat her hand.

"Thank you, Dougal. I'm so, so sorry for how I behaved at the pub last time."

Dougal waved away her apology. "Dinnae fash, lass. We've all been there."

"Some of us more often than others," said Harriet, with a look at Dougal. He merely grinned and raised his pint glass to her in salute.

"So, how are you getting on with your energy work, Hunter?" asked Harriet.

"Better, I think. At least, Ryder hasn't complained." Hunter looked over at her sister, and was surprised to find her and Mackenzie still deep in discussion. She smiled, and turned back to Harriet and Dougal. "How are things with you, Dougal?"

Hunter thought she saw an emotion flit quickly behind Dougal's eyes, almost as if there was something that he didn't want to tell her. He then quickly covered it up with a smile, and said, "Och, aye, things are going the same as they usually do."

They were interrupted as one of the members of the band turned on the microphone and started to address the crowd. "Hello and good evening, folks. Lovely to be back here in

Burley." There was a round of applause. "We are going to play four dances for you, then we will have a break, do another four and then it's the most popular three dances that we will repeat. You know how it works!" Everyone clapped. "This evening, we will start with something simple. We'll do the Gay Gordons. Everyone, up and in a circle with a partner!"

Dougal held his hand out to Harriet, who rolled her eyes. "Fine," she said, "but I'm not going to dance with you all night, Dougal."

"I wouldn't impose on the fair lady," replied Dougal in a very good highbrow English accent. That made Hunter laugh out loud. She looked over at her sister, whom she knew wanted to ask Mackenzie, but he was looking down into his pint. "Come on, Ry, dance with me," said Hunter, holding out her hand.

"Okay!"

They made their way to the dance floor, and joined the other couples standing in a circle. The sisters copied the poses that the others were waiting in, which had the ladies on the outer edge, their arms to the left and holding onto their partner's hands. Ryder decided that she was the man for this dance, and so Hunter took the outside position. She had danced this before, and knew what to expect. Ryder just grinned, happy to try anything new.

The callers explained the dance to them and took them through it step by step, first without the music. They then had a trial run, with the band playing at half speed while the caller gave them instructions. By the end of the second run, Ryder had got it down pat. On the third try, the band played at full speed, and the sisters had a grand time doing the four different sequences. After the song ended, the caller said that they will try it again, but this time on the last pass, the ladies were to switch with the partner behind them. This caused a little chaos, but it was also fun. Hunter had the first round with her sister, and then danced the second with Dougal, who was behind her with Harriet. After she had danced a round with Dougal, she danced another round with an older gentleman who had a long, white beard and a tweed waistcoat. He smiled at her and gave her a wink as she left to go dance with another partner when the round finished. Hunter found herself dancing with Doris, who smiled at her and said, "Hello, dear. Lovely to see you here, tonight." Doris was a good dancer. The older woman smiled at Hunter and added some extra flourishes, which made Hunter step up her game. They quickly high-fived each other before Hunter danced the last round with the person behind. It was one of the men that Ryder had introduced to her earlier this evening, and she smiled as she danced with him, helping him to remember the steps and calling them out softly to him when he got confused. The dance ended, and the man bowed to her and thanked her. She gave a small curtsey and a smile.

Ryder came running up to her. "Oh. My. God. That was so much fun!"

"It is, isn't it?" said Hunter.

Dougal and Harriet joined them. "I wonder what the next dance will be?" asked Harriet.

"Okay folks, let's try something a little trickier," said the man at the microphone. "Probably best to do this one before we've had a few drinks," he said, which got a laugh from the crowd. "It's time for a Trip to Tunbridge!"

She heard a few people applaud, and Hunter decided to give this one a go as well. Ryder had already found another partner, and so Hunter looked around. The older gentleman that she had danced with earlier came up to her. "A lady should never be in want of a dance partner," he said, and held out his hand. Hunter smiled, and took it. She was excited, as she had never danced this one before. She caught a quick glance at Dougal, who was sitting this one out. Harriet was game, and had asked a man at the next table to dance. He agreed, and they took up their positions. Hunter noticed that Dougal's expression had shifted from his usual jovial smile to one of consideration, and perhaps even consternation.

"This dance is a Regency dance, from 1793," the caller said. A little thrill coursed through Hunter. She loved all things Regency. Her favourite book was, of course, *Pride and Prejudice*. She heard her sister down at the other end of the hall give a small squee of delight. Ryder was more a fan of the movies than the novels, but still, it made Hunter smile. The caller explained the dance, which was quite complicated. They began as before, without music as they learned the steps, then at half tempo and finally dancing it in full. As Hunter moved between the rows of people with her partner, she couldn't help but feel like she had stepped back in time. It really was very Jane Austen-esque, even if she was dancing with a septuagenarian instead of Mr Darcy. They were dancing in groups of threes on either side, with ladies on one side and men on the other. The dance began with the chosen partner for the main section, but then switched over to dance with others in a quick circle at the corners. It was confusing at first, but Hunter soon got into it. She felt very much like her heroine, Elizabeth Bennett.

Next it was the Hunsdon House, a dance performed in a square. This one was danced first with your partner, and then with others at the corners, followed by much going in and out, back and forth. Hunter knew this dance, and so it wasn't too difficult for her. She danced this one with Harriet, and in her square of eight, most of the dancers were women. Hunter guessed that a lot of the men had given up after the Trip to

Tunbridge. The women were still game, and the two men who were part of their square had obviously danced this before as well. Hunter felt good; her dress was flowing around her, the people were lovely and the music was fabulous. She couldn't stop smiling as she danced, and she was truly enjoying herself.

The fourth dance was a waltz, and so couples could come up and dance as they pleased. Hunter went back to the table with Harriet, but gazed longingly at the dance floor. She felt someone come up beside her, and turned to see Dougal looking down at her. "I believe I owe you a dance, milady," he said, holding out his hand. "We never did finish the one we had started at the pub," he continued, with a wink.

Hunter laughed and took his hand. He led her out onto the dance floor. She saw Harriet and Ryder come out too. Hunter was sure Ryder had never waltzed in her life, but Harriet was already giving her sister instructions. *Good luck, and have fun,* thought Hunter towards her sister.

This is so awesome, she heard her sister reply in her mind.

The music started, and Dougal began to lead Hunter around the floor. Hunter was surprised; Dougal was actually a good dancer. She was able to relax in his arms, and trust him to lead. She looked out over his shoulder at the other couples, and smiled. Harriet and Ryder were having a great time, and Ryder was doing her best to be graceful, but still managing to step on Harriet's feet. An older couple swayed gracefully past, looking for all the world as if they had grown up doing this, which they probably had. Dougal's soft voice in her ear cut into her thoughts.

"I saw Jack the other night, after I took ya home from the pub." Hunter tensed up, and she felt Dougal give a little squeeze of reassurance in the centre of her back where his hand lay.

"Something is up, lass. I don't know what, but something is up with him."

Hunter turned to look at Dougal's face for a moment. She saw concern in his blue eyes. She looked away, and finally said, "Whatever it is, he brought it on himself."

Dougal spun her around in a few dizzying circles, as the music swelled. "I'm not so sure, lass," he said. "I think there's something else at play there. Jack's no' the man ta love ya and leave ya." Hunter remained silent as they glided and swayed around the floor. "He was plannin' on taking ya over to Ireland, you know," Dougal continued. "And then something happened, I don't know what. But he loved you with all his heart. I think he still does."

Hunter found that her left hand was gripping Dougal's shoulder tightly. She tried to relax. "Then why did he leave? Why is he with Courtney now?" she managed to say in an even tone.

She felt Dougal's sigh across her right shoulder. "Honestly, I don't know. But don't close the door on him yet, lass."

The music came to a long, slow end, and Dougal gave her a graceful twirl, holding her by the hand. He bowed gallantly, still holding her hand. Hunter gave him a little smile, and said, "Thank you, Dougal."

"It was my pleasure," he said, leading her back to the table.

The caller went up to the microphone. "All right, folks, we are going to have a fifteen-minute break, and then we'll be back with some more dances." People dispersed, going to the bar to get refreshments, or sitting down at the tables. Hunter took a seat at the table where Mackenzie still sat. Ryder and Harriet came up to join them. Dougal said that he was going for another round of drinks, and they put their order in. Harriet tried to give him some money, but he refused and went to the bar.

"That was so much fun," said Ryder grinning. She was looking a little hot and sweaty, but happy. She grabbed a napkin and wiped her forehead. "Who knew that a waltz was so hard, and such good exercise? I can feel it in my legs." She stretched out her legs and wiggled her purple-booted feet.

Harriet fanned herself with a coaster from the table. "Phew! Yeah, it's great exercise. And at least no Fae King is trying to kill us in here," she said wryly.

Mackenzie looked at her in surprise. Ryder saw his look, and grinned. She leaned in close and said softly, so other tables couldn't hear, "I guess you don't know, do you? Hunter, over there, is half Fae. Turns out, her father is the brother to some Fae King in the Otherworld. Said brother's in a snit about it, and tried to kill us all in the ritual that we did to free our mother from his evil clutches."

Mackenzie's eyes widened. "You're putting me on," he said softly.

Harriet shook her head. "I wish to hell we were."

Mackenzie looked around, making sure no one was near them to overhear. He leaned in close to Ryder. "Tell me more," he simply said. Mackenzie was a Buidseach, a type of Scottish Witch. Dougal had told the sisters a while back that his brother had magickal powers, even though Dougal himself lacked any sort of magickal ability, instead inheriting the 'brains and the brawn' as he liked to put it. Mackenzie listened intently, and Ryder relished in telling the story again.

"That's amazing," he said, when she had finally wound down.

"It's totally badass," said Ryder.

Dougal came back with their drinks. "Here ya go. Hope I remembered correctly." He passed them out around the table.

The Veil Between the Worlds

"Those were some pretty swish moves you had up there, Dougal," said Ryder. "Where did you learn to dance like that?"

Dougal's face reddened. "We all learned to dance when we were younger, at cèilidhs. They're pretty much similar to this."

"You should definitely have a go with him, Ryder," said Hunter with a smile. She was trying to push what Dougal had said to her about Jack out of her mind. "If they do a waltz again, do it!"

Ryder looked over at Dougal. "You heard her. It's a date," she said with a grin. Dougal just turned even redder and rubbed the back of his neck.

Soon enough, the band came back on and the caller came up to the mic. "Alright folks, it's time for the Black Nag! Take your partner and line up in two rows of three pairs each." Everyone at the table was shocked when Mackenzie asked Ryder if she would like to dance with him. "A world of yes," she breathed, and took his hand as he led her onto the dance floor.

A man Hunter did not know came up to the table, and asked Hunter for a dance. He looked to be around thirty, and was very handsome. His light brown hair was styled in a trendy, shaggy cut that fell around his forehead, ears, and down the back of his neck. He had electric blue eyes and a strong, chiselled chin covered in what Ryder liked to call 'designer stubble'. *What the hell*, thought Hunter. She smiled and took his hand as he led her up. As she glanced back at the table, she saw Dougal and Harriet watching her with a look of disbelief on their faces. Dougal quickly grabbed Harriet's hand, and she made no protest as he brought her up to stand near Hunter and her new partner.

The caller explained the dance, which was complicated at first, until the music kicked in. Once the music was going, it was much easier to remember the dance, as the steps just flowed with the melody. Hunter smiled at her charming partner. He wore a patterned, dark blue shirt that matched her dress. The first few buttons were undone, giving Hunter a little glimpse of tanned and toned skin beneath.

There was a lot of hand holding in this dance, and as their hands touched, Hunter could feel a warm, slightly tingly sensation. It reminded her a bit of Jack, when their energy sometimes mingled. Hunter was a little uneasy about the tingling from a stranger at first, but soon got used to it. Maybe he too was from one of the magickal families here in Burley. She could feel his eyes on her when the ladies wove in and out of each other on their side, and she in turn watched him do the same on the men's side.

When they came back from the walk, they then had to pass each other. As she turned around her partner, Hunter felt a pulling on her long hair. "I'm so sorry!" her partner said, as he looked down at his cufflink, before they had to separate. "I think we got caught up," he said on their next pass.

Hunter smile. "Not a problem"

As they took hold of each other's hands and swept up the line, he said, "You have the most beautiful hair."

Hunter could feel a blush coming to her face. "Thanks," she said, looking down as they trotted back down.

"Do you live around here?" he asked, as they passed each other once again.

"Perhaps," she said, with a sly smile on the second pass.

"Mysterious. I like it," he said as they passed each other again. They then waited for the people to dance at the corners, and Hunter also stole a glance at the other couples. She saw Ryder and Mackenzie up at the front, looking really good together. When she looked at Dougal and Harriet near to her, they seemed to be frowning at her. She also caught a glance of

Doris standing with her group of ladies by the bar, and her expression was one of disapproval.

Hunter and her partner then had to hold hands and turn around each other twice, repeating that again on the other side with the other hand. "What about you?" Hunter asked, as they circled each other.

He smiled, a very charming smile. His electric blue eyes looked deep into her own each time they held hands, and the tingling returned. "Yes, I live near Burley. You're new here."

Hunter smiled back. "Yes, I am."

"Welcome to Burley," was all he said, before they parted again.

The dance finally ended, and everyone clapped. Hunter's partner gave her an elaborate bow, and she laughed as she curtsied in return. He came up to her and smiled a dashing smile, running a hand through his hair to push it out of his eyes. "Can I buy you a drink?" he asked her, with a slow, sexy smile.

"Hey, Hunter, you promised me the next dance," said Harriet, stepping up and putting her arm around Hunter's waist.

Hunter looked at the man before her. "Maybe next time," she laughed, as she was drawn away by Harriet.

As they stood waiting for the other couples to come up, Harriet leaned in close. "Do you know who that was?" she asked incredulously.

Hunter shrugged. "No idea."

"That's Alexander Hardwick."

Hunter felt a shiver run up her spine. A Hardwick. That meant that he was, indeed, from one of the magickal families in the area, and a powerful one at that. A family that had a bit of a dark reputation in the magickal community. She had met one of the Hardwicks before, Alice Hardwick. She was Courtney's best friend. "Shit," was all Hunter said.

Witches of the New Forest

"Yeah. Don't even go there."

"I wasn't going to go anywhere, with anyone, you know," said Hunter, feeling a trickle of anger spark in her heart. "It's all still a bit raw and early. I'm not that kind of person."

Harriet took her hand and gave it a squeeze. "I never said you were. Just be careful around Xander. Like all the Hardwicks, he's bad news."

Hunter nodded and reigned in her anger. Her friend was only trying to look out for her. The caller came up to the mic and said, "Alright everyone, let's do Sadler's Wells."

Hunter had done this one before. She liked the way that the dance moved up the line. Harriet knew this one too, and they had great fun dancing and weaving in and out. Each time they came together, they shared jokes. "Why is it good to eat a Witch's soup?" asked Harriet. Hunter shrugged as they turned around each other. When they took hold of each other's hands to do a turn, Harriet said, "Because it's newt-ricious!" Hunter laughed. The next one Harriet had was, "Where do Witches bake their cakes? In the coven!"

Hunter had a go next. "What do Witches put on their bagels? Scream cheese!"

Harriet retaliated. "What did the Witch do when her broomstick broke? She witch-hiked home!" Hunter groaned at that one, and the dance ended. They all clapped, and Hunter stayed on the dance floor for another dance. Harriet stayed with her, and Ryder and Mackenzie came up too.

The caller smiled, and said, "Right, if you've still got the energy, it's time to Strip the Willow!" They heard a young man call out from the bar, "Where's Willow?" His mates around him punched him on the arm.

"This one is *fast*," said Harriet. Hunter agreed. She had only done it once, long ago, and remembered it being utterly chaotic.

She grinned though, and was going to give it her best shot. They lined up in two rows with their partners. The caller directed them, and then the music began slowly. It was all good until the band began to speed up, and then speed up, and speed up some more. That's when it got messy. Harriet was good, and helped Hunter when she lost her direction. Mackenzie did the same for Ryder, and they all spun around, laughing and having a great time.

When the dance ended, Hunter considered sitting out the last one. But when the caller came on and said, "This last dance you might know from the 2005 movie of *Pride and Prejudice,*" Hunter totally changed her mind. The man looked around at the crowd and said, "Find a partner and let's party like it's 1799!" Everyone laughed at his little joke. "This is called, The Young Widow."

Hunter and Ryder just looked at each other, grinning. "We are *so* doing this," Ryder said. A young man that Hunter recognised from the pub asked Ryder for this dance. She waved at her sister and watched as she gleefully took her place in the line. Dougal came up and asked Harriet for this dance, and she agreed. That left Mackenzie and Hunter, and Hunter was surprised when Mackenzie asked her for this dance. He was so polite, and she said yes willingly.

Mackenzie was a good dancer, and he knew this dance. Hunter remembered most of it from the movie, and she had to smile when she watched her sister. The two sisters had to dance with each other for a bit, and Ryder just shouted excitedly, "This is the best dance ever!" at her. Hunter threw back her head and laughed along with her sister. It felt good, like something was slowly starting to release deep within her.

Hunter caught a glance at Dougal and Harriet, and noticed Dougal watching Harri intently. Hunter smiled, finally understanding what was going on there, even if Harriet had no idea. Hunter looked around the room as she waited for her turn in the dance, and clapped along with everyone else. Her hands missed a few beats though, when she looked over to the band and saw Jack standing by the side of the stage, with a pint of beer in his hand, watching her with those green eyes of his.

Hunter had to quickly come back to the dance as she and Mackenzie were up, and had to dance down the line. *What the hell was Jack doing here?* thought Hunter.

Jack's here? she heard her sister reply in her mind.

By the stage.

A few seconds passed, before Hunter heard her sister say, *Huh*, in her mind. Hunter looked over at Mackenzie, who was standing opposite and clapping while others took their turn. He was watching her with a knowing look in his eyes. He simply nodded, and then turned his gaze back to the dancers. Hunter realised that he must have some sort of telepathy as well.

The dance ended, everyone laughing and clapping at the end. Hunter was still a little distracted. Ryder made her way over to her sister and put a hand on her arm. "Are you okay?" she asked softly.

"I'm good," Hunter replied. "I'm going to sit down for a bit."

"I'll come with."

The sisters went to their table and sat down, while Harriet went up to the bar with Dougal to get some drinks. Mackenzie excused himself, and went outside for a moment to get some fresh air. The band were taking another break, but reminded them that they were coming back on for three more dances soon. Hunter just sipped at the soda that Harriet brought to her, and kept quiet as the conversation flowed around the table about the dances. She tried not to look for Jack, or think about what

The Veil Between the Worlds

Dougal had said to her during the waltz. It was just easier right now to remain angry at Jack for what he had done.

After ten minutes, the band came back. "Okay folks, we are going to do three dances over again. Those will be the Gay Gordons, Trip to Tunbridge and Strip the Willow. Get your partner and let's begin! Hunter watched as Dougal took Ryder up to dance the Gay Gordons. She and Harriet sat this one out, deciding to watch the dancing for a change. Dougal smiled down at Ryder, and they looked cute together, with his tall, brawny six-foot three frame next to Ryder's five-foot six body. They danced really well together, and Hunter was pleased that Ryder had remembered the dance so easily.

After the dance had ended, and before the next dance was called up, someone not from the band came up to the microphone. "Would the owner of the red convertible Mercedes please go outside onto Pound Lane? They are towing your car." Hunter heard a man swear, and then she saw the handsome man that she had danced with earlier, Xander Hardwick, running for the door. Some people laughed, while others shouted "Go, Xander!"

The next dance was then called up, which was Hunter's favourite, Trip to Tunbridge. Her view of the dance floor was suddenly blocked by a tall figure standing in front of her. She looked up, right into Jack's face. "May I have this dance?" he asked softly.

Hunter's heart beat fast in her chest. Should she refuse? She hadn't had time to think about what Dougal had said. She wasn't ready for this. But Jack simply stood there, his hand extended. Hunter swallowed, and without realising it, said, "You may." She took his hand, and he led her out onto the dance floor.

You sure about this, sis? She heard Ryder in her head.
Nope, but it's too late now. Don't worry. I'll be fine.

Hunter stood on one side with the ladies while the men faced them opposite. Jack looked at her, those green eyes seeming to take everything in. Hunter steeled her heart against his gaze.

The music started, and the first couple took to the floor. As they danced up and down the rows, Jack just watched Hunter, as if drinking her in. She couldn't help but look back, her resolve weakening. She was glad when a dancer from the first couple did their twirl with her, just to break the tension between her and Jack. Soon enough, it was their turn.

As she and Jack walked around the outside of their row, Hunter stole a quick glance and saw that Jack was still following her with his eyes. They came back up on the outside, and then Jack took her hand to lead her down the middle of the rows.

"You look beautiful, tonight," he said softly, as they moved down the rows. They turned, and made their way back up.

"Thank you," was all Hunter said, before they parted again. She and Jack walked around the back of their respective rows, and met in the middle again only to part and dance with the corners. They walked around again, and finally met up in the middle once more. Jack took both of her hands and drew her near as they spun around.

"Is everything okay at home?" he asked.

"Yes," was all Hunter managed, before they had to separate.

They danced again with other partners at the corners, and while they had to wait again, Jack's eyes never left her. She felt a warm wave of green energy come from him, reaching out towards her. She longed to fall into that energy, but she stopped herself just before, and drew up a red wall of anger, blocking him. She saw him flinch in response, and his brow furrowed slightly as he considered. When they came together again, he took her hands as they twirled and asked, "Why did you do that?"

They had to break apart again, and wait as another couple danced. Hunter just looked at Jack, and mouthed, *You know why*.

She had to take his hand again and move up the row. "Hunter, I'm so sorry," he said, before they parted once more to stand at the top of the row while the other partners danced, before they themselves had a turn with other partners. They stepped away from each other, and then came back together for a final turn.

"I'm sorry too," said Hunter, her voice laced with anger. They parted, and stood looking at each other while the song ended. Jack and the other men along the line bowed to their partners. He came up to Hunter to take her hand.

"Please, Hunter, just give me time," he said softly, squeezing her hand gently. He led her back to the table without a word. The others had already taken a seat, and were watching them.

"Hey, Hun," said Ryder as she stood up to meet them. "Jack," she said, her voice flat.

"Ryder," said Jack softly. He nodded to everyone at the table, and then excused himself.

"He's got some nerve," said Ryder softly as she and Hunter sat down together.

"I don't want to talk about it," replied Hunter, taking a sip of her drink.

Harriet leaned over. "Don't let it spoil your evening," she said. "You had a good time tonight, remember?"

Hunter nodded, and faked a smile. "You're right. I did."

The caller came back up to the mic. "Thank you all so much for having us here tonight. We raised over £1,500 for our charities tonight. Well done, everyone!" There was a big round of applause. "We will play a final waltz, for any couples who would like to come up and dance one last time." Hunter bent down to pick up her bag and head out, but her sister's hand was upon her arm. She looked up and found Police Constable Hart standing at their table. He greeted them all and looked at Hunter. "Hello, Miss Williams," he said. "Would you like to dance?"

Hunter, too surprised to say anything, simply nodded. He took her by the hand, and they got into hold on the dance floor. The music started, and PC Hart, or David as everyone called him, started to lead her adeptly around the dance floor. "So, Miss Williams, have you enjoyed the dancing tonight?" he asked with a smile.

Hunter looked up at him. He was around her age, with brown hair, blue eyes, and a little dimple on his left cheek when he smiled. He had been the officer who had aided them at the scene of the car crash, and who had also checked up on them afterwards in hospital. He was also the one who had responded to Jack's break-in at his cottage. David seemed like a nice guy; friendly and professional. His expression was usually very serious, but when he smiled it totally changed his face, making him very approachable and switching him up from handsome to downright hot. "Yes. Yes, I've enjoyed it all very much," Hunter said, a bit uncertain and her head still spinning a bit from her encounter with Jack. "Oh, and please, call me Hunter," she said.

"I heard about you and Jack," said David. "I'm sorry to hear it. But it looks like you have remained friends."

"What? Oh, the last dance." Hunter didn't know what to say about that. Even she didn't know what it had been all about.

There was a slightly awkward silence, before David said, "What do you think about Burley?"

"It's – it's a lovely place."

He leaned in a bit closer to her ear. "And what about the magick?" he asked softly.

The Veil Between the Worlds

Hunter stiffened, and pulled back to look at him. He *knew*. He knew about the magick that abounded here in this little village. She tested him, just to make certain. "It is certainly a magical place," she said warily, turning her head to look over his shoulder again.

"You come from one of the five families," David whispered softly in her ear.

Hunter's grip tightened slightly. "You know, don't you? How do you know?" She leaned back to look at his face again.

David smiled, and the dimple appeared on his cheek. "It's in my family. Not the magick, but the knowledge of just what Burley is," he said quietly so that only Hunter would hear. "My grandfather knew, and when I entered the police force and began working here, he made sure that *I* knew about the families here in Burley."

"Oh," said Hunter, a little smile coming to her face. "We met your grandfather last month. He's a nice man."

"We actually have a special department, you know. Me." Hunter giggled at that. "I deal with all the 'paranormal disturbances' in the community, at least the ones that get reported."

"Do all the families know that you know?"

"Only the heads of the families know what it is that I do here in Burley."

"Then, why – why would you tell me?"

"You're the head of the Appletons now, Hunter. Even if you go by your father's name, that of Williams."

"Oh," Hunter said lamely. She chewed on her lip, wondering if she should tell David about her mother's return.

"And because I'm interested in you, Hunter. I find you very beautiful. And I'd like to get to know you better."

Hunter was stunned by this declaration, but was saved from responding as the music ended and the band thanked everyone for coming. She pulled away from David. "Thank you for the dance, David."

"It was my pleasure. Would you like to go out for a coffee next week? Tuesday?"

"Um, I guess that would be okay. I'm – I have to say, I'm a little messed up, I guess, from everything. So can we go just as friends?"

"Not a problem. I'll see you at Lovey's, at 2pm?"

"Sounds great. See you then." Hunter smiled and moved away quickly, not knowing what to say. She was totally flummoxed by the situation, and completely unprepared for what David had just said, both regarding his job and his feelings for her. She wasn't ready to see anyone right now, and the way her heart was so broken, probably never again.

"Hey Hun, nice moves out there," said Ryder, coming up to her and taking her arm. "Come and sit with me for a bit. Tell me all about Officer Studly."

Chapter Nine

Harriet, Ryder, and Hunter all went back to the cottage. Ryder asked Harriet if she wanted to stay over, so they could watch some movies; specifically, *Pride and Prejudice*. Harriet agreed, and soon they were all sitting in the living room, Ryder and Harriet with some gin and tonics, and Hunter with a glass of red wine.

"That was just the best thing ever," said Ryder dreamily.

"So, what did David, or should I say, PC Hart talk to you about?" asked Harriet, a knowing look on her face. Ryder made kissy faces next to her.

"Just about the dance."

"Really? That was a lot of talking, just about the dance."

Hunter took a large sip of wine from her glass. "Um, he also kind of asked me out for coffee."

"There it is!" cried Ryder with glee.

Hunter shook her head. "No, no, no. There is nothing there. I told him I would go, just as friends."

Harriet and Ryder looked at each other for a moment, before turning back to Hunter. The looks on their faces were plain: they weren't buying it. Hunter just shrugged. "Seriously, I'm not dating anyone for a long, long time after the Jack fiasco. If I'll ever date again."

"Well, you were quite popular tonight, I have to say," said Ryder with a grin.

"Yeah," replied Hunter sarcastically. "That old guy with the beard was totally hot."

Ryder rolled her eyes. "I'm talking about Xander Hardwick. And PC Hart. Oh my god. His last name is even Hart. Dr Love! Paging Dr I. M. N. Love!"

Now it was Hunter's turn to roll her eyes. "It's Hart, not heart with an 'e'. It's an old English word for a buck or a stag." She ignored Ryder, who began to snore as she pretended to fall asleep during Hunter's explanation. "Just watch the damned movie."

The ladies got comfy on their seats, and cued up their Aunt Ivy's old DVD player. "Matthew Macfadyen was *the best* Mr Darcy," said Ryder.

They all gave simultaneous, girly, sighs.

The next morning Hunter was sitting at the breakfast table in the kitchen, reading up on Fae lore. She had made pancakes and coffee, and had already eaten when Harriet and Ryder came downstairs. "Mooooorniiiing!" sang Ryder as she entered. She grabbed Harriet and they waltzed around the kitchen table.

Hunter looked up from her studies. "Morning. I don't think I've ever seen you this happy, this early before."

Harriet let Ryder go with a twirl. Ryder landed against the kitchen counter and sagged down it onto the floor in a mock swoon. "Oh, Mr Darcy…"

Harriet laughed, while Hunter turned her attention back to the books. "I made pancakes," Hunter said. "They're in the microwave; just give them a quick zap."

"Oooo, yummy!" floated Ryder's voice from the floor. Hunter heard a scuttling sound, and the pantry door opened. There was some rummaging, and a hand with a bottle of maple syrup appeared on the table next to her. "I got maple syrup!"

Harriet sighed and pulled Ryder up off the floor. "That is so American, maple syrup and pancakes," she said.

Ryder stood up with a look of shock and horror on her face. "You have offended me and my country! Maple syrup is a *Canadian* thing, I'll have you know! The Americans just stole our idea, like they have so many others."

"I believe it was the Algonquians who are first credited with harvesting and making maple syrup," said Hunter, without looking up from her book. "And they lived in what is now known as both Canada and the US, but mainly Canada. In the unceded regions we now know as pretty much everything east of the Rockies in Canada, and also New England, New York, New Jersey, etc."

"Thanks, professor," said Ryder, who rolled her eyes and turned on the microwave to warm up the pancakes.

"I keep forgetting that you're a Professor of History," said Harriet, coming to stand behind Hunter and look at what she was working on.

"Mmm hmm," said Hunter, still writing down notes.

"Well, we'll leave you to it," Harriet said, giving Hunter a small pat on the shoulder. Hunter felt a sharp jolt of energy going through her shoulder, which pulled her away from her studies. She looked up at Harriet, who was grinning down at her.

"Why did you do that?"

"Oh, so you felt that, did you?"

"Yes, of course. What was that?"

"That's me, pushing energy into you, when you're not expecting it."

"Well, why would you do such a thing?"

Harriet leaned against the counter and crossed her arms over her chest. "Sometimes, when you're around other magickal practitioners, they can push their energy onto or into you. Sometimes knowingly, sometimes unknowingly." The microwave beeped, but Ryder was now watching the two women, totally engrossed in the conversation. "I was just wondering," continued Harriet. "Did you feel any sort of energy exchange between you and Xander last night, while you were dancing?"

Hunter looked down at her book for a moment, trying to comprehend where all this going. "Well, um, yes, I did feel a kind of tingly energy every time out hands touched."

Harriet nodded. "And did it feel good, or did it feel bad?"

Hunter shrugged. "I don't know. It was just a weird, tingling sensation."

"Have you ever experienced this sort of thing before? Maybe with Jack?"

Hunter considered for a moment. "Well, yes, of course. When our energies melded together it was soft. It was warm; glowing. His energy is green and strong, but comforting, like an old oak tree."

Harriet's eyebrows raised. "Just be careful. There are lots of real, magickal practitioners here in Burley, and you never know what somebody is sending you."

"I think I've kind of dealt with that already, at least once last night. When Jack and I were dancing, I could feel a wave of his green energy reaching out towards me."

"How did that feel?"

"I wouldn't know. I put up a wall so that it couldn't get to me."

"But you didn't with Xander."

Hunter shook her head. "I didn't know who he was."

Harriet sighed and sat down at the table. "Maybe you need to protect yourself a bit more on a regular basis. You are half Fae, Hunter. You will feel and be able to work with energies more so than other magickal practitioners. You are probably also more susceptible to other people's energies than your regular Witch, Druid, or whatever. It would seem that your powers are increasing, and not only might you be a magnet for anyone who wants to use or abuse that power, but you might also be sending out your own energy unknowingly too. And so, you must be responsible, and find a way to contain that energy."

"You mean, like zipping up your chakras?"

Harriet smiled. "Good! You've been reading that book. Yes, having a good control on your energy centres will definitely help. By 'zipping up' you won't appear so... bright and shiny, I guess you could say, to others who might want to abuse your energy in some way. Or vamp it, or whatever."

Hunter sat back, a little shocked. "Is that what you think happened last night?"

Harriet shrugged. "With Xander? Maybe. It wouldn't surprise me. With Jack? I don't know. He's always been a stand-up kind of guy. Did you feel anything when you danced with Mackenzie?"

Hunter thought for a moment. "No, not a thing," she realised.

"That's probably because he's containing it, putting up a barrier so that his energy doesn't affect others. He is being responsible with his energy, and he's got quite a bit of it too, from what I can see in his aura."

Hunter just shook her head and looked down, trying to process this new information. "And I've got to be responsible with my own energy too," she said softly.

Harriet reached out and put her hand on Hunter's shoulder. "You've done really well so far, what with the healing of your auric and psychic wounds. We all have to be responsible, and take how our energy affects others seriously. All of us magickal practitioners here in Burley have an obligation to be responsible with our powers and our energy, if we want to keep and maintain this magickal place."

Hunter looked up and nodded at the young woman next to her.

Ryder plopped down the pancakes on the table in front of them, and said, "With great power, comes great responsibility. Now, let's eat pancakes."

After breakfast, Hunter wanted to go for a walk, but she didn't want to go out on the heath in case Jack was working there today. Instead, she decided to go into the woods at the back of their property. It was a warm day, and so she just wore a light camisole tank top with a pair of cargo shorts. She twisted her hair up and clipped it in place, and then called out to her sister, "I'm going out for a walk!"

"Okay! Where are you going?"

"Out back, not far."

"Be careful! Take your keys and phone!"

Hunter sighed, and went back upstairs to grab her phone. She hated how everyone was always so needful of having their phones on them at all times. But she also realised that in her case, it was probably a good idea to have a portable means of communication. She wasn't sure just how far her telepathy with her sister ran, and so having the phone would be good idea. *You know, in case my uncle, or any other magickal creature decides to pop by and attack or something*, she thought wryly.

As she left the cottage, she took in a deep breath. The air smelled thick and green, as if it was going to rain later. Hunter made her way to the forest edge, and stepped under the canopy of the tall beech trees. She ran her hands down the smooth bark, looking up at the majestic, elegant shapes that stretched up towards the sky. She sighed and continued walking, thinking how lovely it was to be outside in the forest, and not be eaten alive by bugs. In the Canadian summertime, humans were a free lunch for every biting insect that had ever existed. But here in England, it was rather different. And quite pleasant.

Hunter walked down small paths that she had never taken before. They were mostly animal pathways through the wood, deer trails and the like. She followed one that had footprints of fallow deer all the way to a little stream that bubbled among the rocks. Hunter stretched up her arms and took in a deep breath, feeling her heart relax a little. Last night had been so full of different emotions. She hadn't even begun to process them, and she decided that today, she didn't have to. She was just going to be in the moment, and to reconnect with nature.

She tried to still her mind of all thoughts. It was constantly churning with information, studies, emotions, plans, and a host of other things that kept swirling around and muddying the waters of her psyche. She sat down on a rock by the stream and just watched the water, not thinking of anything and allowing her mind to settle, so that all the detritus could sink to the bottom and let everything else run clear.

She dipped her fingers into the cold, clear water, relishing in the feel of the water sliding across her skin. It had been such a long time since she had just stopped and used her senses, without thinking, without judgement. She soaked in the sensation with a smile, inhaling the scent of the water, the damp earth and rocks, the forest, and the hazy sunshine that coloured the air. She listened to the water and the few birds in the area, singing quietly in the heat of the late morning. A crow cawed overhead, and a dragonfly skittered past to land on a rock further upstream in a patch of sunlight. Hunter straightened up and put her hands in her lap, closing her eyes.

Everything was so calm here in the forest. Here amongst the trees there was no hurry, no pressing need, no worry to crease her brow. She simply sat and enjoyed the peace.

Witches of the New Forest

After a long while, Hunter opened her eyes and stretched. She stood and looked around, surrounded by peace. She felt a pull to follow a trail across the stream, and so she headed down it. Her mind felt rested, and her shoulders had dropped significantly. She hadn't realised just how tightly she had been holding herself these last few weeks. She refused to think of the reasons why, not wanting to spoil her walk.

The trail eventually came out into a small clearing. In the clearing rose a circular mound. Hunter pondered this for a moment. It was most unusual that there were no trees growing on it. She walked around the edges, and then she realised that she had come across an ancient burial mound; a tumulus. She knew that there were Bronze Age barrows all over the New Forest area. This must be another one, off the beaten track. She pulled out her phone and took some photos of it, with a wry smile at her earlier condemnation of phones. She then pocketed it back in her shorts and climbed the mound to see it from a different angle.

The mound was slightly dipped in the centre, probably from subsidence. Hunter wondered if this mound had ever been excavated. There might be all manner of treasure beneath her feet, as well as the remains of people who walked these lands over five thousand years ago. Hunter stood upon the barrow and let her mind wander, thinking of what life must have been like back then, wondering who had been buried here and why.

A slight breeze stroked her bare skin and blew some wayward curls across her face. She brushed her hair aside as she looked around. A mist had started to gather beneath the trees, which was odd, considering it was midday.

Hunter's heart suddenly beat faster in her chest. She recalled that a mist had appeared on the heath during the ritual that they

The Veil Between the Worlds

had done when they had found her mother. A mist that had accompanied a very powerful being from the Otherworld.

Right on cue, a figure emerged from the mist at the trees' edge, and began to walk up the barrow towards her. Hunter got out her phone and dialled her sister, but then saw that there was no signal. She swore softly and put the phone back into her pocket.

The figure was cloaked and hooded, moving gracefully up the mound towards her. Hunter grounded and centred her energy quickly, pulling up extra energy from the earth in case she needed it. "You have nothing to fear from me, Hedge Witch," a soft, male voice said, as if he had sensed what she was doing.

"Who are you?"

The figure began to walk around her, circling her slowly. Hunter had a vague sense of déjà vu. The mist crept up the side of the barrow, until she and the figure were in a small circular space within it. Hunter considered just running away, but in the mist she didn't know where she would go, or where she might end up, either here or in the Otherworld. She also wanted more information. She pushed aside her fear and embraced her growing confidence instead. She felt like she was coming into her own power lately, and so she stayed. A flash of anger crossed her heart, at how she was always beginning to feel like she was under some sort of attack. She used that anger to put up a red wall of energy between her and this being, much like she had done with Jack at the dance.

The figure stopped and turned to look at her. She couldn't see much within the depths of the hood, but got the impression of a handsome, almost androgynous face. "Such anger," he said softly, almost as if musing to himself. "Be careful with that anger, Hedge Witch. It will lead you to your own destruction. Anger will be your ruin."

Hunter felt her heart rapping against her ribs, as well as her anger rising even further. "You will not speak to me like that," she said, raising her chin and feeling power flow through her.

The figure cocked his head. "So, it is true. You are so much alike."

Hunter's eyes flashed in anger. "Stop speaking in riddles."

The figure before her laughed softly. He then said, "It's our nature, my little Cailleach Fál. We cannot go against our natures." His voice was soft and smooth, like honey.

"Just tell me what you want," said Hunter, the heat of her anger making her skin hot and her face flush.

She thought the figure smiled, deep beneath the shadowy hood, though she could not see him clearly. "I want many things, Hedge Witch."

Hunter decided to try another tack. "Why have you come here? Why are you speaking to me? And who are you?"

The figure gave a soft, short laugh beneath the hood, and began to circle her once more. "Three questions you have asked, and three answers you will receive. I have come here to warn you; that if you follow the seven-pointed star, it will lead you to your ruin. We share some interests, and in your mission I wish you to succeed. I am your ally in this matter, though you know it not. He stopped his pacing, and turned to look at her again. "Does this satisfy you, Hedge Rider?"

Hunter shook her head slowly. "No, it does not."

"What a pity," said the figure, stepping back and dissolving into the mist.

Hunter stood on the mound even as the sun came out, burning away the mist with an unnatural speed. *Gods, what is it with this place?* she thought. She both loved and hated Burley, with its magick and magickal creatures. There was always something to contend with, something that pushed and challenged her until she felt like her nerves were on breaking point. Whether it was a love that had gone wrong somehow, strange Fae creatures, or other magickal practitioners possibly making their moves on her - it was all just too much. She threw her hands up in exasperation and simply shouted out her frustration of it all in a very unladylike manner.

"Fuck!!!"

As she came back into the cottage, she took off her hiking boots in the porch and opened the front door. It had been locked, as Ryder had a double shift at the pub today. She stepped into the quiet house. It was empty and cool, and Hunter relished the peace inside as she closed and locked the door behind her. At least no one could get to her in here, she thought.

She hoped.

She sighed and made her way to the kitchen, where her book and notepad were still on the table. She sat down and began to make notes of her encounter with the strange, Fae being, recalling everything that he had said to her. Hunter sighed again.

Just another day in Burley.

The following day passed without incident. Hunter spent the day studying, and Ryder had left early to go to the market in Portsmouth with Harriet. She hadn't seen Ryder since Sunday morning, as her pub shifts that day had her coming home late, and then she had left early this morning for market. When Ryder returned in the evening looking tired, Hunter debated whether or not to tell her of the encounter that she had experienced the day before in the forest. She decided to tell her sister, and showed her the notes that she had made.

"Huh," said Ryder. "This whole number three business, is that important?"

Hunter looked at her notes. She then saw that she had, indeed, asked three questions, and the mysterious stranger had responded with three answers. "The number three is actually very important in faery folklore," Hunter mused softly. "Interesting."

"I saw something you did not," said Ryder in a childish, singsong voice.

"Very good, Ry. Very good."

"So, what are you going to do?"

"What do you mean?"

"Are you going to try and contact this person again, whoever or whatever he is?"

Hunter shook her head. "No, I don't think so. Whatever message he had was quite specific. Namely, the seven-pointed star. He said not to follow it, for whatever reason. I don't know. Sounds to me like he's trying to throw us off our course."

"The seven-pointed star that you and Mom found, the one that came from your father's coronet."

"That's right. The Fae can be very tricky. In folklore, they love to lead people astray. He's probably in league with Lanoc, and trying to put us off our game. I think we're on to something with the star, and they don't like the fact that we're getting close."

"Tricky bastards," said Ryder. "Well, I'm off to shower and go to bed. It's been a long day. Night, Hun."

"Night, Ry."

Chapter Ten

Hunter slept in the next morning. She had been up late, studying and trying to discover more about the Fae, their motivations and how to handle them, should she come across the one that she had just encountered, or any others from the Otherworld. Her anger at being toyed with by the strange Fae on the mound, and also being attacked by Lanoc on two earlier occasions only fuelled her fire, and she used it to push herself further. She had promised not to do a hedge riding while Elspeth and her mother were away, but she was sorely tempted. They needed more information.

When Hunter awoke, it was to a rainy and dim mid-morning light. Hunter had slept in her old room, now her mother's room, so that Ryder could come and go as she pleased without worrying about disturbing her. She heard Ryder in the kitchen, and so she rubbed her eyes and got up, staring blearily out the window. Rivulets of rain fell down the panes, distorting the view of the trees in the back that bordered their property.

Hunter sighed again at the challenges that the New Forest, and Burley in particular were throwing at her. Coming into her heritage, not only as a part Fae but also as a magickal practitioner from a long line of Witches, was more than enough to deal with at any given point. However, being confronted by strange Fae creatures and attacked by their leader only added to the pressure that she was under. Throw in a love story gone wrong, and it seemed like her life was a bit of a disaster zone right now.

Oh crap, thought Hunter, suddenly remembering that she had agreed to go for a coffee with Police Constable Hart this afternoon. *Why did I say yes?* She got in the shower and tried to at least make herself presentable, even if it wasn't a date. She had made it perfectly clear at the dance that they were simply going as friends. She didn't want to give David the wrong impression, but she also didn't want to look like a slob either.

When she came downstairs, the coffee was ready and Ryder was humming along to the radio. The Rolling Stones' 'You Can't Always Get What You Want' was playing. "Morning, Ry," said Hunter, grabbing a cup and pouring herself some coffee.

"Morning. You're up late. Burning the candle at both ends and all that?"

"I guess you could say that. I just wanted to swot up on some more Fae stuff."

"Mmm hmm," said Ryder, looking at her sister. "Just make sure to take care of yourself too, you know."

"Yeah, yeah."

"So, you've got your date with Officer Studly today, don't you?"

Hunter sighed. "It's not a date, Ry."

Ryder grinned. "Of course it's not."

"We are just going for coffee. As friends."

"Friends where one has expressed an interest," said Ryder.

"I can't help the way he feels," said Hunter, sitting down at the table.

"And how do *you* feel?"

Hunter looked up at her sister. "Honestly? I don't know. I'm not going to date for a long, long time. Right now, I don't want to date or see anyone or be in a relationship ever again. What I had with Jack was special. What I *thought* I had with Jack," she said, correcting herself.

"You still danced with him the other night, though."

Hunter stood up and looked out the kitchen window. "Yes, I did. He caught me off guard. It's difficult, because I can't just abandon the feelings that I have for him so easily."

"Maybe you shouldn't abandon them," said Ryder softly.

Hunter turned to face her sister, a spark of anger rising in her. "What, so you are taking Jack's side in all this?" She could feel the heat rushing up to her face.

"God no. He broke up with you. All I'm saying is, maybe there is a reason, one that he's not sharing."

"Oh, there's definitely something he's not telling me. And it probably has to do with his feelings for Courtney, and how he never abandoned *those* feelings."

"Maybe," said Ryder. "But perhaps it's time to have a talk with him?"

"We already talked. He just asked me to give him some more time. Well, he can have all the time in the world," said Hunter, putting some toast in the toaster and slamming the handle down. "I'm done with men. They all just want something from you, and as soon as they get it, they leave. Even if you give them *everything*." Hunter felt close to tears, and she pushed them down. "He's had weeks now to think about it, and I'm done."

She felt Ryder's hand on her shoulder. "Whatever happens, I'm always on your side," she said.

"I know."

Hunter drove up to Lovey's Tea Room. She parked in the main village car park, and walked the short distance over. She pulled up the hood of her rain coat, as it was coming down in buckets. As she entered the building, she saw that it was fairly empty. The weather was keeping the tourists to the bigger towns, where they could pop into shop after shop to avoid the rain. She spotted David sitting by the window off to one side, and she drew down her hood. "Hello," she said as she came up to the table.

He stood up and smiled at her. "Hello, Hunter. I'm sorry about the weather."

Hunter gave a small laugh. "I'm sure you'll try harder next time."

He laughed at that, and waved at her to take a seat. "Can I get you some coffee? Or tea?"

"Um, sure. I'll take an Earl Grey, please."

"Anything to eat?"

"Not just yet. I had a late breakfast." David nodded and went to the counter to place the order. Hunter watched him as he moved between the tables. He was tall, just over six foot, with powerful shoulders and slim hips. His short, brown hair was casually rumpled, and he was dressed in jeans with a grey Henley shirt, the sleeves pushed up. He came back with a tray that held a pot of tea for both of them, and two cups with saucers.

"Tea must always be drunk out of china cups," Hunter said with a smile.

"Really?" said David as he sat down. "I usually just grab the nearest mug."

Hunter shrugged as she took a cup and saucer from the tray. "It's just something Elspeth always says."

David nodded. "Elspeth is a remarkable woman."

"She certainly is. I guess that she is the head of the Caldecotte family?"

David nodded. "Yes, she is."

"So, she knows about you then."

David looked Hunter in the eye. His blue eyes twinkled as he smiled. "Yes, she does."

Hunter poured herself a cup of tea, and also one for David. "That must be difficult, keeping a secret like that," she said softly, even though there was no one around them to hear.

David gave a little sigh, and offered Hunter some milk. She waved it away, and he poured some into his cup. "It is, and it isn't. While I do get the occasional call for certain... incidents, most of the magickal community take care of things on their own."

Hunter looked at him over the rim of her cup. "How does that make you feel?"

David smiled. "A little superfluous, actually." His dimple showed when he smiled, which Hunter thought was cute. "But actually, when I am let in on some of the goings on, it really is very interesting."

Now Hunter's interest was piqued. "Are you allowed to talk about any of it, or is it strictly confidential?"

David put his teacup down and looked out the window that was steaming up with the humidity. "Technically, no, but as my department doesn't technically exist, then there's that consideration."

"Is it lonely?"

That question seemed to surprise David, and he turned back to Hunter. "Lonely? Hmm. That's an interesting question." He thought about it for a moment. "I guess, perhaps, yes. I have no colleagues to talk to about these matters; only the people who are directly involved. I can't even share things with the other heads of families, as what happens is under strict confidence. It's only with their permission that I am able to share details. I can, of course, investigate, but I am not at liberty to divulge information to those who are not involved."

"Don't worry, I won't ask you for any juicy gossip," said Hunter with a grin. She saw David smile at that, and he gave her a look that, if she hadn't already been heartbroken, would have stirred something within. His face quickly changed to one of concern.

"Well, you've had your fair share of trouble already while you've been here," he said. "I wish I could have helped more in what had happened to you. At least we found the other vehicle."

Hunter choked for a moment on her tea. "You what?" she finally managed to squeak.

David handed her a napkin, and waited for her to settle. When she waved at him to continue, he looked at her closely. "Jack didn't tell you?"

"Tell me what?" asked Hunter, with a sinking feeling.

"We found the Hummer, on the Hardwick estate."

Hunter felt like the floor had fallen out from under her. Her stomach did a little dive, and she felt blood rushing in her ears. "Oh god," she said, feeling unwell.

"Hunter? Hunter!" David jumped out of his seat and knelt before her. "Put your head between your knees. You're white as a ghost, and I think you're about to faint." Hunter did as he instructed, and put her head between her knees. She looked down at her damp boots, and tried to breathe. Finally, the rushing in her ears faded, and she felt a little steadier. She pulled up slowly, and David put his hand on her shoulder. He leaned in and said, "Are you okay?"

Hunter nodded. "Yes. I-I'll be okay. I am okay," she corrected herself. David remained there for a while longer, waiting for the colour to come back to Hunter's face. "I'll go and get you some water," he said finally, and went to the counter where the staff were watching with interest and concern. Hunter

The Veil Between the Worlds

now felt a blush coming to her cheeks. *Gods, I nearly passed out in front of everyone. How embarrassing.*

David came back with the water. "Here you go," he said softly. Hunter took the water and sipped.

"I'm so sorry. I don't know what came over me there. It really shouldn't surprise me," she said.

David raised an eyebrow. "What shouldn't surprise you?"

"That the truck was on the Hardwick estate. It kind of makes sense."

David leaned back for a moment and studied her. "What do you mean?" he asked. Hunter looked at him, and knew that he had more information, but wanted to get her take on it first.

"Well, Jack and Courtney are back together. I guess he's covering for her, or her friends, or something." As she said that, her heart broke all over again. A tear escaped and rolled down her cheek.

David handed her another napkin. "Hmm, interesting. But I'm not sure that's the reason."

Hunter dabbed at her face, willing herself *not* to break down right now. She had already nearly fainted, now she was crying in front of this man? *Pathetic*, she told herself. She remained silent, not trusting her voice at the moment.

David leaned in towards her and gently took her hand. "Jack was the person who called it in, Hunter."

Hunter looked up at him. "What?"

David squeezed her hand. "Jack called it in. He found it just before the summer solstice, in a disused barn on the estate. He said he was doing some work there, and had come across it, and immediately he phoned it in."

Hunter's mind was reeling. Just before the summer solstice. Right when he began to act differently, and just before he pushed her away. "But, what does this mean?"

David leaned back and withdrew his hand, taking a sip of his tea. "It means that we investigated the Hardwicks, all of them. Turns out, the truck was supposed to be Alice's surprise birthday present, from her father. She states that she had no idea that he was even getting her a vehicle for her birthday. She had an alibi for that evening too. All the other Hardwicks were accounted for as well. None of their fingerprints were on the vehicle. The father said that he had the truck delivered straight to his garage on the estate. He said he hadn't even known it was missing. When you've got over a dozen vehicles in your luxury garage, you might not notice when one goes missing, I suppose. Especially if it is not currently being used. We've had to put this one down to vehicle theft, and joyriding." He watched Hunter for a moment. "I'm only telling you this because you were involved in the accident. I had no idea that you didn't know. I thought Jack would have told you straight away."

Hunter shook her head. "No, he didn't."

"But what's this about Jack and Courtney being together?"

Hunter looked down at the table. Something was going on here, and she didn't want to drop Jack in it, even if he deserved it for breaking her heart. She had to figure this out before she started getting others in trouble. She reminded herself that she was, in fact, talking to a police officer. "Just a rumour that I heard, recently," she said with a shrug, avoiding eye contact.

"Mmm hmm..." said David, expecting more.

"I don't really know much about it. They weren't together at the dance, the other night." She looked up and saw David considering this fact.

"No, they weren't. And why would he call it in, if they were an item?"

The Veil Between the Worlds

Hunter looked up at David. "No, he wouldn't. He would want to protect her, not land her in it, I guess." A small hope began to bloom in her heart.

David sighed and leaned forwards onto his elbows. "Is there anything you want to tell me, Hunter?"

Hunter looked at him, and felt a blush rising to her cheeks. She looked down. "I wish I had more to tell, but I'm afraid I don't. I'm just as in the dark as you are. I suppose it could have been joy riders, out at night after having stolen the truck."

"You suppose it could be, but could it also be something else?"

Hunter forced herself to look up at him. "Honestly? I don't really know. This is all still so new to me."

David's features softened and he took her hand again. "I'm sorry, Hunter. My cop hat came on there for a moment. I didn't mean to make you feel bad in any way, or to interrogate you."

Hunter managed a small smile. "That's okay. It's just been a crazy few weeks, you know? I didn't even know about my family's... secret, until my sister and I came here to settle the estate."

David looked surprised. He squeezed her hand once more and let it go, taking another sip of his tea. "Wow. I had no idea."

Hunter shrugged. "Like I said, it's been a bit crazy." David picked up the teapot and refilled her cup, then his. She needed to change the subject, quickly. "So, enough of the accident. Tell me more about yourself."

Hunter spent the next hour with David, listening to him share stories about growing up in Burley, his school years and joining the police force. She told him about how her family had dealt with her mother's disappearance, and the role that she had taken on in caring for them. She then spoke about her education, and her job as a university professor. She made sure to keep referring to her mother in the past tense, as she hadn't really discussed it with Elspeth or her mother as to whether the 'special unit' of the local police force should know. Elspeth would be aware of David's role in the magickal community, but her mother wouldn't. It was all such a mess, and until she could have the time to think it all through, she needed to be careful.

David really was a nice guy, and she enjoyed his company. But her thoughts kept returning to Jack, and what might be going on there. She tried to push them to one side, and keep focused on the conversation at hand. Again, she needed time to process all this.

At around three-thirty, after another pot of tea and some cake, Hunter said that she had probably best be getting home. She wanted to make a home-cooked meal for her sister, who was working hard lately, and she was worried that her sister wasn't eating as well as she should. David smiled and said to give Ryder his regards, and walked her to her car. The rain had let up, and Hunter smiled at David as she fished out her keys. "Thank you again for the tea and conversation. It was nice. I don't really get to socialise all that much."

David leaned on her car. "Why not?"

Hunter shrugged. "I guess I'm just not really all that sociable. Never have been."

David looked her over quickly, before saying "We are all different, with different needs. You will find your place in this community, and there is a place for you're here, if you want it. Know that, Hunter Williams." He pushed himself up and leaned forward to give her shoulder a small squeeze. "You take care. Can I call you sometime?"

Hunter smiled. "I'd like that. It's nice to have another friend here."

The Veil Between the Worlds

PC Hart smiled, and said, "I'll be in touch." He turned and walked away down the car park, his hands in his jeans pockets. The sun decided to come out, and lit up the area with sparkles from the fallen rain. Hunter sighed, and then got in her car to drive home.

She had a lot to think about.

Chapter Eleven

Hunter decided that she needed more information, on all manner of things. *Just what was going on with Jack? Was he with Courtney or not?* The fact that he had called in the discovery of the truck seemed to indicate that he wasn't with her. But then why were they seen together at the pub that night? Hunter turned it over in her mind for the whole drive home. Her heart flip-flopped a dozen times before she made it to the cottage.

As she pulled into the driveway, she decided that she needed other, much more important information first. There were more pressing matters at hand than her messed up love life. She couldn't waste time wondering about Jack. They needed to know more about the Fae, and get some information on her father and his possible whereabouts. Trying to rescue him was the most important thing right now.

Even if her heart disagreed.

Hunter got out of the car and pulled her house key out of her bag. As she walked up the pathway, she decided that she would do some sort of ritual to try and find out how to get more information. She had promised Elspeth and her mother that she wouldn't do any hedge riding while they were gone, but were there other things that she could be doing it the meantime?

As she turned the key in the lock, she thought back to what her mother had talked about when they were discussing possible sources of information. Elspeth had asked Abigail about her familiars. Her mother had told them how her familiars had helped her to find spots where the veil between the worlds was thin, where she could cross over into the Otherworld.

Why shouldn't I try and do the same?

Hunter closed and locked the door behind her, dropping her keys into the small bowl by the door. *I can do a ritual to find my own familiar, and perhaps they will be able to provide me with the information that I seek. Or at least point me in the right direction.* Hunter set her bag down on a chair, and ran upstairs to her room to grab some books. She brought an armload downstairs to the dining table, where she began to study everything about the Witch's familiar.

She learned that the familiar could have many different uses and forms. Some Witches used their familiars to spy on others and get information. This was the most prevalent in tales about Witches, but Hunter learned that there was something much deeper, hidden beneath the surface of the Wicked Witch who spied on her neighbours. No, the familiar was something that was not a slave to do one's bidding, or which was used solely for nefarious means, but rather a good and trusted friend who could guide the Witch to help her on her own spiritual journey of empowerment.

Often the familiar was conflated with the spirit realm in the books that she was reading. In some books, when Witches contacted the spirits, they were also contacting their familiars. Hunter sighed. The word, spirits, could also really mean just about anything in this world or the Otherworld. It was all so vague, and that irritated her.

Regardless of the exact classification of a familiar, whether it was a spirit, an animal, a plant, or a magickal being from the Otherworld, the familiar was there to help the Witch as she sought out more information on her world and the Otherworld. Hunter saw that there was no established ritual to contact one's

Witches of the New Forest

familiar, but there were certain clues that she could follow to create her own ritual.

She got up and left the books for a while so that she could make some dinner for her and her sister. As she put the ingredients together in the kitchen, she also went over ingredients for her own ritual that she would perform. She noted what they had in stock in the cottage, and what she could use, both in the kitchen for dinner and also magically for her ritual.

When Ryder came home at 6pm, the sisters sat in the kitchen and had their meal. "I'm glad Jenny could give me a ride home today," Ryder said.

"You can always call me and I'll pick you up, you know."

"Yeah, I know. But I knew you had your date with Office Studly today, and needed the car."

"It wasn't a date, Ryder."

"Whatever. Man, was it ever busy at work today," said Ryder, piling the pasta onto her plate. "When the sun came out later this afternoon, so did all the tourists. Sunny, summer days in Burley are just crazy! Who'd have thought that so many people would come to such a tiny little village?"

Hunter took a bite of her pasta and thought about it for a minute. "Well, I guess it's because of the Witchy tourism. It's something to 'tick off the list' when one is visiting the New Forest for the first time."

Ryder poured herself a glass of wine and took a big swig. She put it down, saying, "Yeah, but come on. There's like, three or four witchy shops here and the pub. That's it. And then they sometimes complain about it. About how they'd been duped into thinking they've come to Witchcraft Central, where they expect everyone to walk around in robes, riding brooms, or cackling over cauldrons."

The Veil Between the Worlds

"Better that, than finding out the real truth about this place," said Hunter.

Ryder shrugged. "I guess. I wonder how Elspeth does it, you know? She's like, this amazing and powerful Witch, but all the tourists see is a retail shop owner, selling witchy stuff."

Hunter nodded. "Yeah, they have no idea that she is actually supplying all the legacy Witches here with what they need for their magickal work."

"I know, right? It just, it sometimes does my nut in, you know?"

"Does your 'nut' in?"

"Yeah, does my nut in."

Hunter laughed. "You're already talking like a Brit," she said.

"Oh, piss off."

"There it is again!"

Ryder sighed. "Well, when in Rome and all that…"

Hunter leaned over and took her sister's hand. "I really appreciate everything that you're doing, Ryder. The money from your work does help, and until we know what we're doing here in the long-term, it's best for us not to dip too deeply into the inheritance. If there is anything that I can do, anything that you'd like me to do, please just say."

Her younger sister smiled, and took off her trendy, red glasses, rubbing her eyes. "Nah, I'm good. You need to study. That's where your strengths lie. We've got some big stuff coming up when Mom and Elspeth get back home, and you're needed for that. We're cool. And this pasta is amazing. Well done!"

"I figured you probably hadn't eaten home-cooked food for a while."

"The pub food isn't too bad, but it can be a bit heavy on the deep-fried junk, and little choice for veggie options. Which reminds me, I've got to see about getting some exercise. I haven't really done anything since we got here. I'd like to get back into mountain biking, and I've heard that there are some pretty amazing trails around here. Also, I could use it to bike into work, on that path that leads into the village. That way we wouldn't need to schedule around the car so much."

Hunter nodded. "You should totally do that. Buy a bike, second-hand even. Isn't there a bike shop in the village?"

Ryder nodded as she ate. "Yeah, there's one near Harriet's place, just down the road. Maybe I should pop in and see if they can sell me anything, or put me in touch with someone who knows."

"Sounds like a plan," said Hunter. "Are you working tomorrow?"

"Yup. All week, afternoon and evening. There's a bug going around and staff are dropping like flies, so we are short-staffed on the already short-staffed list of people trying to keep everything running. It's a mess. But we're managing. Just."

"You're a natural, behind the bar," said Hunter with a smile, remembering how her sister dealt with the 'punters'.

"It's fun, you know? You get to meet all kinds of folks. I'd rather be working behind the bar than serving food. Tourists are nicer to you at the bar," she said with a grin.

"I envy you, sometimes. How you can just chat so easily with people."

Ryder went and topped up her wine. "We play to our strengths. You're the professor, I'm the bartender."

"You are much more than that, Ry."

The Veil Between the Worlds

The following day, Ryder left mid-morning to spend some time with Harriet before her shifts at the pub, and Hunter decided that she would do her ritual. She was excited, and hopeful for finding her familiar. She was aware that magick didn't always work straight away, but she had to try it out. They had nothing to lose, and were in desperate need of more information.

The more that Hunter thought about the encounter that she and her mother had, inside the standing stones of the Otherworld, the more she grew wary of it. It couldn't just be as simple as hedge riding to the Otherworld and finding her father by solving a riddle. The words of the Fae man that had approached her in the wood kept coming back to her. Could he be telling the truth about the seven-pointed star, or was it as she had first suspected, and he was merely trying to throw them off the scent? She knew that the Fae were tricky, and loved to lead people astray. But she was also aware that they sometimes helped others, just as when they had brought her mother's body back, after keeping it safe for so long. Hunter needed to know more, and as Elspeth wasn't inclined to give her any more information on dealing with the Fae (other than warnings not to), she decided that perhaps her familiar might be able to point her in the right direction. *If* she could find her familiar, or call one to her.

She went into her mother's room, and looked at the seven-pointed star that lay on the dresser. She ran her fingers over it, trying to see if there was anything there energy-wise that she could pick up on. Still there was nothing, no energy emanating from it. Her mother had said that she thought it was Aedon's, but when Hunter picked it up there was no sense of any energy there that she could discern. She honestly had no idea if she would be able to feel her father's energy, as she had never known him. She had never really tried to sense energy in objects before, apart from the one time she had sensed Jack's energy in his drum that night at his cottage. She sighed, pushing that thought from her mind, and went back to the room that she had been sharing with her sister, to assemble her tools.

She brought out the cauldron, pentacle plate, and the small wand. She sat on the floor, and sprinkled some protective herbs in a circle around her. She hallowed the compass, and got to work.

She lit a small, charcoal disc and placed it inside the cauldron. She then placed the cauldron on the pentacle plate. While she waited for the charcoal disc to get hot, she grounded and centred her energy. When she was ready, she took out a pinch of mugwort and charged the herb in the palm of her hand with her energy. She then breathed over it softly, and said, "Herb of the Witch, help me to discover my true familiar." She placed the mugwort on the charcoal disc, where it released a pungent smoke.

Next she took up a piece of paper, and wrote down her request again. She pushed some more of her energy into the paper, and breathed on it as well for good measure. "Lord and Lady, grant my request to find my familiar," she said softly. She then placed the paper in the cauldron, where it caught alight and sent up a plume of smoke. She pointed the wand at the smoke, and swirled it up and outwards, saying, "Take this message where it needs to go, my familiar to find, my knowledge to grow." The smoke seemed to take on a shape, which vaguely resembled a deer, before it quickly dissipated.

"It is done," said Hunter softly. She sat in the compass for a while longer, simply enjoying the quiet and the solitude. She eventually closed down the circle, got up, and made some lunch.

The Veil Between the Worlds

After she had eaten, she decided to go for a walk. It was a nice, warm day; perfect end of July weather. The sky was blue and there was a slight breeze. Hunter wore her cut-off denim shorts, and a white t-shirt. She tied up her hair in a ponytail, and slathered on some sunscreen. Pulling on her hiking boots, she locked the door and headed out onto the heath.

She decided to avoid her usual route, and instead chose paths that she had never walked before. She felt confident that she would be able to find her way back, often checking behind her to look at the paths from a different perspective for her return route. She knew which direction the road and the cottage lay, as well as the village, and so she walked with confidence. She kept an eye out for adders sunbathing on the path, but only came across tiny little lizards that scurried away in the blink of an eye. The heather was starting to come out, and bees buzzed everywhere alongside other pollinating insects. The purple of the heather and the scent of the blossoms was absolutely beautiful, and like nothing she had ever experienced.

The heat on the heath was rising, making the land shimmer in slow waves. The dry, arid soil pushed the waves of heat upwards, and Hunter soon found herself seeking out the cool shade of the trees. She followed a small track that led to a patch of woodland, and sighed in contentment as she walked beneath the canopy of oak and birch. She didn't meet a single soul these paths, as they were not on the usual walking routes, and she thoroughly enjoyed the solitude.

She came upon a little inclosure, which was the name for a cleared area of woodland here in the New Forest. In the centre of the inclosure stood a lone tree, with a stone-like object beneath it. The inclosure was fenced, but she followed her instinct and found an opening nearby, which she used to enter and explore the area further. She approached the small, twisted tree and discovered that it was a hawthorn tree.

A faery tree, she thought. Hawthorn was a tree deeply connected to the faeries, and the surrounding folklore stated that if one sat or slept beneath a hawthorn, they would meet the faeries. Hunter looked around cautiously, for she did not want to meet any Fae out here on her own. As she got closer to the tree, she started to make out the object lying beneath it.

She stepped up carefully, and saw a squat, square structure in the ground with a wooden lid that was open. She peered down into it and saw that it ran deep into the earth. She thought she saw a flicker of water, and so she looked around for a small stone and dropped one in. She heard a splash, and then considered what she had found.

It appeared to be an old well. Wells were human structures often placed upon natural springs. And so, Hunter had found an old spring by a hawthorn tree. Her heart began to beat faster, and she took a step back. *Oh no, this could be a portal to the Otherworld.*

No sooner had she come to that realisation, than she heard something coming towards her through the brush and the low-lying bracken. She looked up and pulled in a sharp breath. There, walking towards her, was a pure white deer.

She was beautiful, and stately, as she calmly made her way over to the well and the tree. Hunter stood transfixed. When the deer was a stone's toss away, she stopped and regarded Hunter with dark, knowing eyes.

Hunter swallowed, unsure of what to do. Was this some sort of Fae creature? She remembered from her studies that deer were often called 'faery cattle'. Additionally, white deer were similar to the mystical unicorn in some traditions, having the power of transformation, or signalling a transformative event to come. As she pondered this, the white hind lifted a foot and stamped on the ground, with a shake of her head.

"Oh dear god," thought Hunter as another thought dawned on her. "Are you my familiar?"

The white hind merely dipped her head in a slow bow. Hunter's blood raced in her veins, and she felt like her heart would burst. *Could my magic have worked so quickly?*

The beautiful doe took another step towards her, and then looked pointedly at a spot between the well and the hawthorn tree. She then turned her gaze back to Hunter.

"Are you trying to tell me something?" Hunter asked. The deer merely dipped her head in a slight nod. "What is there, between the well and the tree?"

The deer simply turned her gaze back to spot, and stamped her foot again. Hunter took a cautious step forward, not wanting to startle the deer. The white hind remained where she was, only a few feet away. Hunter made her way towards the spot that the deer indicated, but was careful not to stand directly on it. Her inner instincts told her not to get directly between the well and the hawthorn. As she looked closer she saw a shimmer in the air before her, one that was different to the heat haze of the heathland. This shimmer had a slight, silvery sparkle to it, almost like water in sunlight.

"A portal to the Otherworld," breathed Hunter. She remembered her mother's words then, about how her familiar had helped her to find places where the veil between the worlds was thin. *Was this such a place?*

Hunter turned back to the white hind. "Why have you shown me this place?" she asked.

The deer looked deep into Hunter's eyes. Hunter heard a whisper-soft voice in her mind, saying, *This is where you need to be.*

Stunned, Hunter's only thought was, *But why?*

This is a safe place to cross over. One where you will not be seen.

Hunter pondered that for a moment. What did it matter if she was seen? Then the realisation dawned on her. This was a place where she could get to the Otherworld, without alerting Lanoc. She remembered the ritual on the barrows, where she had called her mother through from the Otherworld. That hedge riding had resulted in an attack from Lanoc, with his trademark thunderstorm and lightning bolts. Hunter was aware that burial mounds were often traditionally associated with the faeries, and so it must have been was a place that Lanoc knew well. As well, ever since then the cottage had probably been under surveillance of some kind. Lanoc would have been made aware when she and her mother "flew" out from the cottage to the Otherworld.

But it seemed that there were other places in the New Forest where the veil was thin. Lanoc himself may have used such a place when he had attacked her while she was out walking with Ryder and Jack in the forest that day. Could this place she now stood in be some sort of 'back-door' portal to his realm, one where they might find more clues as to her father's whereabouts?

Is this a safe entry to the Otherworld, where I might find more clues, and find my father? she asked.

It is.

Hunter looked at the unimposing spot with new eyes. She saw bell heather growing around the well, the 'faery bells' of the little blossoms. The hawthorn still had some flowers on it, while at the same time sporting fruit in the small haws or berries. A tree that fruited and flowered at the same time was definitely a faery tree, according to the old lore. Hunter took another moment to consider. *And if I were to go through, how would I find my way back?*

You will know, she heard the doe's soft voice in her head. *If your intentions come from a place of love, you will know where to go.*

Hunter reached out gently towards the shimmering portal, just barely visible. As her hand touched it, it flared to life with a bright, white light. She jumped back in surprise, withdrawing her hand, the light instantly dying away. All that remained was the shimmer before her.

It will not harm you.

Hunter looked at the white deer. She felt like she had a million questions, but was unable to form them into any coherent thought.

Never forget, it is in your blood. You are coming home.

With those final words, the beautiful white doe turned and trotted off into the shade of the forest that surrounded the inclosure. As she neared the fence, she lithely bounded over it and disappeared into the trees.

Hunter released a breath that she didn't know that she had been holding until that moment. Her knees felt a little shaky, and so she sat down beneath the shade of the hawthorn.

You are coming home. Those four words rang in her head. Not only was she coming into her magickal powers as a hereditary Witch, but she was also half-Fae. She belonged to this land, her mother's land, just as much as she belonged to her father's world.

The Otherworld. The full realisation of being half-Fae hit her.

It was no wonder she had always felt different. It was because she *was* different. She truly belonged to two very different worlds. And she had power of her own to welcome and embrace in both of these worlds. Before it had just been something to consider in her mind, but now she truly felt it in her heart.

Hunter sat for a long time, beneath the hawthorn tree near the well, coming home to herself.

Chapter Twelve

The rest of that week passed quickly. Ryder had bought a second-hand mountain bike, and was enjoying cycling into work. She also tried one of the marked bike trails in the New Forest, 'The Old Railway', from Brockenhurst to Burley. Hunter had driven her up to Brockenhurst, and from there Ryder had cycled home on the trail. She said it was amazing, and that Hunter should come with her next time. There was a bike hire in Burley, where Ryder had bought her bike, but Hunter declined.

Instead, Hunter used every spare moment to study, while Ryder interspersed her studies with work. Hunter decided to keep the secret of her familiar close to her chest for now, as she was still coming fully into the realisation of just who, and what, she was. At the end of the week, Elspeth and Abigail came home.

When the two women entered the cottage late one night, they were happy to discover the sisters at the dining table, books and tools spread out around them. "Hello, ladies. Been studying?" asked Elspeth as she held open the door for Abigail to enter with her suitcase.

"Hello, my loves!" sang Abigail as she entered the house. "Oh, we had a wonderful time! But it's so nice to be back here with you." She went up to her daughters, and gave them each a hug. Elspeth closed the door and followed behind.

"And how are you two feeling?" asked Elspeth.

Ryder smiled, and said, "We're ready for anything. We've been studying and practicing for months now."

Elspeth smiled in return, but shook her head. "The true Witch never stops learning," she said.

Ryder shrugged her shoulders. "Yeah, I get that. But still, we are much stronger than we were before. I've been working on sending energy to Hunter, and setting up protective shields. Hunter's been doing a lot of research."

Elspeth leaned over to look at the books. "Research on what, my dear?"

Hunter looked up at the older woman. "On the Fae," she said, waiting to hear the older Witch's reaction.

Elspeth merely patted Hunter's arm. "That's good, dear." She turned to Abigail, and said, "Well, I'm off home now. I have to get in early to the shop tomorrow, and see to everything that needed doing while I was away." She went over and hugged Abigail. "It's been good to get to know you again, Abigail."

Abigail smiled back. "And you, Elspeth. Blessings." She walked the older woman to the door, and let her out. As she closed the door, she spread her arms out wide. "Ah, it's good to be home!"

As Hunter got ready for bed, she mulled over Elspeth's reaction to her research on the Fae. *That's good, dear,* was all that the older Witch had said. *In a condescending tone, too*, thought Hunter. *In fact, in a* very *condescending tone.* As Hunter climbed into bed, she lay there wondering about that encounter. Did Elspeth not consider Hunter's abilities to have improved in her time here? Did she not fully understand what Hunter's heritage truly meant? Did she completely disregard Hunter's three university degrees, and the work that she had already done in historic and folkloric circles?

Hunter also had a feeling that Elspeth was holding back information from them, information about the Fae. She had presumed that it was for their own safety, but now that Hunter was coming into the full realisation of her heritage and her own power, holding back that information took on a totally different tone. Just what was Elspeth hiding?

Maybe she and Jack are not too dissimilar, she thought. *They present one face to the world, while there is a whole other side that they keep secret, as if they were playing some sort of game. Well, I can play that game as well!*

Ryder came into the room from the bathroom, and got into bed. "Mind if I read for a while?" she asked Hunter.

"Actually, I do. I just want to go to sleep, Ryder." In reality, what Hunter wanted to do was to think in the peace and quiet of the darkness, but she wasn't going to tell her sister that.

"Okay," said Ryder, a little uncertainty in her voice. "Are you alright?"

"Just fine."

"Okay. Night, Hun."

Hunter didn't reply. She was already considering what she was going to do. She felt like a foray into the Otherworld was something that she needed to do. And do it on her own. With her Fae blood, perhaps she would not be so noticeable to the other inhabitants of that realm. Perhaps she could even take the seven-pointed star with her, and try to find the location that had been described in the riddle they had heard at the standing stones. She could scout out the area, before she took her mother there.

She considered again whether using the seven-pointed star and following the riddle to the location was a trick or not. The Fae man had warned her, but after even more consideration Hunter suspected that he was aligned with Lanoc. He had a condescending manner to him, which made Hunter think of how her mother and Harriet's parents had described Lanoc. How Lanoc hated humans because he thought they were beneath him, and corrupting his brother. The more Hunter thought about it, the more she came to the conclusion that she was deliberately being misled, and that she was truly on to something with the star and the new portal that her familiar had shown her.

It was time for Hunter to enter the Otherworld on her own.

The next day, Hunter had wanted to get back out onto the heath, to go to the well and the tree. But Abigail wanted to spend some time with her girls, and so Hunter stayed at home. Ryder had the day off, so they sat outside and talked about Abigail's vacation in Cornwall. The old oak tree had been pollarded by some tree surgeons that Thomas had recommended, the branches cleaned up and stacked on the edge of the lawn to provide a shelter for insects and small animals. Hunter was sad to see the oak tree's damage, but hoped that it would make it through. The tree surgeons were fairly positive about the outcome.

Abigail spent around twenty minutes, just talking of her vacation with Elspeth. With each minute, Hunter could feel her frustration growing within her. After a few more minutes of this, Hunter's exasperation came to the surface. "That's all well and good, Mom, but what about our mission here? What about finding my father?"

Abigail's face fell. "I haven't forgotten, Poppet. I know that you both need to train up before we do anything further. After what had happened the last time, we need to make sure that we are strong enough before we carry forward with this mission to find your father. I, more than anyone, want and need to see him released."

The Veil Between the Worlds

Hunter felt taken aback by her mother's words. Hunter was, after all, *his* daughter. Why did her mother say that her feelings mattered more in this regard? Hunter felt anger rising in her, and she used it to shield her thoughts and emotions from her mother and sister. She simply sat back, and let the hot waves wash over her, as her mother and Ryder continued talking.

"Hunter? What do you think?"

Hunter was brought out of her thoughts by her sister, who was looking at her intently. "What?"

"Harriet says that she'd like us to go out tonight. Are you up for it?"

Going out was the last thing that Hunter wanted to do tonight. She said as much.

"Well, maybe Harri can come here instead. What do you think? We haven't seen her since the dance."

"We could invite Elspeth too," said Abigail. "She'll probably need to wind down after her first day back at the shop. We can make it a Ladies' Night."

Hunter stood up and shrugged. "Do what you want. I'm going in to study." She left her mother and her sister outside and went in to hit the books, as well as plan her next hedge riding.

Harriet and Elspeth came over for dinner, and the five women sat at the dining table, enjoying a meal that Abigail had made. Harriet had brought a couple of bottles of wine with her, and they talked and laughed around the dinner table. All except for Hunter, whose thoughts were elsewhere.

Finally, Elspeth spoke out. "Hunter, my dear, whatever is the matter? You haven't joined in any of the conversation tonight, and you appear to be totally distracted. Is there something wrong?"

Witches of the New Forest

Hunter looked at Elspeth. *Oh yes, there is plenty wrong,* she thought to herself. *Your brother dumped me, you think I'm just a 'baby Witch' and you're hiding something from all of us.* "Nothing is wrong," she said, feeling the heat flush to her face. She was never any good at lying.

Elspeth leaned across the table to take her hand, but Hunter pulled away. "Hunter, what is bothering you?"

Ryder cleared her throat. "She hasn't had the best of times here, lately, what with everything going on," she tried to explain.

Hunter's anger flared up. "I'm right here, Ryder. I don't need you talking about, or for, me."

Ryder looked at her sister, startled. "I'm just trying to help."

"Well, don't," said Hunter, cutting off her sister. "I'm fine, okay? Leave it."

Harriet looked over Hunter's head, her eyes unfocused. After a moment, she came back to herself, and looked at Hunter. "Um, Hunter, your energy is a mess."

Hunter swung her head around to glare at Harriet. "No, it's not. I've been working hard on it."

Harriet stood up and walked towards Hunter. She held out her hands, as if trying to sense something.

"Leave me alone!" said Hunter, pushing back from her chair and standing up. Her anger at having her opinion of herself being so casually overlooked flared up, and she felt a full-on rage coming.

"Hunter, please, calm down," said Elspeth in a soothing tone.

"I will not calm down! Stop telling me what to do! I'm a thirty-five-year-old woman, and I know myself better than any of you!"

Harriet stopped, and looked at Elspeth. Elspeth nodded, and stood. "Hunter, please sit down."

The Veil Between the Worlds

Hunter looked around the table. Her mother looked shocked, and Ryder, for once, had nothing to say. "I will not," she said evenly.

"Very well," said Elspeth. She waved her hand, and Hunter's chair hit her hard against the back of her legs, forcing her to sit. She felt a push of energy pressing down on her, keeping her seated and in her chair. Elspeth sat back down, and picked up her wine glass. She took a leisurely sip, before putting it down again. She then looked straight into Hunter's eyes, and said, "I think you may have been spelled, my dear. You are not acting yourself."

"How would you know?" said Hunter, struggling against the pressure that was keeping her seated. "You know very little about me."

Harriet came closer. "Hunter, your energy is all weird. It's not like it was before. Remember, when I saw your energy as golden, and shifting? Well, that was a healthy, if somewhat different aura, probably due to your Fae heritage. But now? When I look at it, it's all red, and there are some dark shadows around it too. I'm worried about you, Hunter. This may indeed be some sort of spell, you know."

Hunter almost laughed at the absurdity of it, but stopped herself. A small sliver of doubt crept into her mind. Was she under some sort of spell?

"Please, let me take a look," said Harriet. "May I have your permission?"

Instinctively, Hunter wanted to say no. But she took a moment to consider it, and slowly she nodded her head. "Alright, go ahead. Knock yourself out."

Harriet came up behind her, and held her hands out over Hunter's head. She hissed slightly as she came into contact with the edge of Hunter's aura. She felt around, not doing any healing work but instead doing an assessment. After a few moments, she sighed and stepped back.

"I think you *are* under a spell. But it may be one of your own making. It's hard to tell, as you've been doing so much energy work on yourself."

"What do you mean, Harriet?" Hunter asked her friend impatiently.

"It looks to me like you've been using the energy techniques that I taught you, and which you further studied, to shore up your power, strengthen your energy, and protect yourself. But the energy that you've been using is all wrong."

"How so?" asked Ryder softly, looking at her older sister with concern.

"There are all sorts of energy that we can use in our magick. We can tap into pretty much any kind of energy, and colour or strengthen it with our emotions. Hunter's energy here is full of anger, and I think she may have used that as a kind of coping mechanism, to fill her aura, protect herself, and the like."

Hunter's rage exploded. She broke free of Elspeth's magick and shot up, her chair falling backwards behind her. "Well, aren't you all the experts of me!"

Elspeth sat still in her chair. Her voice, when she spoke, was calm and quiet. "Hunter, does this seem like normal behaviour to you?"

Hunter's inner fires dampened down a bit, and she took a moment to think. In fact, she needed a lot more time to think. "Perhaps not. I don't know. Just leave me alone right now," she said in a soft, but determined voice.

"You've been through hell, Hunter," said Ryder, coming up to her sister and putting a hand on her shoulder. "It's no wonder that you're pissed off. But we are here to help you. You get that, right? We only want what's best for you. If I was acting all weird, I'd hope you'd call me out on that. I'm always here for you, Hun. I'm always on your side." She looked around the table at the other women. "I think maybe we should call it a night. Thank you all for coming."

Elspeth and Abigail stood up. Abigail looked uncertain, but Elspeth was nodding. "It has been a long day. Hunter, I am sorry for using magick against you, but I was worried about you. I *am* worried about you. I only want what is best for you."

Hunter nodded, only half-believing the older Witch's words.

Harriet approached Hunter again, and touched her lightly on the arm. "You take care of yourself, Hunter. If you need me, for anything, you know where I am." Harriet then nodded at Ryder, and went to get her things.

Abigail looked at her two daughters for a moment, and then saw Elspeth and Harriet to the door. "Take care," she said, as they left. She closed the door softly and turned to face Hunter and Ryder. "I'll clean up," she said, coming back to the dining table. "You girls just relax."

Hunter blew out a long breath. "No, Mom. You and Ryder go relax. I've got this." She immediately felt bad about the scene that she had caused, and wanted to make amends. "Please, let me get this."

Ryder nodded, understanding her sister's apology. "Come on, Mom. There's a good murder mystery on tonight." She took her mother by the arm and led her out to the sofa, leaving Hunter to clear the table and sort out the dishes.

Later that night Hunter sat in the window seat of the room she shared with her sister, watching the moon rise over the distant trees. Usually the cool light of the moon made her feel good, but tonight she was still on edge. She felt like she had been patronised by everyone, and made a fool of at the dinner table, especially with Elspeth's magick. Hunter's anger rose, and she swore softly as she stared out the window.

She was tired of everyone treating her as some sort of 'newbie'. *I have studied my ass off for months now, and if there was an exam on 'Beginner Witchcraft', I would have aced it*, she thought. She knew that she was far from being any sort of 'Expert Witch', but she still had achieved quite a few things in her short time as a Hedge Witch. She had done a hedge riding all the way across the New Forest, without even knowing what hedge riding was. She had enspelled an entire pub full of people with her singing (albeit unknowingly). She had helped to protect her sister and Jack from a malevolent Fae entity in the forest. She had found her mother's spirit and had called it through from the Otherworld. She had met another Fae and walked away from that encounter, seeing through his deceit. And now she had called her familiar to her. She had probably seen and done more Witchcraft in these last few months than most Witches did in their entire lives. But she was still being treated as a *newbie*. There was no thought or regard for her Fae heritage, for her inherent magickal skills. Everyone treated her exactly the same as her much younger sister. She was not a young twenty-year old. She was a university professor with a career of her own. She had three degrees under her belt, and she knew something about folklore. Even if she hadn't known about magick (with a 'k') and the magickal community here in Burley, she still *knew things*.

She wrapped her indignation around her and used it to shield her from the judgements that surrounded her. She felt like she could hear what others thought of her clearly, in her mind. *Newbie. Tourist. Baby Witch. Foreigner. Outsider. Loner. Weird. Socially Awkward. Nerd.* All of these thoughts, coupled with what Jack had done to her (which was the same thing that all her previous boyfriends had done to her), hardened her heart against the world.

Well, it was time to show them all.

Chapter Thirteen

Hunter got up at 3am, and quietly moved about the cottage. She had left her sister sleeping in the room they shared. She silently snuck into her mother's room, and took the seven-pointed star from the dresser, without waking her. Hunter crept down the stairs, and went into the kitchen pantry. She had packed a bag the night before with some water, snack bars, peanut butter and jam sandwiches, and apples. She stashed her phone into the bag as well, just in case. She pulled on her backpack, and was out the door in no time flat.

Hunter wore black leggings, a black long-sleeved t-shirt, and had a large, lightweight, grey scarf around her neck. She wore her leather hiking boots. Her hair hung loose around her shoulders. She didn't know why, but she wore the antler pendant that Jack had given her. Even though their love hadn't lasted, she was sure her love of the deer would stand the test of time.

It was dark out on the heath, so she turned on the flashlight that she had taken from the kitchen drawer. She used it to walk across the road and down the paths that she had taken earlier that week. It was much more difficult in the dark as things did not appear the same, and she had to turn around several times after missing her trails. At around 4am the sky starting to lighten, and soon she was able to put away the flashlight and continue in the dusk.

She made her way to the hawthorn tree and the well; the portal to the Otherworld. As she approached it in the twilight hours, her heart began to race. A small voice in the back of her

The Veil Between the Worlds

mind asked, *Why are you even doing this?* Hunter ignored that voice, and reminded herself of her ability and her heritage. She could do this.

She stood by the tree and touched the bark of the trunk. It was firm and rough beneath her fingers. She ran her hand carefully along a branch, avoiding the thorns. Her eyes traced the crazy patchwork of branches that twisted every which way above her. It was mesmerising. Hunter pulled her eyes away from the branches, realising that she was falling under the faery tree's spell.

She had work to do.

She took a sip of water from her bottle, and settled her nerves. She had not brought any tools with her, as there didn't seem to be one that would fit any role in what she was about to do. All she needed was herself.

She heard a sound from off to one side, and looked up. There, standing on the edge of the inclosure, she saw her familiar. The white hind stamped her foot, and seemed to shake her head. *Are you telling me not to go?* thought Hunter. It didn't make any sense. *You showed me the way before. Why do you not want me to go now?*

Now is not the time, she heard in her mind.

Hunter looked at her beautiful familiar, glowing in the dusk before dawn. *Will you come with me?* she asked.

The white doe stamped her foot again. *No, I must remain here.*

Hunter looked at the white hind. *Why is that?*

I will be needed here, she said.

Is there anything you want to tell me, before I go then? asked Hunter, miffed that her familiar wouldn't accompany her.

Now is not the time.

Hunter sighed in exasperation. Time was wasting away. She wanted to cross through the portal while it was still twilight. She felt that it would help her on her way, going through a liminal place at a liminal time. *I have to go,* she said to her familiar. *And I am going now.*

The white hind said nothing, and only looked at her with those dark, knowing eyes.

Hunter shrugged and turned away, walking towards the portal. It was time.

She tested it with her hand as she had the last time she had been here, and the white light flared up around her. She reached all the way in, and then pulled her hand back out. Everything seemed okay. Hunter did the same with a leg, and was satisfied that it was safe; or as safe as can be. Her heart pounding, she took a step forwards, and walked through the portal.

Her vision was blinded by brilliant white light. She took another step forwards, unable to see but feeling it was the right thing to do. Suddenly the bright light faded, and she found herself in the Otherworld.

Before her stretched rolling hills, dotted with woodland. Just beyond the rolling hills lay a vast forest. The sky was a pale blue on the horizon, but faded to twilight above her head. She could see stars directly overhead, and gave a small gasp.

The stars were different here.

She couldn't recognise any of the constellations. After a few moments, she began to get a crick in her neck from looking up, and so she turned her gaze back to the horizon. She thought about where she needed to go. She pulled off the backpack and took out the seven-pointed star. She replaced her pack over her shoulders and held the star out in front of her. She thought of the riddle that she and her mother had heard in the stone circle, and whispered it softly.

*"At the rising sun,
A bridge there will be,
Where day meets night,
That is where I will be."*

Suddenly she felt a pull in her solar plexus, a tugging sensation that wanted her to move forwards. The seven-pointed star seemed to glow slightly. She turned around to check the portal, and create a memory of where it lay in her mind for her return. As she turned around, she noticed that the star stopped glowing. She then turned to face the direction that called out to her, and the star began to glow again.

Interesting.

The star and her instincts would lead her, she was sure of it. She pulled the straps of her backpack tighter, and headed across the rolling hills towards the forest. The light slowly increased, and she wondered if the sun fully rose here in the Otherworld. She had read accounts and stories over the years in her studies, of people who had either travelled to or come from faery lands, describing them as a place where the sun never rose nor set. Instead, the lands of faery existed in some sort of perpetual twilight. She looked at her watch, and noticed the time. It should be sunrise just about now, she thought. She then looked more closely at her watch, and saw that the second-hand on her watch had stopped moving. She wondered if the Otherworld did strange things to devices, like watches and other technology. She resisted the temptation to get out her phone, and kept on walking.

There were paths that led up and down the rolling hills, and she followed them as the star and her instincts directed. She saw no one, only a few birds: blackbirds, crows, and even a phalanx of swans flew overhead. That made her stop in her tracks, and her heart open. They were so beautiful. The swans were heading in the same direction she was, and she thought that was a good sign. She was looking for a place where there was water, certainly. She needed a bridge, and a bridge usually ran over water.

It felt different here in the rolling hills, than it did in the standing stones. There, she had felt like she was sometimes walking through water, and at other times light as air. Here, she felt normal, though everything seemed brighter, clearer and more defined than in her world. There was an air of magick and mystery all around.

The sky lightened around her, and soon the stars slowly winked out. There was still a feeling of perpetual twilight, however. After Hunter had walked for about an hour, she stopped and sat down on the edge of the forest. She could see crows flying in lazy circles in the distance, enjoying the thermals. They slowly circled towards and then over her, continuing out over woodland. Hunter took this as a good omen.

She pulled out her water flask and ate a sandwich, followed by an apple. She hadn't expected the Otherworld to be quite so similar to the 'real' world, or *the world she lived in*, she supposed she should call it. No world was 'more real' than the other. She thought about how relaxed she felt here, and how peaceful it was. No cars, no noise, except that of nature. For her sensitive soul, it was bliss. She often felt the modern world was just too busy, too noisy, too distracted. Here she could sit and think in peace.

As she put her water flask and sandwich tin away, she pulled out her phone, just out of curiosity. She wondered how electronic items would work here. Her watch had stopped; how would her phone react?

The Veil Between the Worlds

She got it out and turned it on. When the lockscreen came up, there was a picture of the seven-pointed star on the lock screen. *How odd, I never put that there,* she thought. She swiped up and unlocked the phone, and saw again the seven-pointed star on her home screen, with nothing else. She tapped on the picture, to see if anything would happen. When nothing happened, she shrugged and put it away. She was glad devices didn't work here. She longed for a world without them, in all honesty.

Abigail woke early, and went downstairs to make some tea. She noticed that some dishes were already out. She went to the porch to peek through the door outside, and saw that Hunter's hiking boots were gone. She surmised that her eldest daughter had gone for a walk on the heath, and had taken some food with her. Hunter had always liked to get out early for walks, and so Abigail softly closed the door and returned to the kitchen to make a cup of tea.

She then spent a couple of hours in the garden, before she heard the back door slam shut. She looked up from where she was weeding the garden, and saw Ryder approaching. Her youngest daughter was still in her pyjamas, and she looked around blearily with a cup of coffee in her hand, her hair mussed up from sleep. "Hello, Peanut," said Abigail cheerily.

Ryder stopped at the edge of the garden that her mother was working on. "God, you and Hunter are so alike. Why must you all get up at stupid o'clock every morning?"

"It looks like your sister when out for a walk," said Abigail. "Can I make you some breakfast?"

Ryder shook her head. "I'm good. I'll get something later."

"Are you working today?"

"Yup. Double shift again, 11am to midnight."

"Hunter can probably give you a lift in, my love, when she gets back. And pick you up tonight."

Ryder shrugged and took a swig of her coffee. "S'okay. I've got my bike. The path from here to the village is good for cycling, and I've got a good set of lights. I'm probably safer on the path than I am on the road," she said with a slight shudder, remembering the accident. "Plus, I like the fresh air after work."

"Are you sure? Hunter will probably be home soon, and you can ask."

"No, I'm good."

Hunter decided it was time to get up and continue her journey. She did wonder at not having seen anyone in the whole time she had been here. As she shouldered her pack, she wondered just how big the Otherworld was, and if it was similar to her world. Was it a sphere in space, like the earth?

She thought about how quickly her mother had gotten to her destination when they had done their hedge riding. It seemed like this journey that Hunter was on was taking a lot longer. Was there something that she could do to perhaps shorten it?

Just as she was having that thought, she heard a noise behind her. She spun around, and saw a woman approaching her from the edge of the forest. She had long, wavy blonde hair, and was wearing a silver-coloured, flowing gown. She looked like something straight out of Tolkein's world.

Hunter stood there, a slight breeze blowing her red curls in front of her face. She pushed them aside, and continued to watch the woman walking towards her. She looked human; no pointed ears like the Fae, elves and other creatures were usually portrayed with, at least in fantasy books and films. Hunter checked for other marks, such as a tail, or even a hollowed-out tree trunk for a back, as in some Scandinavian folklore of Fae creatures. She couldn't see a tail, nor could she see the woman's back.

The woman laughed then, and spun around in a circle, showing her full body, gown flowing around her. She appeared perfectly normal, and human. But Hunter had a feeling, deep down, that she was from the Otherworld, and not a visitor, as she was.

"You are correct, my dear," the woman said, reading her mind.

"Who are you?" asked Hunter.

The beautiful woman, still smiling, simply said, "I am a messenger. I have some advice for you, to help guide you."

Hunter took a moment to think. "But I have a familiar already."

The woman looked around. "Oh, really? Where is she?"

Hunter pursed her lips, thinking how she should respond. "She chose not to come."

The woman took a step closer. "Why would that be? You shouldn't be alone, out here."

Hunter took a cautious step back, wanting to keep some distance between herself and this woman, until she was sure of her intentions. "Why is that?" she asked, trying to buy time to think.

"Because, *he will find you.* He does not like your kind."

"My kind?"

"Human."

"I am not human," said Hunter, testing the waters.

The woman considered her for a moment. She leaned closer, and gave another small laugh. "No, no you are not. But he will hate *that* even more."

"How can you tell what I am, just by looking at me?"

The woman smiled and waved her hand airily. "If I was in your world, would I not stand out?"

Hunter thought this over. Yes. Yes, she would most definitely stand out.

"Your human nature, or half-human nature is visible to us. Just as our Fae nature is obvious to you. You have seen us before, though we are able to cloak ourselves from those who have not the gift."

"I don't understand," said Hunter, confused.

The woman began to circle her, her hands clasped behind her back. "We came when you called to us, Hedge Witch. We came when you sang. We followed your song."

Hunter tried to think back to when she had sung a song. "I still don't understand."

"You sang, to all those people, even while you called to us. So we came, five of us, to answer your call. You are the one that we have been waiting for."

Hunter's brain finally clicked into place. "The pub. When I sang, and did a hedge riding there. You, you were the strange group that came in, which no one else saw! I hadn't dreamt that up!"

The woman stopped, and looked at her with a smile. "No, Hedge Rider, you were not dreaming. We cloaked ourselves from others, so that we would only be seen by those whom we chose."

"But why? Why did you come over?"

"You called to us."

"No, I didn't."

The woman took another step closer. She was almost within touching distance. Hunter braced herself to flee.

The woman reached out, and Hunter flinched. The woman's smiled wavered for an instant, and then she smiled again. "Your hair," she said, looking at Hunter's long, red curls. "I only wanted to touch your beautiful hair."

"No, thank you," said Hunter, taking a step back from this strange woman.

There was an awkward silence, as Hunter couldn't find anything to say. The beautiful woman just stood there, looking at her with large, hazel-coloured eyes. Finally, she said, "Turn back, Hedge Witch. This is not the way."

Shocked, Hunter put a hand to her heart. "What do you mean?"

The woman looked around, as if hearing something. "I must go. Goodbye, Hedge Witch. I hope to see you again." She smiled, and then stepped back, fading from sight into the shadow of the trees.

Hunter looked around her, to see if anyone was approaching. The woman's sudden disappearance made her uneasy. But she saw nothing except the rolling hills, and the forest in front of her.

Hunter blew out a deep breath that she had been holding in. *Well, that happened,* she thought wryly. She wondered why the woman had told her to turn back. *Was she in league with the Fae man that had approached me in forest, earlier that week? What if he was part of her group? Could he be that strange, blond man that was watching me in the pub? What if they all were in league with Lanoc, and trying to turn me from my quest?*

From what she had learned in her studies, and which was pretty standard in all faery folklore, was that not everyone on the Other side were true or helpful. Some of the beings that she might encounter were there to challenge her. Others might aid her, while others might seek to harm her outright, cause her to lose her way or to trick her. She didn't feel any malice from this strange, beautiful woman, but neither did she trust her. Hunter decided that she could only trust her own instincts, and those were to carry on. She was certain that she was on to something important. She pulled out the seven-pointed star again, and felt a draw towards the forest. As she stepped beneath the canopy of tall trees, she saw a path laid out before her, winding through the trunks into the deep, green, mysterious forest. She smiled, and walked on.

It was lunchtime, and Abigail was starting to worry. Hunter still had not returned. She called Ryder on her phone. "Hello, Peanut. Have you heard anything from Hunter, yet?"

"Hunter's still not back?"

"No," said Abigail. "I'm starting to worry."

"Do we know how long she's been gone?"

"I have no idea. She wasn't here when I got up this morning, around 6 o'clock."

There was a pause. "So, Hunter's been gone for over six or seven hours now. That's long, even for her."

"Should we call somebody?"

"Just a sec." There were sounds, like Ryder was walking quickly somewhere. "Okay Mom," she said softly. "I'm here. We can't call the police, because they think *you're* still missing. That could compromise the entire magickal community. Maybe we should call the ranger station, to see if anyone has seen her?"

"Good idea."

"I know who to call."

"Thanks, Peanut."

In the middle of the lunch rush, Ryder quickly scanned her contacts list, and hit Dougal's number.

"Hey, Ryder. What can I do for you?"

"Hey, Dougal. Are you at work at the moment?"

The Veil Between the Worlds

"Yeah?"

"Good. Um, it looks like Hunter went out for a walk this morning, early, but she's still not back. She's been gone for at least six or seven hours now. She's never gone for that long. Is there anything you can do?"

There was silence for a heartbeat. "Six or seven hours you say?"

"Yes."

"Any idea which direction she might have headed?"

"Honestly, no. We were all asleep when she left."

"And you don't know what she was wearing?"

"No."

"Damn. Okay, I'll let the other rangers know, and we'll check the main areas and trouble spots. Don't worry. We'll find her."

"Okay, Dougal. Thanks."

Dougal picked up the walkie-talkie from the stand at the ranger station where he was filling in some paperwork. He pushed the button on the radio, and spoke into it. "Hey, everyone, heads up. This is really important. We have a missing person, out on the heath near or around Burley. A woman, long, red hair, about 5ft, 10, around thirty-five years old. She's been missing for over six or seven hours. I don't have a description of what she was wearing. Last known point, Pound Lane halfway between Burley and Thorney Hill. You know how this works. Radio back to me with any information."

There was a moment of silence, before the radio beeped. "Dougal?" It was Jack's voice, and he sounded worried. "Is it Hunter that's missing?"

"Aye, I'm afraid so."

There was another moment of silence. "On it. I'm at Burbush car park with an ATV."

Another beep sounded. "Dougal? This is Janine. I'm at the wildcrafting site, with the truck. I'll have a look over here."

Another beep. "Dean here. I'm near Holmsley car park, with an ATV. I'll scout out the eastern side.

"Roger that," said Dougal. He put a pin on each location that they had called from. "I'll stay here, waiting with the map. Radio in where you've been, as you go."

After another half hour of walking, Hunter began to sense a change in the air. There was a feeling, a kind of heaviness, similar to what she had experienced during her last hedge riding with her mother. The air felt thicker here, and suddenly her ears popped. *That's better,* thought Hunter. *I must be getting close.* From the look of the light in the sky far above the treetops, it appeared to be around dawn. The cries of the crows sounded over her head now, and soon she found herself heading slightly downwards. She thought she heard the sound of water, like a babbling brook nearby. She walked on, and a few minutes later she saw a stone bridge before her. It spanned a brook that ran through the forest, disappearing down the small hill and into the trees.

She was in the right place, she was sure of it. And at the right time.

She looked around, but she found no clue as to what she needed to do. She sighed, and picked up the seven-pointed star again. "What do I do now?" she asked it. The star was silent, the glow gone. There was only the sound of the crows calling in the distance now, the wind softly sighing in the trees and the laughing tinkle of the water than ran through the forest. Hunter felt deflated. She had no idea what to do. She walked out onto the bridge and considered her options.

Ryder's phone rang again. "Heya. Any news?"

"The star. Aedon's star. It's gone," her mother said.

"What?"

"It was right here on my dresser. And now it's gone. You don't think..."

Ryder swore softly.

"You don't think that Hunter took it, do you?" her mother asked.

"Most likely."

"Why would she do such a thing?"

Ryder frowned. She then spoke softer, and her voice was slightly muffled. "She has been acting weird lately. Something isn't right. And now both she and the star are missing. I'm going to call Elspeth."

Ryder hung up, and quickly scanned for any new messages, but there were none. She scrolled through her contacts, and then hit the button.

"Hey, Elspeth? I think we have a situation here."

Chapter Fourteen

Jack hopped onto the all-terrain vehicle, tore out of the car park and rode down the track. His heart was in his throat at the thought of Hunter gone missing. He followed the main tracks directly to the nearest hotspot where people often got into trouble: Whitten Pond. When he arrived, he saw a family of four there. He parked the ATV and went straight up to them. "Excuse me, but have you seen a woman with red hair, 5ft 10, thirty-five years of age?" The family shook their heads. "If you do, can you please call the ranger station at this number?" Jack handed out a card, and they said they would. "Thank you," he said, and hopped back onto the ATV to do a tour around the pond. The family watched him as he rode around, avoiding the boggy areas with the vehicle and instead getting out on foot where necessary.

After he had completed his physical check of the area, he stood at the water's edge, getting a *feel* for the place. He rooted his energy into the ground, and stretched out his awareness. Nothing felt out of place. Quickly, he ran back to the ATV and pulled out the radio from the clip at his belt. "Whitten Pond, no sign of her."

"Thanks, Jack."

Jack pulled away quickly and drove over to the next pond. As he pulled up and got off the four-wheeler, he heard the next call in. "Avon Water, all clear."

"Cheers, Dean."

A few minutes later, "Shears Brook. Clear."

The Veil Between the Worlds

"Thanks, Janine," came Dougal's voice over the radio. "Ronnie's coming in to do the northern part near Burley, from Moorhill Road downwards. Geoff's out of the country, on holiday, so it's just us five."

Jack ran his hands through his hair, frustration taking over. *Where could she have gone? Was she hurt?* He continued on his rounds, visiting bogs, cottage ruins, sandpits and other hotspots where people were likely to get into trouble. He radioed them in, and alerted everyone he saw along the way, handing out the ranger station's number. The radio kept beeping, with other co-ordinates being checked off, and still no sign of Hunter. He and the other rangers continued to search.

Suddenly, a thought came to Jack's mind. He hauled his ATV to the ranger station, driving dangerously fast. When he got there, he saw Dougal come out. "Jack – are you gonna come in and get a bite to eat?"

"No, Dougal. I have an idea. I'll be back soon."

Dougal just watched in silence as Jack jumped into his jeep and drove off.

Jack pulled up to his little gatehouse cottage. He slammed the door of his truck, and ran into the house. He strode towards his bedroom, and pulled back his dresser. Tucked between the dresser and the wall was a small, wooden box. He grabbed it and shoved it into a backpack, and then headed back out.

He drove to his sister's place, and pulled up into the driveway. In the late afternoon light he got out of the jeep with his bag, and he saw Elspeth come to the door with her phone to her ear. She waved him inside. Jack followed.

"Okay, thank you. I will call you if I hear anything in the meantime." She lowered her phone and turned to face her brother. "Well, Jacob. It's about time you decided to talk to me."

"Not now, Ellie. I've been looking all over for Hunter. But then I had an idea. I found this, early this morning. I was going to bring it to you tonight after I finished work, but after everything that's happened, I suddenly had an idea, and I think it might help us in our search."

Elspeth eyebrows raised. "Just what have you brought, Jack?"

Jack reached into his bag and pulled out the box. He strode into the living room, and placed it on the coffee table. Opening the box, he said, "This."

Ryder swore for the millionth time as she paced behind the bar. She couldn't leave her shift, as there was no one to cover for her. She couldn't just up leave, right in the middle of a super-busy shift in the peak of tourist season. She would get canned for sure. She kept checking her phone for messages, and calling her mother and Elspeth for updates. She also kept trying Hunter's phone, but the line just went dead each time.

It was now early evening when Jack pulled up to the ranger station. He saw Dougal's truck was still there, and a police car had parked next to it. Jack knew that the other rangers were tired after the long day and had gone home, and so didn't hold it against them. A search at night was dangerous for everyone. There was only so much that the park rangers could do, and they could really only do it safely in the daylight. They would be better able to find her in the daylight the next day. Jack went straight to his ATV. Dougal and PC Hart came out of the station. Dougal hollered at Jack, "Where're ya off to, now?"

Jack pulled his backpack onto his shoulders. "The Deer's Circle."

Jack drove quickly to the place where he and Hunter had first met. He had to drop off the ATV alongside a bigger track, before he could head to that area on foot. The trails were small here, only wide enough for one person. As he jogged up to the spot where he and Hunter had first met, and last argued, he felt a deep sadness in his heart. He didn't know what he would do if anything happened to Hunter. He scanned the area but saw nothing. He decided to also send out his energy, to see if he could feel Hunter anywhere nearby. He knelt down and placed his hands on the soil, rooting himself energetically in the earth, and went on the alert for anything wrong in the area. Everything seemed normal.

Suddenly, he heard a loud thud next to him.

He looked up and saw a beautiful, white deer. She was standing within arm's reach. How she had approached him without his knowledge he didn't know, but there she was. She looked at him with large, dark eyes, and suddenly Jack's heart leapt up.

This must be some sort of messenger, he thought. He slowly stood, not wanting to startle the deer. He knew from Celtic mythology that white hinds and harts were very special, and often belonged to the Otherworld. Jack looked at the hind before him, and said softly, "Do you know where Hunter is?"

The deer bowed her head once, and turned to walk away. Jack reached into his pocket and pulled out his phone. "Dougal?"

"Yeah, Jack," Dougal said softly. It sounded like he was walking somewhere. "Hang on." There was a slight pause. "Okay, I'm alone now. Come back here before ya collapse, ya bloody eejit. You'll do her no good if you keel over, ya know."

"Dougal, I'm with a white hind. She's leading me."

There was a long pause. "Ya dinnae say? Hell mend ye, ya bloody Druid. Alright. I'll let your sister know."

As Hunter walked out onto the bridge, she felt the heaviness in the air all around her. It was like wading through molasses, or treacle. She held out her hands before her, still holding the star in her right hand. She could feel energy in this spot, energy that resonated with her. It was strong, and it felt right. She wondered if perhaps it was her father's energy that she could feel. She neared the centre of the bridge, and a sliver of sunlight escaped through the trees.

The sun was rising.

Suddenly, a mist appeared all around her, rising up so quickly from the ground that she had no time to do anything but draw in a sharp breath. It was difficult to move, and her heart began to race. She used all her strength to look down at the star in her palm. It flashed brightly, and then crumbled away to dust, blown away on the rising breeze.

It was a trap.

She had been tricked.

Jack followed the white hind through the growing dusk, and eventually came to a fenced inclosure. He hadn't been here for a while, and looked across the open area. The white hind jumped easily over the fence, and then turned to look at him. He quickly climbed the fence and dropped down the other side. The deer led him to the centre, where a hawthorn tree stood by an old well.

"I don't remember this tree being here," Jack said softly to himself.

The deer stamped, and caught his attention. She walked over to the hawthorn, and looked to a spot between the well and the tree. Jack followed, and tried to see what it was that she was looking at. "There's nothing there," he said.

The deer stamped her foot again, looking at him and then turning her gaze back the same spot she had been looking at before. She nodded her head as she gazed at something that he could not see.

Jack slowly walked up to the hawthorn tree. He ran his fingers across the rough bark and then, in the last of the evening's light, noticed a long, red hair that had caught on a low branch. It glowed in the rays of the setting sun.

"Hunter," he said, his resolve strengthening. He turned to the white hind. "Where did she go?"

The deer simply stamped her foot a third time, and looked between the well and the tree. Jack walked on a few more steps, and suddenly felt a strange energy coming from the area. He reached out with his hand to try and feel it better, and then a white light blinded him. He dropped his hand, and the light disappeared. "What the hell?" he said, raising his hand once more. Again, the light flashed, and he withdrew his hand.

"Oh my Goddess," Jack breathed. "Of course. The well, the faery tree. This is a portal." He looked back at the white hind, who stood there, watching him. She nodded her head once.

Jack took a deep breath, turned to the portal, and walked through.

The mist enveloped Hunter, until she could see nothing else. She called out, but there was no answer, only the echo of her own voice. *Damn it*, she thought. *Who was I kidding? I'm not Witch enough to deal with this stuff. I've walked right into a trap like a fool.* In the mist there was no sound, no scent, nothing.

A moment later she heard a chuckle of laughter near her. "Who's there?" she said, trying to sound confident, but there was slight tremor in her voice.

"Hello, Hedge Witch." A voice that she thought she recognised drifted towards her.

"Where are you? Show yourself!"

"As you wish." Out of the mist came a cloaked and hooded figure. It walked towards her gracefully, lifting its hands and pushing down the hood. Hunter's heart thudded in her chest. She knew him, she recognised him, she remembered him.

"It's you…"

The white light flared all around him, and Jack was momentarily blinded and confused. He felt he must push on, and so he did, and then half fell out into a new world. His head spun and he fell to his knees, dizzy. It took several minutes for his body to adjust, and then he slowly raised his head. Before him, a vast expanse of rolling hills stretched before him, dotted with woodlands and a large forest just beyond.

"By the Lady," Jack breathed in wonder. He got to his feet, and began to feel steadier. He looked around, taking it all in. He was actually, *physically*, in the Otherworld, and it took him a few moments to come to terms with that. He then shook himself, and shrugged the backpack off his shoulders. He placed it on the ground, and took out the wooden box.

Opening the lid, he lifted out some sort of doll. It had long red woollen hair, and was bound tightly with red cord. Stitched to the woollen hair were several strands of real hair, long, auburn curls just like the strand he had seen on the hawthorn tree. Jack picked up the poppet with a look of disgust, and then took in a deep breath. He closed his eyes for a moment, raising his own energy, and then spoke into the early dawn's light:

"As you are bound to her,
Now you must serve me.
Lead me to her now;
So shall it be."

He felt a kind of tugging sensation in his hand, and the bound poppet's energy urged him down the path. He quickly packed away the empty box in his backpack, lifting it onto his shoulders once again. The poppet's energy tugged at his hand once again, and he began to jog down the path and across the rolling hills, towards the forest.

"Who are you?" asked Hunter.

The man smiled at her and cocked his head to the side, as if amused. "We have met several times now, Cailleach Fál. I feel as if we are old friends." His blond hair curtained at his forehead, and his grey eyes held hers. He was beautiful, in an androgynous way; slim and slight. He walked up to her, his gaze never leaving her own. "Why did you come here?" he asked, raising an elegant eyebrow.

"The star showed me the way," Hunter simply replied.

The man before her sighed, and closed his eyes in exasperation for a moment. When he looked at her again, there was steel in his gaze and also in his voice. "Did I not tell you? Why did you not listen to me?"

Anger burst in Hunter's heart. "Why? Why did I not listen to *you*? Maybe it's because you talk in riddles. Maybe it's because you delight in obscurity. Maybe it's because you are Fae!"

Both eyebrows now raised. "And that's a problem, Hedge Witch?"

Hunter glared it him. "I thought you were in league with Lanoc," she said through gritted teeth.

The man before her tutted softly. "Such anger. I warned you before, little Hedge Witch. That anger will be your ruin. And your pride."

"What are you talking about now?"

"You are more like him that you realise. Especially if you keep this up."

Hunter's hands balled into fists. "Are you here to mock me? Is that what this is? Are you Lanoc's minion, or something?"

Anger flared in the strange, eldritch man's eyes. "Far from it," he said, forcing his words to come out smoothly. He closed his eyes again, and took a deep breath. "We are on the same side, you and I," he said, as he opened his eyes and stared right into her soul. Her heart fluttered in her chest at his gaze. It seemed one that was full of longing, and promise. "I am here to help you. This one time, Hedge Witch. I had a feeling you would disregard my advice, and come here. So I have been waiting to help you."

Hunter nearly told him that she didn't want his help, but stopped herself. She reined in her anger, accepting that she needed this strange man's help. "Are you friends with the lady in the silver gown?" she asked, trying to get more information.

He smiled, and walked up to her, moving with cat-like grace. He reached out and stroked her long, red hair. She still couldn't move, otherwise she would have slapped his hand away. "Beautiful," he said softly to himself.

"Are you friends with her or not?" Hunter said, almost shouting.

He pulled back and studied her once more. Finally, he said, "We are on the same side. Not everyone agrees with Lanoc, my dear."

The Veil Between the Worlds

"What does that mean?" said Hunter angrily.

"As I said when we met earlier, Hunter, I am your ally. We share the same interests. I am here to free you from this trap. Are you satisfied?"

Shocked, Hunter didn't know what to say. *And how did he know my name?*

"You could express your gratitude, you know," he said slyly.

Never say 'thank you' to a faery, the words came back to her. She had come across this saying several times in her studies. She calmed herself down, so that she could think more clearly. She needed to be careful around this being. She did not want to be indebted to him in any way. But she realised that she already was, to some extent. She searched through her mind for the correct thing to say. "May there always be friendship between us," she remembered at last.

The man before her gave a disappointed sigh, before he turned that charming smile on her once again. "Very well." He raised his arms over head, placing the backs of his hands together. He threw his head back, and then he suddenly drew his hands swiftly down, towards the ground. As he did so, the mists parted and Hunter felt more real, more solid once again.

She half-fell onto the stones of the bridge. She could hear the water beneath her, and smell the scent of the trees around her. She looked up to the strange man before her. He suddenly looked away, into the trees, worry creasing his brow. "Who are you?" Hunter asked again softly.

"Your friend," he said, stepping quickly away and disappearing into the fading mists. Hunter slowly stood, but nearly jumped out of her skin when she heard his voice at her ear. "Now go! Before he finds his trap has failed!" Hunter whirled around, but no one was there.

"Damn you, whoever you are," she muttered. She then felt the wind picking up, and looked at the swaying treetops. Clouds scudded across the sky; low, dark clouds rumbling with thunder. "Oh, hell no," she said, and then ran into the woods.

Jack had to slow to a walk as he approached the forest. He hadn't eaten since lunch, and he was beginning to get tired. He pushed on, the poppet in his hand tugging him towards the wood. He stopped at the entrance for a moment, to catch his breath.

"She needs you."

A woman's voice sounded at his ear. He spun around, and saw a woman with long, golden hair and a silver gown standing near him. "Go to her, now. Before he finds her. She is lost, but you can find her." She stepped back into the trees, and disappeared.

"Damn," said Jack, and he raced into the trees as fast as he could go.

Hunter sped through the tree trunks. She thought that she had taken the path back the way that she had come, but the path she had chosen dwindled to nothing more than an animal track. She stopped and spun around, trying to get her sense of direction back. The wind was still picking up, and leaves began to fall around her. She needed time to think, but there was no time. She just kept running, even as the rain began to fall. Anger filled her once again; anger at the Fae, who never gave a straight answer, anger at Lanoc, for trapping her, but most of all, anger at herself, for allowing herself to be tricked. *Stupid, stupid, stupid!* she repeated over and over again, as she ran through the trees.

She needed to get back to the portal, but had absolutely no idea where it was or how to get there. She knew that she was forgetting something important, but in her fear and haste there was no way she would remember. Small branches caught in her hair and scratched at her face and arms, and still she pushed on, feeling the storm approaching.

And with it, her doom.

Suddenly, she heard a shout. "Hunter!"

She whirled around, trying to discern where the voice came from. She knew that voice.

Jack.

"Hunter!" Again he called, and she could finally see him, standing on top of a small ridge, looking down at her. She ran towards him, even as he scrambled down to her. When they met she stopped and bent over double, trying to catch her breath.

"Jack! What are you doing here?" she gasped, hands on her knees. She was utterly confused as to why, and how, Jack was here in the Otherworld.

"I could ask you the same thing," he said, his voice raised to be heard above the wind. "We've got to get out of here, now!"

"That's exactly what I've been trying to do," she said bitterly. "I can't find the way out."

Jack grabbed her arm. "I know the way."

Hunter pulled away from him. *What if this is just another trick?* she asked herself. She saw that he was holding something in his left hand. "What is that?" she asked, pointing to the thing he was holding.

Jack looked down at the object he held. "I used it to find you." He tucked the thing into a pocket of his cargo trousers. He then came towards her and held her gently by the shoulders. "Hunter, please, follow me. I know the way."

Hunter looked at him, the rain beginning to fall heavily around them. His green eyes looked into hers, and she could see the love that he had for her, still there. Confused, she shook herself free from his grasp. "Why should I follow you?" she said, anger growing in her heart. "You left me, Jack. You left me for your ex-girlfriend." The hurt and betrayal made her anger rush to the surface. "I thought we had something special. And then you just throw it all away, as if it didn't mean a thing." Her voice caught in her throat, and she stopped herself before she started to cry. She *would not* cry in front of him.

"Hunter, I had to. I had to draw Courtney away from you."

"What? Why? That doesn't make any sense!"

Jack's pained eyes held hers. He took several steps back. He then removed the item from his pocket so that she could see it properly. "I found out that Courtney and Alice caused the car accident. And this morning, I found this. It's you, Hunter. They have cast some sort of spell on you. I used this poppet to track you, knowing that it was bound to you. And now, please, you have to come with me. I can't lose you again, Hunter."

Hunter looked at the thing Jack held. It was indeed some sort of poppet, with long, red hair, bound in red cord. As Jack's words sank in, she raised her eyes to his, not knowing what to say. Jack then replaced the poppet into the box, tucking it away in his backpack. He shouldered it and came to stand in front of her again.

"I can't lose you again, Hunter," he repeated. "I won't lose you." He held out his hand to her, the wind whipping around them, the rain now pounding heavily and soaking them through.

Hunter's world stopped. It felt like she was at a crossroads, or a precipice. Whatever she decided now would change her life forever. She looked at Jack, conflicting emotions rushing through her. Anger still waged its war on her heart; anger that was pitted against the love that she still held for Jack. And suddenly she understood. Anger wasn't *her*; she wasn't an angry person by nature. And then another thought dawned on her. The pride that had led her to this fall, again, that was not her. These emotions, pride and anger, may have originated with her, but to consume her as they had?

Anger will be your ruin, the Fae man had said to her. Twice now.

Hunter gave a single, gasping sob as she realised what had happened. She reached out her golden energy to him. She was met halfway by his green energy, and when they met it swirled around them, cocooning them from the storm. She opened her heart to him, tears falling down her face. She reached out her hand.

"Take me home, Jack."

Hunter and Jack ran through the forest, hand in hand. The rain still beat down on them, and the storm followed. As they cleared the trees, they looked out over the rolling hills. Hunter pulled them to a stop. "We'll never make it," she said, despair taking over. Tears began to fall again. "I'm so sorry, Jack. I'm so, so sorry. You should never have followed me here. I can't bear it," she said, weeping.

"Hunter," he said, sweeping her into his arms. "I would follow you to the ends of the earth. I have never stopped loving you. I have watched over you day and night, every chance I could. I will never leave you again."

Hunter looked up into his green eyes. Lightning crashed into a tree nearby, blinding them momentarily with its flash. When she could see again, she looked up into his gorgeous green eyes. "I love you, Jack."

"I love you, Hunter."

They then felt a shift in the air next to them, and a tinkling sound like tiny bells sounded above the raging storm. Hunter squinted through the rain, and saw a silvery shimmer appear right beside them. She then remembered the words of the white hind. *If your intentions come from a place of love, you will know where to go.* She turned to Jack. "This is it! Come on!" She tugged on his hand, and pulled him through. A brilliant white light flashed and went out, just as lightning hit the very spot where they had stood.

Ryder looked again at the clock behind the bar. It was 9pm, and still no sign of Hunter. "That's it," she said, and rang the bell. "We're closing early tonight, folks! Come on, out you get!" She was met with questions and smart remarks. "I mean it!" she shouted, ringing the bell.

Jenny, the other bartender, came downstairs from her apartment above the pub. Her hair was mussed up, and Ryder concluded that she must have fallen asleep on the couch. There were dark circles under her eyes, and she looked tired, as they all did after having pulled double shifts all week. "What's going on?" Jenny asked.

Ryder looked at her. "Hunter is missing. I need to go, now."

Jenny looked at her for a moment, studying her face. She then grabbed hold of the bell, and rang it. "Closing time! Now!" She turned to Ryder. "Go," she said softly. "Go now. I'll close up."

Ryder nodded her thanks, and ran out the door. She unlocked her bike and hopped on it. She pedalled furiously up the hill, past the hotel and out towards the outskirts of the village. She was breathing hard when she got to the top, but she kept going as fast as she was able. She ducked onto the path that followed the road to the cottages, pouring out her frustration as her legs pumped the pedals. Her lights were good, and they shone through the darkness. She was about three-quarters of the way home, when suddenly she felt a deep dread falling upon her.

Fear filled her heart, and she slowed her bike down, her breath misting in the air.

Something was out there.

She heard a low growl, and then the sound of chain, clinking on the ground. *This can't be good,* thought Ryder. The sound came from the path before her, and she suddenly spun her bike around and starting pedalling back the way she had come. She heard something running behind her, growls and hot breath at her heels. She didn't turn to look; she just kept pedalling as fast as she could.

But she was not fast enough.

She felt hot, searing pain in her leg, and she screamed as she was pulled from her bike. She was thrown to the ground, and then something jumped on top of her. In the darkness, she couldn't make anything out, but it sounded like a large dog. She felt its jaws snapping the air just in front her face, and instinct took over.

She grabbed the thing and rolled, but it still came out on top. Where she held it, her hands burned as if she was holding hot coals. The stench of sulphur was in her nostrils. Still she held on, pushing it away from her. She felt hot, fiery energy rising within her. Fuelled by her fear and adrenaline, she released it through her hands with a fiery blast that blew the thing off her, to land several feet away along the path. Still on her back, stunned and panting for breath, Ryder looked up through the dark treetops, seeing the stars overhead.

The thing yelped and scrambled. Ryder turned her head to look at it, and watched as the shadowy form turned to smoke, fading away into the darkness.

Slowly she stood, her leg on fire. She looked down, and saw that it had been badly mangled. There was nothing she could do for it; she needed help straight away. She pulled out her phone, but it had been smashed.

A screeching sound came from overhead, and Ryder looked up to see a barn owl in the tree above her. It launched itself into the air, and flew low over her head. She head a woman's laugh, as it disappeared into the night. "*Next time*," the same voice said into the darkness.

Ryder limped to her bicycle, and barely managed to get a leg over it. Her other leg wasn't working properly, and so she sat in the saddle and pushed along the ground with her good leg, helping to move her along. The nearest place that she could get help was Elspeth's cottage. Her head was pounding, and with each passing minute she felt weaker and weaker. That last quarter of a mile felt like hours. No cars passed her on the road that ran alongside path. It was just her and the darkness, her light having also been smashed in the fall.

Breathing heavily, she finally saw the lights of Elspeth's cottage. She got to the driveway, and fell over. She lay there on the gravel, wondering if she had the energy to make it to the door, or whether she would just die here, in the driveway. With an enormous effort, she pulled herself along the drive with her arms, her strength fading fast. Her head was swimming with the effort, and she had to stop once to throw up. She pulled herself up to the door and scraped at it with her hand, before losing consciousness in the darkness.

Hunter and Jack fell through the portal together, landing at the base of the hawthorn tree, next to the well. It was full dark around them. She felt Jack's arms around her, and he pulled her towards him so that his body cushioned their fall. She landed on top of him, and heard him give a small grunt. She rolled off quickly, and reached out to him. "Jack? Are you okay?"

The Veil Between the Worlds

"Yes," she heard him say. She heard him sitting up. Her eyes still hadn't adjusted to the darkness.

"Why is it so dark?" she asked.

"Because it's nighttime," Jack replied. Her eyes began to adjust, and she saw Jack heave himself up to his feet. "You've been missing all day, Hunter." He held out his hand to her, and she took it. He pulled her up.

"But I've only been gone a couple of hours, at most," she said, surprised.

Jack pulled her close, and held her to him. He put his chin on top of her head, never wanting to let go. "You've been missing for over thirteen or fourteen hours, maybe even longer now," he said softly. He stroked her long hair. "I was so worried." His voice caught on those last words, and she could feel his arms trembling.

"I'm so sorry, Jack," she said. "I had no idea."

Suddenly, both their phones started to blow up with messages. They parted, and took off their backpacks. "What the hell is going on now?" asked Jack softly as he reached into his bag.

Hunter pulled out her phone. There were voice messages and texts, from her mother, Ryder and Elspeth. She brought her phone to her ear, and listened to the latest message from Elspeth.

"Hunter, if you get this message, wherever you are, please come to Lymington Hospital right now. Your sister has been badly hurt, and she needs you."

Hunter nearly dropped her phone. She looked at Jack in the darkness, and could just make out the shock on his face as he read a similar message on his phone. "Ryder," she whispered, and her phone then dropped from her numb fingers. "Oh no, what have I done?"

Jack shot off a quick text, and then bent over and picked up her phone, placing it in her pack. "Come, Hunter. We've got to go. I'll take you." He zipped up her bag, and shrugged his own pack on. He then swung her bag over his shoulder too. Grabbing her hand, he began to lead her across the inclosure.

"No, there's a place over there where we can get through," Hunter said numbly, pulling him towards the gap in the fence. They went through, and Jack used his phone as a flashlight as they made their way to the ATV. Once there, Hunter pulled on her own backpack sat behind him. She hung on as they drove to where he had parked his jeep. Hunter began to sob, frightened for her sister. Her arms wrapped tightly around Jack's waist, she pressed her face into his strong back and wept as they rode through the night.

When they arrived at the hospital, they found Harriet waiting for them at reception. "This way," was all she said, and led them through the winding corridors to the ICU. Halfway down a corridor, they could see some people standing outside a larger room, marked with a sign above it that read: 'Intensive Care Unit'. Hunter looked at a clock on the wall as they passed, and saw that it was nearly 3am. As they approached, they saw Elspeth and PC Hart standing there, talking in low voices. "She's in there," said Harriet. Jack and Hunter entered the unit, and a nurse at a desk by the door spoke to them. "Who are you here to see?" she asked.

"My sister. Ryder Williams," said Hunter softly.

The nurse nodded and looked at Jack. "Are you immediate family?"

"No," he said.

"Then I must ask you to wait outside, please," said the nurse, gesturing to the door. Jack looked at Hunter and took her hand, giving it a small squeeze. "I won't be far. I'll be waiting for you," he said. He had dark circles under his eyes, and his face was pale. Hunter looked down for a moment, overwhelmed with everything that had happened. "Thank you, Jack," she said softly. She glanced back up at him, and he nodded once, before turning away and heading out the doors. Hunter could see Elspeth and PC Hart still talking together, and Harriet off to one side, looked worried. Then the doors closed.

"This way," said the nurse, guiding Hunter to a corner of the room where an area had been curtained off. The nurse pulled the curtain open slowly, and motioned for Hunter to come in. She then closed the curtain behind her.

What Hunter saw almost made her heart stop beating right in her chest.

Ryder lay on the bed, pale and unmoving. Her leg was in a cast, and was elevated. She lay there, deathly still.

Elspeth came quietly into the curtained area. "Hunter, thank all the gods that you're back. I found her, outside my door, badly hurt. They've allowed me to stay with her until you arrived." She lowered her voice. "Please, you've got to find her."

In a daze, Hunter walked up to her sister's bed. Ryder looked so small, so fragile, lying there as if she were dead. Her breathing was slow and shallow, her chest barely moving. "What happened?" Hunter asked softly, wondering if all this was some sort of bad dream.

"She was attacked as she rode home from the pub. She hasn't regained consciousness since we found her outside my door. Please, Hunter, see if you can find her."

"What do you mean?" asked Hunter, still in a daze.

Elspeth lowered her voice to a whisper. "Her spirit isn't here. I believe she is lost, somewhere. Your mother tried from the cottage, but was unable to locate her. But you can. I know you can."

"Can what?"

"Your mother said to follow the thread from her body, and bring her back. It's our only hope."

Hunter, still not able to believe this was happening, found herself moving up to her sister. She took up Ryder's hand, which had a heart rate monitor strapped to a finger, and an IV drip. "Ryder," she said softly, her voice breaking. "Ryder, what happened? Where are you?"

She felt a soft, whooshing sensation, much like the first time she had ridden the hedge. This time, her physical body remained standing, while her spirit flew along the thread of Ryder's soul, out of the hospital and into darkness. Stars whirled overhead, and suddenly she found herself on a dirt path, with trees to her right and an open space on her left. She took a moment to look around, and realised that she was on the path from the village to the cottages, next to the road. "Ryder?" she called out. "Ryder, are you here?"

There was a soft glow in the darkness. "Hunter? Is that you?" Ryder's voice came from the faint light, as if from very far away.

Hunter focused on the light, and saw Ryder's spirit, shimmering in the shadows. She walked towards it. The early, pre-dawn light was beginning to lighten the eastern sky before her. "Ryder? Can you see me?"

Her sister looked at her, dazed. "I – I don't know what happened. Or where I am."

Hunter held out her hand. "You've been attacked, Ryder. You've got to come back to your body now."

Ryder tried to take a step towards Hunter, but found that she couldn't move. "I – I can't," she said, fear rising in her voice.

The Veil Between the Worlds

"Ryder," said Hunter firmly. "You can do this. Draw up energy from the earth, and take my hand." Hunter walked towards her sister, her hand outstretched. She feared that if Ryder's spirit had been separated from her body for too long, that she would never find her way back. "Take my hand, Ry. You can do this."

Her sister looked at her, her pale spirit form fading in and out. "I'm so very tired, Hunter," she said, her voice getting softer, and sounding more distant.

"Just take my hand. Let's go home," said Hunter. She reached out, and brushed against her sister's hand. "It's time to go home, now."

Ryder's spirit nodded, and she reached out and took Hunter's hand. Hunter grabbed it tightly, even as she felt the whooshing sensation taking them both back along the spirit thread, all the way back to Ryder's body in the hospital room.

Hunter slammed into her body, and staggered. She turned her gaze to her sister, and suddenly saw Ryder take a deep breath, and open her eyes.

"Ryder!" cried Elspeth, leaning in. "Thank the Lady, you're back!"

Hunter could feel nurses rushing into the room behind her, but she was only focused on her sister. Ryder turned to Hunter, her eyes wide. She took another breath, and another. Hunter gently squeezed her sister's hand. "Hey, sis," she said, tears falling from her eyes.

Ryder looked up at Hunter with a haunted look in her eyes. "Courtney says, hi."

Chapter Fifteen

The doctor came into the curtained off area soon after the nurses had reported Ryder's awakening. The doctor looked her over, and checked her vitals on the monitors. She asked Ryder several questions, and made notes on a clipboard that she held. When she had finished her examination, she said, "You've had a lucky escape, Miss Williams. You had lost a lot of blood, and were very weak. What you need to do now is to rest, so that your body can recover from the hypovolemic shock due to the loss of blood. You'll stay here in ICU until we are certain that your body is able to cope with the trauma." The doctor looked at Hunter and Elspeth. "You both are welcome to stay with her, if you'd like."

"Thank you," said Hunter. The doctor nodded, and then left the small, curtained area.

Hunter looked at her sister, "Ry, what did you mean, Courtney says, hi?" she said softly.

Ryder looked at them both. Her face was pale, and her eyes were too large in her face. "I heard her. I heard Courtney's voice. I'd recognise it anywhere, after the crap that she pulled at the pub a while back." Ryder closed her eyes, as if just speaking was very tiring for her.

Elspeth took Ryder's hand in hers. "You just rest, Ryder. We will sort all this out later, when you are better."

Ryder's eyes flitted open. "Stay safe, Hunter," she said, before she closed them again and dozed off to sleep.

The Veil Between the Worlds

Hunter left the ICU to let everyone know what was going on. Elspeth said that she would go outside and discreetly call Abigail. When they walked out of the unit, she saw Jack was sitting on a bench, conversing with PC Hart. Harriet was sitting next to Jack, her hand placed on his back. Jack sat bowed over, his head in his hands, elbows on his knees. He looked up when he heard the doors open, and then he stood when he saw Hunter walk out towards them.

Harriet and PC Hart also turned to her. Harriet rose, giving Hunter a small, hopeful smile. "How is she?" Harriet asked.

"It looks like she'll be okay," said Hunter. She saw Harriet's face instantly relax, and Jack gave a sigh of relief. "She'll be in this unit for two to three more days, before she's moved out to another ward."

Harriet nodded. "That is good news."

Jack came up to her and gently touched her elbow. "How are you, Hunter?" he asked softly, his green eyes searching her face.

"I've been better," said Hunter, her voice beginning to tremble. Tears slid down her cheeks. "This is all my fault."

Harriet came up and wrapped her arms around Hunter. "Nonsense," the younger Witch said, giving Hunter a squeeze. She then pulled away, holding Hunter by the arms. "We have all made mistakes, and we did not take notice of the warning signs. We should have been more vigilant. I'm so sorry, Hunter. *I* should have known. I should have seen that something was happening."

Elspeth came back into the corridor outside the ICU. She heard Harriet's words to Hunter, and patted Harriet's arm. "Now is not the time or place for this discussion," she said. She looked to PC Hart. "David, I believe you needed to talk to Hunter?"

Witches of the New Forest

David nodded, and walked forward with a quick glance at Jack, before turning to Hunter. "I'll need to ask you some questions, Hunter, if I may. Is now a good time?"

Hunter nodded dumbly, still a little dazed by everything. David took her by the elbow and led her away from everyone. "May I buy you a coffee, and we can have a chat?" he asked gently.

"Yes, okay," she said. He led her down a few corridors to a quiet cafeteria. There were only a handful of people there, mostly hospital staff during the wee hours of the morning. He took her to a table away from the few others that were there, and asked her what she would like to drink. She told him a cup of coffee, and he nodded and went up to the counter.

Hunter watched him as he walked away. He looked so different in his uniform. She wondered what the police would do, or could do, in this situation. She said as much when he returned, putting the drink and a date square in front of her.

"You look like you need to eat something," he said with a small smile. He sat down, and gestured for her to eat. "Please, go ahead. I can wait."

Hunter gratefully ate the date square, and took a few sips of her coffee before she sat back and looked at David. He calmly drank his own coffee, looking around at others in the room before his gaze settled on her again.

"Better?" he asked.

"Yes, thank you."

"I'm glad that you're back. You had us all worried."

Hunter looked up in shock. "What? Oh, no – you weren't out there looking for me, were you?"

David nodded slowly. "The park rangers were out, and both Elspeth and Dougal called me when it began to get dark. What happened, did you get lost or something?"

"Um, that's a long story, actually," said Hunter. She felt awkward talking to him about what had happened, and she wasn't sure she wanted to go there with him just yet.

David seemed to sense this, and so he simply said, "All that matters is that you're back. If, or when, you want to talk, you know where I am."

"Thank you," Hunter said softly.

"You look tired, Hunter. So I'll keep this brief." He leaned in towards her, and spoke softly so that they were not overhead. "So, to answer your earlier question, in my capacity as a regular police officer, all I can do is investigate what would appear to be a wild dog attack. But if you have any further information that you would like to give me, I'll see what other avenues might be available."

Hunter looked at him, knowing that he spoke in his capacity as the one and only member of the village's 'special unit'. "Ryder hasn't been able to say anything much, yet. All she said was that after the attack, she heard a woman's voice, a voice that she recognised as Courtney Peterson's. Apparently, all Courtney said was, *'next time'*."

David blew out a breath and leaned back in his chair. "Damn it. This just keeps getting more and more complicated."

Hunter reached out and touched his hand. "Is there *anything* you can do, David?"

David looked at her, an intensity in his eyes. "I'll just have to pay Courtney Peterson a visit, though in a professional, mundane capacity. Ryder says that she heard her voice at the scene of the incident. That could easily be dismissed legally. In my other capacity, well, Courtney isn't a member of the five families around here. This is totally unprecedented." He then dropped his gaze, and patted Hunter's hand. When he looked up at her again, his blue eyes were apologetic. "I'm not sure how much I'll be able to do on any of these fronts. The last time I interviewed the Hardwicks, they all had tight alibis. Miss Peterson will likely be the same."

"It's obvious that she's out for us, and has been for some time now," said Hunter. "Jack also believes that she and Alice had put a spell on me, too."

David's hand gripped Hunter's. "What? How? What did they do?"

Hunter shook her head. "I don't know yet. I don't have all the details. All I know is what Jack told me."

David nodded slowly as she spoke. When she finished, he said, "Right. I will also interview Jack and the Hardwicks more thoroughly."

"Maybe we should all get together, when we can, and talk about this? It might make more sense, and we'll all be up to speed."

David nodded, and released Hunter's hand. "Okay, that's a good idea. Call me when Ryder comes out of the hospital, and we will all arrange for a time to talk. I think I'm going to have to let the rest of your family, and Jack, know just who and what I am, with regards to the Burley police force. I need to let them know that they can come to me, with anything, and not wait to get information from the heads of the families only. This is a much bigger thing than I think has possibly ever happened here in Burley. If families are going to start open hostilities with each other, that could have a huge impact on everyone in the community." He looked Hunter in the eyes, and said, "This could be a very dangerous situation."

Hunter felt tears welling up again. She berated herself. Was there going to be a time when she talked to this man, without feeling like she was going to pass out or break down? "I'm so sorry, David. This really is all our fault. If we'd never have come here, none of this would ever have happened."

David stood up and moved to kneel in front of Hunter, taking her hands in his. "Don't *ever* think that, Hunter. Evil exists everywhere. This is not about you, but about someone in this community who has crossed some serious lines. If it didn't involve you, it would have involved someone else."

Hunter looked into his blue eyes and simply nodded. His intensity and seriousness was so very different from when they had last seen each other at the tea shop. She began to wonder just how many people in this little village lived a double life. Elspeth with her shop, who was a powerful Witch and leader of a local coven of hereditary Witches. Jack, a Druid, whose secrets she had yet to learn about, as they hadn't had any time since he found her to discuss it. Her mother, with her lost love who turned out to be Hunter's real father. And now this police officer who knelt before her, his earnest gaze on her. *Was anyone who they appeared to be?* she wondered.

"Okay, David. I'm sorry."

"We will sort this out, Hunter. You have my word."

Jack came into the cafeteria, looking to get a cup of coffee and some food. He had barely eaten anything all day, and was fading fast. When he came into the room, he saw PC Hart and Hunter together at a table. David was kneeling before Hunter, holding her hands. A wave of jealousy swept over Jack, and he walked up to them. "Is everything okay here?" he asked, with a little edge to his voice.

David stood, and smiled down at Hunter. "Yes, everything will be fine. Don't worry, Hunter. We will sort this out. Just let me know when Ryder is back home, and we will go from there. I'll file this tentative report, and wait until both you and your sister are able to talk. And if you need anything, anything at all,

Witches of the New Forest

you know where to reach me." He looked over and nodded at Jack, then turned and left.

Jack stood and watched him go, not saying a word. Hunter looked up at Jack, wondering why he was scowling as David walked away. "Jack, is something wrong?"

He sat down heavily in the chair that PC Hart had used. "I don't know Hunter. You tell me."

Not understanding that remark, Hunter's brow furrowed as she tried to figure it out. She was tired, and she needed to get back to her sister. "I – I don't know, Jack."

Jack's features softened. "It's been a long day, Hunter. Let's get back to your sister." Hunter nodded. Jack stood, and led her back to the ICU. "Elspeth and Harriet have gone home now. They'll be back tomorrow." He took Hunter in his arms and held her for a moment. "I'll be right here, if you need me."

Hunter looked up at Jack's face. He looked very tired, and pale. He needed to go home and get some rest. "Jack, you've been out looking for me all day, and you need some food and some sleep. You're about to collapse yourself."

"Are you sure? I don't mind staying." He swayed a little, and Hunter tightened her arms around him.

"Go, Jack. I'd rather you went home and took care of yourself."

Jack looked at her for a long moment. "Okay. But you take care of yourself too, Hunter. Make sure you rest, okay?"

When Hunter looked into his beautiful green eyes, all her previous feelings for him came rushing back to her. She leaned her head on his shoulder, and put her arms around his waist. "I will, Jack. Thank you. For everything."

He kissed the top of her head, and then let her go. He cupped her cheek with his hand for a brief moment, before he turned away and walked down the corridor, his hands in his pockets

The Veil Between the Worlds

and his head down, shoulders slumped wearily. Hunter sighed, and turned back to the ICU, going back to sit with her sister.

Ryder was in the ICU for a couple of days, before she was admitted to another ward. She had been given her own room, and she spent the next two weeks there as her body made up for the loss of blood. With every passing day she became stronger. Hunter and Elspeth had taken it in turns to stay with her in the ICU at all times, and then they were with her during visiting hours when she was admitted to the new ward. Harriet also came over every day to check in on her. Ryder spoke to her mother using Hunter's phone several times a day. Jack called Hunter briefly each evening, to get a progress report on Ryder. He didn't keep her on the line, as he knew that she was tired. Hunter was glad of his calls, though she still didn't know what exactly had happened between them, or what was happening now.

No one talked about what had happened to Ryder just yet. They all wanted to make sure that Ryder was out of the woods, so to speak, before they even decided to go there. As well, they could easily be overhead by any of the hospital staff. Ryder agreed to wait until she was better, though it sorely tested her patience. "This denouement had better be worth it, sis," she said quietly one day as she, Hunter and Elspeth all sat together.

Hunter nodded. "PC Hart also wants in on this, so we'll save it until you are home, and we can all be together, in privacy." Ryder nodded, understanding the need to keep this quiet until they knew it was safe to speak, without putting the magickal community at risk.

In the meantime, Elspeth's coven cast a host of protection spells for them all.

At the start of the second week, Hunter, Elspeth and Harriet were all chatting one morning to Ryder in her hospital room about small, unimportant things, when Jack appeared. He pulled aside the curtain that partitioned the room from the corridor, and knocked softly on the wall. "May I come in?" he asked. He held a small vase, filled with wildflowers.

Ryder looked up at the sound of his voice. When she saw Jack, her face registered her disbelief. "What in the hell are you doing here?" she asked.

Hunter stood and walked to her sister' side. "Ryder, Jack was the one who found me, when I went missing."

"He what?"

Jack stepped forward. Hunter looked up at him. His eyes were full of tenderness and emotion. "Ryder, you and your family are in danger. I did what I thought was right." He stepped in close, and continued quietly, to prevent being overhead. "I lured Courtney away, to protect you all. I had to divert her attention from you, so that you would be able to do the work that you needed to do, without her and Alice's interference. I also needed time to find out more about just what it was that they were up to."

Ryder looked at him, her eyes narrowing. "I *knew* you were up to something! You should have told us, Jack," she said sternly, even though her voice broke wearily on those last words.

Hunter held her sister's hand. "When you're better and ready to come home, we'll talk about it more then, okay?" she said to her sister.

Ryder looked at them both, and gave a slight nod. She closed her eyes, and drifted off to sleep again, but not before she said, "I knew you crazy kids would find each other again…"

Hunter asked Jack to come over that night, to talk about what he had told them at the hospital. She couldn't wait until Ryder

The Veil Between the Worlds

came home. Hunter needed to know just what he had meant. She needed to know the truth. Jack came over after his shift, and knocked on her door at 6pm. Hunter answered, and waved him inside.

Abigail immediately came out of the kitchen, and saw Jack. She rushed over to him and threw her arms around him. "Thank you, thank you, thank you for finding my girl," she said as she squeezed him tightly. "We were all so worried. Hunter told me that she had some sort of mishap in the Otherworld, and you helped her to find the way back. I cannot thank you enough for what you have done."

Jack looked surprised at first, and then smiled gently, looking at Hunter over her mother's shoulder as she hugged him. "No need to thank me," he said softly. "I love her, and would do anything for her."

When he said this as he looked over at her, Hunter's stomach did a flip and her heart beat faster. She pushed her feelings down, wanting to know the full situation before she opened her heart to him again. She came over and touched her mother on the arm. "Mom, you're going to squeeze the life out of him if you keep this up."

Abigail pulled away and nodded with a smile. "There is a lot you need to tell us, Jack. I can feel it." She looked over at Hunter. "But I suppose right now you are here to see Hunter. I'll leave you both to it." She went back into the kitchen, where she was preparing some supper.

Hunter looked at Jack, and swallowed. He was as gorgeous as ever, even in his dark work uniform. He had his backpack slung over his shoulder. "Would you like to come out back and talk?" Hunter said, trying to keep her voice even.

"Yes, I would like that very much," replied Jack. He followed her out the back door, and they made their way to the

235

oak tree that had been struck by lightning. Jack looked up at it, and smiled. He reached out and patted the large trunk. "I think you'll be okay," he said whispered softly to the tree.

Hunter led them to the chairs beneath the oak, and they each took a seat. "Well, Jack, where do we start?" she asked, blowing out a long breath.

"Perhaps I should start at the beginning," he said, placing his backpack on the ground beside him. They looked out over the beech woods that bordered the back of the property. Jack took in a deep breath, and looked at her for a moment. She returned his gaze, but looked away after a moment, unsure of what to say or do. So many emotions were running through her, and she was terribly afraid of being hurt again. She waited for him to explain.

"The day after we made love, I found something in my room," Jack began. He looked away into the distance as he recounted his tale. Hunter watched his face, to try and determine whether it was the truth. Nothing in his countenance seemed to indicate otherwise. "After I saw you again that night, I – I was hoping that you would come over again soon, and so I went to flip the mattress over. I wanted you to have a nice, fresh bed to sleep on. When I did, I found something under the mattress." He reached over into the backpack, and pulled out a poppet.

Hunter leaned forwards to see it better. When she recognised it, she hissed softly. "Jack, that's you." Jack nodded. The figure was dressed in clothing similar to what he was wearing now, even with a small replica of the park authority badge on the breast. It had dark hair, and green eyes. Something was wrapped around the doll. "What is that around it?" Hunter asked.

"Some sort of binding, love spell," said Jack. "It didn't have a chance to take effect, as we had set the wards down in the house before we went into the bedroom." Jack turned to look at Hunter. "Besides, I can't imagine anything would draw me

The Veil Between the Worlds

away from you, spell or no. Hunter, you are everything to me. That night that we spent together, my world changed."

Hunter didn't know what to say, and so she remained silent, looking down into her lap. Jack tore his gaze away and continued. "I then realised what was going on. I think Dexter was actually trying to tell me, as when I got home that evening after the cottage was trashed, the first thing he did was run into the bedroom and lie down on the side of the bed where the poppet had been placed. When I found this *thing*, I had a pretty good idea of who was behind the break in. And so I did the ritual that you suggested, to try and find my staff. I also took Elspeth's advice, and asked my spirit guides to help me. They helped lead me in the ritual as I rode the drum beat, like you said I could, and I followed the thread of my energy to the staff. I saw a building on the Hardwick estate, an abandoned barn over on the eastern side of the grounds. So I went over there and investigated in person. What I found was not only my staff, but also the truck that ran us off the road."

"The Hummer," said Hunter. What David had told her was true, and Jack *had* called it in.

"That's right. It was there, and it was unmistakeable. Marks and indentations on the front bumper, where it hit us. Then I also found something more." Hunter looked closely at Jack. His jaw was clenched, in anger and frustration. "I found another altar, where dark magicks had been performed. Similar to what I had seen, last year."

Hunter drew in a sharp breath. "Oh god."

"The remains of a ritual or a spell were still there. A tiny, toy truck like the one I was using was there, along with some herbs. I took my staff and smashed the altar into ruins, before the police came. I didn't want to endanger the entire magickal community, and so I erased all existence of it. I cleaned it all up, and then

Witches of the New Forest

David came after I called him to let him know that I had found the truck."

"Is that Courtney and Alice, working dark magicks together, do you think?" Hunter asked, a chill coming over her.

Jack nodded. "Yes, yes it is. I kept an eye out on the grounds, in abandoned buildings for where they would set up next, and sure enough I found another altar that they had set up, this time in the ruins of a cottage on the northern end of the estate. I tried to figure out just what they were going to do next, but it was difficult. I had to spend time with Courtney, making her believe that her love spell had, indeed worked." Jacked turned to look at Hunter, anguish in his eyes. "It was the most difficult, and the most horrible thing I've ever had to do, Hunter. But I want to assure you that absolutely nothing physical happened between Courtney and I." He turned and looked away, shame on his face. "I made her think that I wanted to take it slowly, and so I managed to keep her at bay in that sense. I don't like deceiving people, Hunter, but I needed to know what was going on. I had to do this."

"Buy why couldn't you tell me, Jack?"

Jack looked at her with those gorgeous green eyes. "Hunter, you are a beautiful, honest soul. Your face betrays your emotions, and there is absolutely no deceit in you whatsoever. I was certain that if you knew, Courtney would see through it. I had to make this hard choice. It was the most difficult thing I've ever had to do. And if I had to do it again, Hunter, in order to protect you and your family, I would, though it kills me."

Hunter thought about it as Jack spoke. What he said was true. She had never been a good liar, and her face did betray her emotions. Jack's declaration about protecting her and her family, no matter the difficulty it put him under, touched her. "Everything that I do is for you," she said softly.

The Veil Between the Worlds

"Yes, Hunter. Can you ever forgive me?"

Hunter reached out and took Jack's hand. "I understand," she said.

"Do you?" he asked, turning to look at her again. "It killed me, Hunter, to see the look on your face when Courtney and I went into the pub that night. I had managed to keep her away for weeks. But that night she was adamant about going. I hoped to all the gods that you weren't going to be there."

Hunter thought about it for a moment. "It probably wasn't about me at all, Jack. Maybe she was there for Ryder."

A look of shock crossed Jack's face. "By all the gods," he breathed. "She was gathering information on your sister. And you just happened to be there."

Hunter squeezed his hand. "Don't worry about that now, Jack. Just tell me everything. Please."

Jack swallowed and looked into Hunter's eyes again. His green eyes now flashed with anger. "It was my own fault, really. Ellie had tried all year to make me understand just what Courtney had done to me last year. But my own pride prevented me from actually seeing what was right in front of my face. I just kept brushing it off, kept dismissing it. Maybe I didn't want to see how powerful Courtney and Alice had become, because it threatened me in some way."

"Jack, have you ever thought that maybe that was part of the spell? To not make you see, or understand? Is that possible, to cause some sort of confusion, or to not allow someone to see clearly what is right before their eyes?"

Jack blinked. "Yes - yes it *is* possible. Damn. I've been such a fool."

"Jack, it's not your fault. You're not the only one who has been the target of Courtney and Alice's spells."

Jack nodded, and squeezed her hand back in reassurance. "But we are free now, Hunter." He released her hand and reached down into his bag again. This time he pulled out a box. "Hunter, please put up your psychic shields. Ground and centre, and be in your own power."

Shocked at his words, Hunter simply looked at him for a moment, uncomprehending. He allowed her the time to make her own decision, and finally she nodded. She closed her eyes and pulled up energy from the earth, and then drew her own energy into her core so that she was centred. She then envisioned a golden light around her body, that hardened into crystal. "I'm ready," she said, her voice steady and sure.

Jack nodded, and opened the box. Hunter peered down into it, and saw that another poppet of sorts was in there. "Ellie neutralised the magick as much as she could, but there still might be some lingering energy. I don't want you to be affected by it." Jack pulled out the doll in Hunter's likeness. Hunter could see it better now, the doll that she had previously seen with him in the Otherworld, the one with long red hair. She blew out a long breath, trying to beat back the anger she felt rising at the sight of the ugly little thing. "That's me," she said, through gritted teeth.

"Yes, it is," said Jack. He turned the doll over to show Hunter. "It's bound in red fabric, which Ellie believes was to mess with your own personal energy and will. When I showed this to her on the night you went missing, she said that you had been acting strangely of late. She took a closer look, and realised that it was a spell to cause anger, and in time, a rift between you, your friends and loved ones."

Hunter's revulsion at the thing Jack held raised a bitter bile in her mouth. She felt like she wanted to spit it out. "Jack, put that thing down on the ground, right now," she said, trusting her instincts. Jack did as he was told, and Hunter slowly stood up from her chair. She leaned over the doll, and drew up more energy from the earth. Humming with power, she said:

By the power of sky, land and sea
This spell is broken, so mote it be.

She raised her foot and stomped hard on the doll. There was a strange, heavy thudding noise, far louder than her foot could ever have made as it came down upon the poppet. In the distance, they heard a shriek, like a barn owl. Hunter leaned in close and spit out her bile onto the poppet. She then closed her eyes, and said, "The beauty and power of the universe destroys all negativity. I am shielded."

A humming sound reverberated throughout the area briefly, before quickly dissipating. Jack looked up at Hunter, astonishment on his face. "Hunter, that was extremely powerful."

Hunter looked down at him as he sat on his chair, his backpack next to him and his own poppet on the ground. "I have been practicing," was all she said.

Jack stood up and reached out towards her. She closed her eyes, willing the surge of energy that flooded through her to settle before she went to him. When she felt its full release, she reached out and took his hand. He drew her close to him. "You have never been more beautiful," he said, as he looked into her face with wonder. A moment, then two passed, and then slowly they leaned in towards each other. Hunter could feel Jack's energy reaching out towards her, even as hers was extending out towards him. She wrapped his green energy with her own golden light, and it swirled around them like sunlight through the leaves of ancient woodland. "Mo grá," he said softly.

"My love," she replied, and kissed him. Their energies glowed in the evening's light, cocooning them in love. Jack pulled her closer, and she entwined her arms around his neck. He ran his hands through her hair. The kiss deepened, and Hunter allowed herself to fall into it for a brief moment, before she gently pulled away. She placed her hands on his arms, and looked him steadily in the eye. "Much has happened, Jack. Let's take this one day at a time, and not rush into anything. My heart was broken, utterly broken last month. I now know that you were only protecting me, but I feel that we should take this slowly. There are still so many things that are up in the air right now."

Jack looked at her, and nodded. "I understand."

Hunter sighed. "We still don't know where we will be, come September. And I'm not sure if I could bear breaking up with you again, if we leave. Things have changed so quickly. There is real danger here, and I don't know if I can risk my family by staying here. There is still so much to be done, and so much to discuss with Ryder. So much has happened since we've been here. So much joy and excitement, and so much danger right now." She realised she was babbling, and paused for a moment to gather her thoughts. "I think I'm going to extend my sabbatical, for one more month, so that I can at least try and find my father. After that, I honestly have no idea what I'm going to do. Will I stay, and be a part of this new, and frightening world, where my loved ones are under all kinds of threat? Or will I go back to Canada, pay off my mortgage, and live a safer, normal life?"

Jack leaned forwards, his forehead touching hers. "I understand, Hunter. Whatever you decide, I will always be here for you, and to support you." He then pulled away, and went to pick up the poppet that bore Hunter's likeness.

"Leave that here," Hunter said firmly. "I will burn it."

Jack nodded, and took up the poppet in his own likeness. "Will you do the same for this one? I trust you and your power."

That simple declaration, made so easily from a man whose power was so much stronger than hers, who had been practicing for decades, touched her heart. "I will," she said, not trusting her voice to more words.

"Thank you. I should go now. Please call me," he said, looking into her eyes.

"I will, Jack. Thank you."

Chapter Sixteen

Lammas had come and gone. Hunter and her mother had celebrated the festival of the first harvest quietly at home. After a fortnight's stay in the hospital, Ryder came home. She was on crutches for her leg, which had been fractured in two places, and had long, angry scars from where she had been bitten. She was going to be on the mend for six to eight weeks, the doctors had told her. Ryder was worried about her job at the pub, but Jenny called her and reassured her that everything was going to be fine. They had pulled some of the staff from a sister-pub in Lyndhurst to cover for her during her recovery.

As soon as she was feeling better and settled in, Ryder wanted the full story. And so Hunter called everyone over one evening. Elspeth and Jack were there, as well as Harriet. Hunter also called PC Hart, much to everyone's surprise. Jack and Hunter sat on the two-seater sofa, a polite distance from each other, which did not go unnoticed. Elspeth sat with Harriet and Abigail on the larger sofa, and David sat on a chair that he pulled over from the dining table. Ryder sat on the recliner, her leg raised.

David's shock at having seen and met Abigail was unsurprising. He quickly adapted, however, and after he had been told the bare essentials of her return, he then briefly explained the role that he had in the magickal community to everyone gathered in the room. He told them how he planned to investigate not only the legal end of what happened, but also in his 'special capacity'.

The Veil Between the Worlds

They all then explained to him further what had happened in June, when Hunter had found her mother. David nodded throughout the story, and approved of their decision to keep this quiet, for the sake of the magickal community. The conversation came to a standstill for a brief moment.

Ryder sat up and looked at Jack. "Okay, Jack. Time to spill the beans. What really went down over the last month?"

Jack sighed, and ran his hands through his dark hair. He recounted the tale exactly as he had told Hunter previously. He told them of how he had discovered Courtney and Alice's dark magickal workings. At that, David sighed. "I wish you had told me everything at the time, Jack," he said.

"I didn't know about you, David. I thought you were just a regular police officer. I wanted to protect the magickal community."

David sighed again, shaking his head. "I understand, Jack. But for me to do my job fully, I've had to protect myself as well. Only the heads of the families knew who I was, and in what capacity. Now you all know, and I am trusting you with that secret."

"Your secret is safe with us, David," said Elspeth firmly. Everyone agreed, nodding and vocalising their support.

Ryder wiggled slightly in her chair. "So, Courtney and Alice have been placing magickal whammies down on Jack and Hunter, right?"

"And you, my dear," said Elspeth.

"Yeah, me too," Ryder said, her face going a shade paler as she remembered the incident.

"What exactly happened to you that night, Miss Williams?" asked David.

Ryder shuddered as she remembered that ride home on her bike. "I was so worried about Hunter. No one had found her yet, and so I closed up the pub early so that I could at least be here with Mom and Elspeth. I got on my bike, and took the path home. When I was close to the houses, I heard this weird sound, and I had a feeling, like something was very wrong, that came over me. I heard a growl, and something that sounded like a large chain, clinking on the ground."

"Goddess alive," breathed Elspeth. "The Black Dog was called in."

Ryder whipped her head around to look at the older Witch. "The who's in the what now?"

Elspeth composed herself quickly. "The Black Dog. In many parts of the country, there is a large, black hound that roams certain areas. Here in the New Forest, we have also had sightings. Sometimes it is beneficent, and helps people out of danger. But when the dog has a chain, it is not just a magickal beast or a spirit of place; it is an evil creature, summoned from the darkest depths. There has been a small spate of such activity here in the New Forest in recent years, dark magicks being used by some practitioners. There have been animal mutilations in Bramshaw, Boldre and also in Linwood."

David nodded. "Livestock ripped to shreds by something, their bodies left behind with an inverted pentagram upon them. Even more recently, a severed deer's head was found in Lyndhurst church."

Elspeth continued. "We, the magickal community, assumed that is was just teenagers, playing at Satanic rites out of boredom, and trying to shock the locals. But with what happened to Ryder, things are indeed taking a much darker turn. The Chained Black Dog can only be summoned by those who have power; real magickal power."

Silence filled the room as everyone took in Elspeth's words. Hunter felt a real dread filling her. *Are we safe here?* she wondered. *I can't stay here with Ryder, not with such dangerous things happening. We have got to leave. How could we possibly stay, when Ryder nearly died, alone and in pain? When everyone that we care about has been attacked by my Fae uncle? When we've kicked off, unknowingly, some sort of feud with others in the magickal community? We should just go back home and forget all this had ever happened. Go back to a life that is 'normal', where magick with a 'k' doesn't exist. Why not just go home? Why not just leave?*

"No," said Ryder firmly.

Everyone in the room looked at her, not understanding. Ryder turned to her sister. "No, Hunter. No, we will not leave."

Everyone then turned to Hunter, whose face quickly blushed.

"Ryder, will you please explain?" asked Elspeth calmly.

Ryder cleared her throat and paused before she spoke. "My sister is worried about the dangers to us here. This Black Dog, these dark magicks; everything. But sis, you can't make the decision for both of us. I've got a stake in this now. I've got a dog in this race, no pun intended. I'm staying, and I'm going to do my best to stop this stuff from happening again. This is our birthright, and our legacy, Hunter. Is it dangerous? Hell yes. But just as you trooped off to the Otherworld to do your thing, I'm going stay and help in whatever way I can here too. That bitch sicked her dog on *me*, and I'm going to see that she gets taken down. She's put us both in the hospital, and now its *personal*."

Hunter looked at her sister, with wonder and then pride. "And I'll be right beside you," she said, with a small smile.

Thanks, Hun.

I love you, Ry.

In the silence that followed, Elspeth sat forward on her seat. "Ryder, please continue with your story."

"Oh, right. Where was I?"

"You heard a growl, and a clinking chain."

"Oh, yeah. So, I turned tail and began pedalling like fuck to get the hell out of there, but it caught up with me and grabbed my leg. I couldn't see anything, but it pulled me to the ground. I managed to keep it off me, by holding it away, even though it burned my hands. And it stank, like sulphur. I rolled, but it rolled with me and came out on top again. I then felt my energy rising, and I manged to blast the thing off of me."

"You blasted it off?" asked Harriet, leaning forwards. "How did you do that?"

Ryder shrugged. "I don't really know. I just felt a build-up of energy, and then *boom*! It came out of my hands and knocked that thing away. It was like, hot, fiery energy. And probably a ton of adrenaline. I turned my head to look at it, and it kind of whined, and then disappeared."

Elspeth leaned back into her seat, a look of concentration on her face as she tried to make sense of Ryder's tale. "And is that when you heard Courtney?" she said finally.

Ryder nodded. "Yeah. There was this loud shriek from the tree above me, and I saw a barn owl fly out from a branch, coming towards me. It flew low over my head, and then I heard Courtney say, '*next time*'."

"Are you sure it was Courtney?" asked Harriet.

"I'd recognise that bitch's voice anywhere. After the nasty things she said to me at the pub when she and Jack were there, I'll never forget it."

Hunter and Jack looked at each other briefly, remembering the barn owl that shrieked and flew over them in the stone circle that first magickal night they had shared. "Damn," said Jack softly.

David interjected. "And so how did you get to Elspeth's house?"

Ryder looked down, clasping her hands in her lap. "I, well, I couldn't really walk, so I pushed myself along on the bike as far as I could. I got to the driveway, and fell off. I then crawled up to the door, and they found me."

Elspeth nodded. "We heard a scraping sound at the door, and the cats immediately ran to the door and started meowing. I opened the door and found Ryder, and called for an ambulance straight away."

"Remind me to thank your kitties," said Ryder with a smile.

"And all this happened while Hunter was… where were you exactly?" David asked, turning to face Hunter.

Hunter blushed again. "I – I was out on the heath, going to a special spot that I had found earlier, somewhere that I could cross over safely to the Otherworld, guided there with the help of my familiar."

At that, the room came alive as everyone started asking questions at once. Elspeth held up her hand and the room quieted almost instantly. "Continue, please, Hunter."

Hunter swallowed. "I – I'm so sorry. I know now that I was influenced by the magick that Courtney and Alice had worked against me, but it's more than that." She looked around the room at everyone. "I know, from everything that I've studied, that I could not have been so enspelled without having left myself open in some way to that magick. In my own pride, I thought that I could do this, that I could take on the mantle of being a Hedge Witch. By my birthright, by my being part-Fae, who was to stop me? I thought I was uniquely qualified to do the work where no one else was.

"I was upset that everyone treated me like some sort of 'Baby Witch'. I had studied for months, and done some pretty incredible things already. I think that my own pride in my accomplishments, as well as learning of my Fae heritage, left me open to their spell with disastrous consequences. I had been using anger to shield myself from pain, from the pain of the breakup with Jack. I guess Courtney and Alice's spell found an easy way into my heart, riding the anger that I had already built. Had I not been so full of myself, of my own pride, I might not have been so easily led. I might have prevented all this from happening, and kept my sister safe." Hunter wrung her hands in her lap, now unable to meet anyone's eyes. There was silence for three, long heartbeats.

"I call bullshit."

Hunter looked up at Ryder, who was glaring at her. "Yeah, that's right. I call bullshit. You *are* powerful, Hunter. I think you don't even actually realise just how powerful you truly are."

"I thought I knew *everything*, Ryder. I thought I knew what was best. I didn't see that I still had a lot to learn. I will always have a lot to learn. I think perhaps Witchcraft is just learning, each and every day. There is no mastery, only understanding that there is so much more out there. I will not let my pride get in the way of my work again, nor will I allow it to be a door for anger and righteousness."

"Well said," said Elspeth softly.

"Hunter, I too have fallen into the trap of my own pride," said Jack quietly. "At first I believed that Courtney had not cast a love spell on me last year. And then cursing me after we broke up. That was *my* foolish pride, not wanting to believe that she had the power to do that sort of thing to me, or that she and Alice working together might have done this to me. And now, once again thinking that I could deal with this situation on my own, and solve this without telling anyone. I realise now that had I just been open and honest with everyone, instead of taking matters into my own hands, Ryder would not have been attacked, and you would not have gone through such heartache.

I've been a fool. And all I can do now is ask if you will forgive me."

"Yes, I forgive you, Jack," said Hunter. Everyone else in the room nodded their assent. "I forgive you everything, because everything that you have said, I have been guilty of as well. For too long I have taken the burden of everything upon my own shoulders, not realising that we are stronger together, all of us: Ryder, Elspeth, Mom, Harriet, everyone. I have learned the hard way when to ask for help, and although self-reliance is a good thing, cutting yourself off from others who can and who are willing to help, who love you, is just a stupid thing to do."

There was another silence, before David picked up the thread again. "So, Hunter, you travelled to the Otherworld?"

"Yes. We needed more information, so that when the time was right for us to locate my father, we would be prepared. Little did I know that it was all a trap, set by Lanoc, my uncle. He must have known that Mom and I would eventually go to the circle of stones in the Otherworld, knowing it was a special place for her and my father. Lanoc set up the fake coronet for us to find. He also must have been the one who gave us the riddle. And so I went to the Otherworld myself, full of myself, in all honesty, thinking that I could get information and perhaps even solve this riddle. I walked right into his trap."

"How did you get out?"

Hunter was silent for a moment. She wasn't sure just how much to say. She knew that Elspeth had some sort of issue with the Fae, and didn't trust them. That contrasted with Hunter's experience of the two Fae that she had recently been in contact with. "I was helped by those who claimed to oppose Lanoc. I was freed from the trap, and then I ran like hell, with Lanoc hot on my heels. And that's when Jack found me."

David turned to Jack. "You found Hunter? In the Otherworld?"

"Yeah, Jack," said Ryder. "How did you do that? Have you got some special Druid mojo for hedge riding too?"

Hunter also turned to Jack. "Yes, how did you cross the veil between the worlds?"

Jack cleared his throat. "That day you went missing, I went out early in the morning to check on the ritual space that Courtney and Alice were using. I had been doing that almost every day, to try and see what they were up to, and to keep tabs on their activity. If I came across anything new, I would go directly to my sister this time for guidance. I didn't want to blow my cover, but I also needed to keep you safe. When I saw what was on the altar that day, my heart stopped.

"It was a poppet, a likeness of you, Hunter. I grabbed it and brought it back to my place, where I placed it in a box and said a spell of my own over it, to try and contain its magick. I also poured salt over it, to cleanse and purify it. I then hid the box and poppet, and was going to take it to Ellie after I got home from work.

"Then you went missing, and I spent the day searching for you throughout the area around Burley. But then I had a sudden realisation. This poppet had been tied to you in some way, in order for it to have succeeded. I thought that perhaps the energy that remained in the poppet could also be used to trace and track you, just like I did with my staff. I used your idea that you gave me when my staff was stolen, and turned it around to use it on this poppet instead. I took this idea to Ellie, along with the poppet, and she neutralised the magick as best she could. There were three strands of your own hair, sewn into the head of the poppet. Ellie said that I could use the remaining energy of the poppet to find you, as it was still connected to you, even though the intention of the spell had been neutralised as best as we could. So I did. I took the poppet out onto the heath, and that's when the white hind appeared."

"My familiar," said Hunter softly.

"No way," said Ryder, grinning. "What's a hind?"

"A doe, a deer," said Elspeth.

"A female deer?" asked Ryder.

"Don't go there, Ry," said Hunter with a warning.

"Hang on a minute," said Ryder. "How did Courtney and Alice get three strands of your hair for their poppet?"

"I don't know," said Jack. "But I'd recognise Hunter's hair anywhere."

Realisation suddenly dawned on Hunter. "Xander," she said softly.

"Huh?" said Ryder.

"Alexander Hardwick," said Harriet. "He danced with her at the First Harvest Dance."

"When we passed each other while doing one of the dances, I felt a tugging on my hair. He made it out like his cufflink had caught on my hair. He took my hair for his sister and Courtney to use in their magick."

"That sonofabitch," said Harriet softly.

"Hang on, was that the guy whose car got towed?" asked Ryder. She then put two and two together. "And right before Jack asked Hunter to dance with him. How convenient." She grinned openly at Jack.

"I can neither confirm nor deny my involvement in that matter," said Jack, with his cheeky grin.

Ryder laughed softly. "So, Jack, to get back on track, the deer led you to Hunter?"

"No, she led me to a portal to the Otherworld, out on heath. Once through the portal, I traced the energy of the poppet to

Hunter. I found her running from the storm, from Lanoc. She was lost, but we made it back here together." He and Hunter looked at each other, and as one, they reached out to take each other's hand.

"Is there anything else that I need to know?" asked David, softly, his eyes turned towards his hands, clasped in his lap. Hunter released Jack's hand. "I don't think so, at least not from me. Ryder, Elspeth? Jack?"

The others shook their heads. David sighed and stood. "Well then, I should be on my way. Thank you for sharing all of this with me. If there is anything else that comes to light, please let me know. I will speak to my grandfather about this, and ask him about the best way forward. He has been doing this for a lot longer than I have, and I'm sure he will be able to advise me how best to proceed." He turned to face Abigail. "It was a pleasure meeting you, Mrs Williams," he said. "I'm glad that you're back, and reunited with your daughters."

Abigail stood as well. "Thank you, Officer Hart. If we find out anything more, we shall be in touch."

David nodded to the room, and then went to the door. "Good night," he said.

Abigail let him out. "Goodnight. Be safe."

The room was silent for a moment, as everyone thought about everything that had just been said. Ryder looked over at Jack, and her eyes narrowed. "So, Jack, you fooled us all pretty good, didn't you?"

Jack looked uncomfortable under her scrutiny. "I-uh, well, yes, I suppose so. I really am sorry. I didn't mean to hurt anyone, I just wanted to keep you all safe."

Realisation dawned on Ryder's face. "That *was* you I saw, that stopped the storm!" cried Ryder.

"What?" asked Hunter.

"When you and Mom were hedge riding, this big storm came up, remember? When the tree outside got struck by lightning? That was *you*, Jack, wasn't it? You stopped the storm, just like you did in the forest that day."

Hunter turned to face Jack. "The strange figure in the backyard that my sister described after we had done the hedge riding – that was you?"

Jack looked a little sheepish. "Well, yes. Hunter, I wanted to keep you all safe, as I said. I have watched over you and the cottage as much as I could in my spare time." He lifted his face to look her in the eye. "Do you remember the rose?"

Hunter looked down. "Yes, I do remember."

Jack gave her a sad smile. "Everything I do, Hunter, is for you."

"And so you were out there, that day, in the treeline, watching over the house," said Ryder softly. "That is just so freakin' romantic." She sighed, wistfully.

"I saw the storm approach, and did what I could do to stop it. I'm sad that the oak tree took the hit, but I think it will recover, in time."

"You saved us, Jack," said Hunter softly.

"I just did what I could to protect you."

Hunter reached out to take his hand again, and held it silence.

Elspeth stood. "I think we all need to take some time to think all this through. Ryder needs some quiet time as well, to heal." Ryder began to protest, but Elspeth held up her hand. "You need to be at full strength, if you are to take on the mantle that you wish to wear, young woman," she said.

"Duly noted," said Ryder, reluctantly.

"In the meantime, I suggest that no one goes anywhere, alone. It would seem that the dark magicks being practiced here are ramping up, and we need to be safe. Now that we have a

Witches of the New Forest

better idea of who and what we are up against, we can better prepare for it. I will be in touch with you all about that, and soon. I'm certain that the coven can help. They've already given us general protection, but now that we know more details, we can be more specific.

"We also have another hedge riding to prepare for," Elspeth continued. "Abigail and Hunter still need to find Aedon, and free him, if they can. There is still much work to be done, and lots of preparation in store. Ryder must heal, so that she can support us, as she is coming into her own power as well."

"Wait, I – what?"

Elspeth looked at her with a smile. "You blew an evil, Black Dog back to its realm. That's no mean feat. Your powers are growing as well, young woman."

Harriet went over to where Ryder sat in the recliner, her leg elevated in its cast. "You're totally badass," she said, giving her friend a gentle hug. Ryder couldn't stop grinning.

"I should go as well," said Jack, standing up. "Ellie, I'm going to stay with you. You shouldn't be alone in the house, and neither should I."

Elspeth nodded. "I'll come with you to get your things, and Dexter. You can stay in the spare room. Harriet, can you stay with your parents, for the time being?"

"I don't think I'm really a target, do you? Does Courtney even know that I exist?"

"Better safe than sorry, dear," said Elspeth.

"Okay. I'll head over tonight. Shall I tell them what's happening?"

Elspeth studied the young woman for a moment. She then nodded. "Yes, tell them. They already know much, and it would be good for the rest of the magickal families to be vigilant at this time. I shall tell Thomas as well, so that he can pass that on to the rest of the Inghams. The Hardwicks, well, they're on their own now." Elspeth's green eyes took on a steely glare. "David will inform Geraint Hardwick, the head of the Hardwick family, of his daughter's behaviour, and also that of his son, Xander. If the Hardwicks can't, or won't prevent their family and their families' friends together from using the dark arts against members of the magickal community, then we most certainly will. If the Hardwick family have all descended into darkness, then that changes everything."

"You don't mean," said Abigail softly.

Elspeth nodded. "A Witch War has begun."

Epilogue

In the evening's light, a police car pulled up into an empty car park high on the moorlands of the New Forest. The door of the car opened, and Police Constable Hart emerged from his vehicle. He took off his cap and threw it into the back seat. He locked the car and looked out over the moorland for a moment, before he set off across the small paths lined with heather and gorse. He made his way across the heath and into the ancient woodland. As the evening shadows lengthened, he approached a small glade in the forest, lit up with the last of the evening's light. At the centre of the glade stood a very strange, oddly twisted tree.

David ran his hands through his short hair, letting out a long breath. He went up to the strange tree, and knelt down beside it. He began to chant, strange words that fell around the glade as the last of the light faded with the setting sun. He then touched the tree with both hands and gave it a slight tug.

Suddenly a tremor in the earth beneath his feet rocked the glade. With eyes widened in surprise and fear, David quickly got to his feet and stood back, watching and waiting to see what would happen. From out of the earth rose a strange, magickal beast.

It was no tree that was in the earth. As the beast emerged, was first appeared to be a tree was really a pair of twisted antlers, the antlers of a great being that had been buried beneath the soil. The beast continued to rise from the earth, and David took even more steps backwards, unable to take his eyes off of the thing that stood before him. When it had fully emerged, it shook off the earth from its coat and turned its large, leonine head towards him.

It's yellow eyes glowed in the dusk. A red mane shone like flame, and it let out a roar, displaying long, sharp teeth. It looked at David and saw deep into his soul. They held each other's gaze for a moment, and then the beast walked off into the darkness of the New Forest.

The adventure continues with Hunter, Ryder, Abigail, Elspeth, and Jack in the third book: The Witch's Compass, available late spring/early summer 2025. Can Hunter and Jack reconcile, after everything that has happened? Will their love see them through the many hardships that still await them? Will Hunter be able to get a better grasp on her pride, her emotions and her powers? Hunter and Abigail still have the daunting task of trying to free Aedon, if they can find him. And what will the sisters do with their legacy – will they stay and continue, becoming fully-fledged members of the magickal community, or will they return back to Canada? Where does that leave the magickal community of Burley, now possibly embroiled in a Witch War that could threaten their very existence?

If you enjoyed this book, please do leave a review. It is the best thing that you can do to help an author continue writing and creating wonderful worlds to explore.

Author's Note

Thank you so much for spending time with me in the little magickal village of Burley, in the New Forest. I have always loved this area with its myths, legends, and magick aplenty. I hope to write many more books within this special setting, with its engaging and interesting characters. The characters write the books for me, and it's a pleasure to spend time in their company. I can't wait to find out what they will do next!

You may have noticed some of the spells and incantations in this book and other books in the series. Many of these, including Thomas' magick and the words that he spoke when performing protection magick, are from the *Carmina Gadelica*: a collection of prayers, songs, charms, blessings, incantations and more that were collected from the Gàidhealtachd regions of Scotland between 1860 and 1909. This material was recorded and translated into English by Alexander Carmichael (1832–1912). Though much of the recorded lore has a gloss of Christianity, it would appear that it stems from a much older Pagan oral tradition that has been passed down through the centuries. For the purposes of this book, I took out the Christian references and substituted them for a modern Pagan context.

As well, in this book, the second half of the chant that Hunter and Abigail used when they first performed a hedge riding together stems from two different sources. The 'Horse and Hattock' spell comes from Scottish folklore, and originally referred to fairies mounting horses and going on nightly adventures. It later became associated with Witchcraft through the detailed confessions of Isobel Gowdie, a 17th century Scottish witch, who said she used it while flying. A *hattock* is a hat, and one should always wear a hat when riding one's horse, or even one's broom! *Pellatis* means to drive forward, or to put to flight. The *thout a thout and tout a tout* section comes from another account of Witchcraft, this time in England, where one Alice Duke in 1664 described Witches who said these words as they flew to and from their sabbath.

If you are interested in learning about modern Hedge Witchcraft or Druidry, please see the books listed at the beginning of this work.

About the Author

Joanna van der Hoeven has written many non-fiction books exploring the traditions of both Druidry and Hedge Witchcraft. Joanna has worked in Pagan traditions since 1991, and has published many books, articles, blogs, and videos on the subject.

Born in Canada, Joanna has lived in England since 1998. She now lives near the Suffolk Coast in a little village nestled in the heathland, with the forest and the sea near to her door. To find out more, please visit her website at www.joannavanderhoeven.com, or see her author's page on Amazon.

Printed in Dunstable, United Kingdom